A PENGUIN MYSTERY

DIRTY SALLY

Michael Simon is a former stage actor who has worked as a stagehand, cab driver, truck loader, disc jockey, proofreader, editor, and ghostwriter. The coauthor of two Off-Broadway plays, Simon has taught at Brooklyn College and New York University. In the late 1980s, he worked as a probation officer in Austin, Texas. *Dirty Sally* is his first novel. His second novel, *Body Scissors*, is available from Viking. He lives in New York City.

Visit the author at www.michaelsimon.info

DIRTY SALLY

A NOVEL

MICHAEL SIMON

PENGUIN BOOKS

PENGUIN BOOKS
Published by the Penguin Group
Penguin Group (USA) Inc., 375 Hudson Street, New York, New York 10014, USA
Penguin Group (Canada), 90 Eglinton Avenue East, Suite 700, Toronto, Ontario,
Canada M4P 2Y3 (a division of Pearson Penguin Canada Inc.)
Penguin Books Ltd., 80 Strand, London WC2R 0RL, England
Penguin Ireland, 25 St. Stephen's Green, Dublin 2,
Ireland (a division of Penguin Books Ltd.)
Penguin Group (Australia), 250 Camberwell Road, Camberwell, Victoria 3124,
Australia (a division of Pearson Australia Group Pty. Ltd.)
Penguin Books India Pvt. Ltd., 11 Community Centre, Panchsheel Park,
New Delhi – 110 017, India
Penguin Group (NZ), cnr Airborne and Rosedale Roads, Albany,
Auckland 1310, New Zealand (a division of Pearson New Zealand Ltd.)
Penguin Books (South Africa) (Pty.) Ltd., 24 Sturdee Avenue,
Rosebank, Johannesburg 2196, South Africa

Penguin Books Ltd., Registered Offices:
80 Strand, London WC2R 0RL, England

First published in the United States of America by Viking Penguin, a member of
Penguin Group (USA) Inc. 2004
Published in Penguin Books 2005

10 9 8 7 6 5 4 3 2 1

Grateful acknowledgment is made for permission to reprint excerpts from the following
copyrighted works: *The Great Gatsby* by F. Scott Fitzgerald. Copyright 1925 by Charles
Scribner's Sons. Copyright renewed 1953 by Frances Scott Fitzgerald Lanahan. Reprinted
with permission of Scribner, an imprint of Simon & Schuster Adult Publishing Group.
"Mustang Sally" written by Bonnie Rice. Published by Fourteenth Hour Music (BMI). All
rights reserved. International copyright secured. Reprinted by permission. "Just Like
Tom Thumb's Blues" by Bob Dylan. Copyright © 1965 by Warner Bros. Inc. Copyright
renewed 1993 by Special Rider Music. All rights reserved. International copyright
secured. Reprinted by permission. "My Generation" words and music by Peter
Townshend. © Copyright 1965 (renewed) Fabulous Music Ltd., London, England. TRO -
Devon Music, Inc., New York, controls all publication rights for the U.S.A. and Canada.
Used by permission. "Who Are You" by Peter Townshend. © 1978 by Songs of
Windswept Pacific o/b/o Towser Tunes, Inc. All rights administered by Windswept. All
rights reserved. Used by permission. Warner Bros. Publications U.S. Inc., Miami, Florida.

THE LIBRARY OF CONGRESS HAS CATALOGED THE HARDCOVER EDITION AS FOLLOWS:
Simon, Michael 1963–
Dirty Sally : a novel / by Michael Simon.
p. cm.
ISBN 0-670-03319-7 (hc.)
ISBN 0 14 30.3531 2 (pbk.)
1. Police—Texas—Austin—Fiction.   2. Austin (Tex.)—Fiction.
3. Jewish men—Fiction.   I. Title.
PS3619.I5625D57 2004
813'.6—dc22   2003065779

Printed in the United States of America

For Dad

A sense of the fundamental decencies is parcelled out unequally at birth.

—F. Scott Fitzgerald, *The Great Gatsby*

DIRTY SALLY

Crack cocaine rolled up Highway 290 from Houston to Austin in 1981, the same route the oil bust rode here in '86 and the stock market crash in '87, so by September of '88 businesses were failing, banks going belly-up, and no one in town was making money except the dealers, lawyers and shrinks. The governor struggled to make good on campaign promises to create jobs and reduce prison overcrowding: new policies made to counter a century of Texan excess left old prisoners languishing for the remainder of century-long sentences on minor drug infractions, while rapists and murderers plea-bargained their way to short terms in county jail. It would take another year till our first drive-by forced the press, and then the cops, to admit that gangs had been creeping around since the city charter was ratified. In every quarter, near-prosperity gave way to frenzy. Secure in my city job, I watched the summer heat plow past Labor Day with no sign of slowing down. Then Dirty Sally's famous legs first kicked up smoke and I learned just what my forty-five thousand a year would cost me.

That's my partner Joey Velez in the picture, first row, second *from right, the big jovial guy with his arm around my shoulders and his trademark chipped-tooth grin. They snapped that shot last Christmas, three months before Joey made The Ultimate Sacrifice—killed in the line of duty. Eulogy delivered by a new police chief he never met, marked in the reception area at police headquarters by the last of a line of plaques, one for every sucker who bit it on the company clock since it was an hourglass. That's me in the Christmas picture, Detective Sergeant Dan Reles—rhymes with "trellis"—Austin Police, Homicide, at six feet even, just a shade shorter than Joey, with the stooped shoulders and busted nose of a mob-friendly boxer, the trade my father raised me to before his fortunes turned and we fled prison-town upstate New York for God's country: Southern gentility, high windows, crack dens, trailer parks, whorehouses, six-month summers, dead cops, beautiful wives, fat lawyers, powerbrokers, future governors and fully lawful plans to take over the world. They're not out to get you, folks say, it's just how they do business. A new breed of power is gestating in the Lone Star State, the world's biggest lab of trial and error, and you're a guinea pig. Your mother and your best friend and everyone you care about gets lost in the soup, the reed you hang onto snaps, you grab that one last thing you believe in, raging at the injustice as you hold the world together with both hands and as the weight of it drags you under, your air bubbles slop to the surface and you know beyond possibility that it's over—the last thing you give up is hope.*

PART ONE

BLACK FRIDAY

Friday, September 9, 1988. 3:30 A.M.
Sands Motel, Austin, Texas

Mice and roaches bustled around her on the rug. She couldn't make out if they were real or not but she noticed a man bouncing up and down on her, all sweat and moans and after-shave. Hmm.

Her eyes lit up a vision, a distant memory of a little girl—her—and a littler boy, giggling in a wading pool. A black charm on a string hangs around the girl's neck. She cradles the boy in her arms as the camera snaps and her vision flashes white.

Outside in the dark, Armand Tejani waited under a palm tree, tapping his eelskin shoes and wiping his heavy palms on his soggy black lapels.

"Come on, man!" he whispered. "How long can this take?"

He rubbed his nostrils, hopped on one foot, eyed the numberless motel room door. Sands Motel, a little bit of Vegas splash right here in South Austin. Whores and junkies didn't amount to much of a tourist attraction—vacationers from Elgin and Abilene abandoned the rotting building years ago to the vermin, mold, drunks and, just now, to a faceless john and one very special girl.

The door finally inched open, the john, his cartoon-broad forehead and narrow chin peeking out, blinking like a freckled mole, a rich, crazy cokehead in a chalk blue seersucker suit. The john closed the door behind him and scampered down a dark side street, clenching and grinding his teeth and checking his fly.

Tejani broke for the door. Finish this one clean, baby, this is the easy part. *Too* easy, for thirty big ones. That's what tipped him off. There was more to be made, lots more. They were paying too well for part one; they'd pay wicked for part two, the part they didn't know about yet. He'd walk off with a fortune, blow town on a blast of 'caine, Vegas, New York—anywhere but Atlanta. Maybe clean up for a while, get some sleep. He hugged the door: silence. Then he turned the knob and slipped inside.

The room stank gag-level. Winos, probably, used the toilet after the plumbing got shut off. A streetlamp shining through the bare window caught a wood roach the size of a woman's thumb, tearing across a gray stucco wall. On a light square of carpet where a bed once stood, the nude girl lay, idly sucking some charm on a string around her neck. Her face showed only a trace of what Tejani saw in the photo: icy blue eyes, blue-black hair, skin like polished gold. Now her skin hung loose on her like someone else's clothes, her black hair twisted against her head and neck, her eyes stared dim and she stank like rotten meat. If he asked her name, she wouldn't understand the question. No trouble tonight. That seersucker john paid her in heroin.

Her glassy gaze finally landed on Tejani. When he snapped off his belt knife, she watched the blade glimmering under the lamppost light. The string around her neck broke, and she choked for a second on the loose charm before she swallowed it hard, the string still tangled around her finger.

Tejani gently lifted the matted black hair away from her neck with the blade and she leaned her head back. The sight warmed him so much that he stroked her hair. He sheathed the knife and instead took the heavy plastic garbage bag from his jacket pocket, pulled it over her head and squeezed it tight around her throat.

First the bag rose and fell with her breath. She struggled feebly and grabbed at her face. Tejani climbed on top of her to pin her arms and legs down as he wrapped the bag tighter around her neck, his pelvis pressed against hers. She kicked out and shook. He felt himself growing hard as her body rose and fell.

Atlanta Federal Prison. 1986. Four crackers hold Tejani down on the toilet floor. A fifth on his back burns Tejani's neck with a cigarette, yelling, "You sent me up for nothin'—for NOTHIN'!" and finally pulls Tejani's pants down and rips into him, growling, "Welcome to the Joint, cop!"

Tejani shook with terror as the stick of a girl writhed under his powerful trunk. He squeezed the bag tighter, forcing the images from his brain when she jolted for the last time, and he came hard against her as her muscles relaxed and she lay still.

Now he'd done what he was paid for. *Little bitch*, he thought, as he wrapped the plastic around her limp body. *Little nobody. You're worth more dead than you were alive.*

1

MONDAY

A Mobster's Lackey

September 12, 1988. 8:00 A.M. 4612 Avenue F

I zero in on the three-on-the-tree gearshift on the steering column of Joey Velez's narco-white Chevy Caprice. I'm riding shotgun as Joey tears northwest on the mountain stretch of Route 2222 in the dark, the road twisting roller-coaster right and left, up a hundred feet in the air and straight back down, the car hanging on by a hair with Joey cackling at the wheel.

"Joey." I try to focus my eyes. "I thought you were dead."

"No, man," he laughs, throwing a wink in my direction. "Pretty near. Wake up, pally, we gotta see someone."

I remember he drove off a cliff on a dark night in March. Then I remember it's March now. The Caprice streaks off the road, arcs into the air weightless as my stomach leaps and the car noses down.

*   *   *

I jolted awake, kicking my feet, wheezing from another rerun of the Joey dream that's punctuated my half-sleep for the last six months. Wake up, it's just a dream. What difference would it make if I'd been with him that night? He would've flown off the cliff anyway and we'd *both* be dead. Or I could have woken him up. Or we would've taken a different road. I threw my arm over my eyes against the sunlight streaking through the venetians.

"I'm leaving your father, I'm not leaving you. You understand that, don't you, honey?"

I'm ten years old, standing in the doorway of my parents' bedroom in our apartment in Elmira, New York, watching her pack.

"Don't you, honey?"

My mother was a glamour gal in the early 1950s, a beautiful WASP with long, silky black hair, sparkling blue bedroom eyes, and at five-eight, a full two inches on my father. With heels and her hair up like a half-raunchy Audrey Hepburn, she towered over him in what I took to be the wedding picture, Dad a skinny immigrant's son, a scrappy street Yid in a borrowed suit. But with her on his arm he felt like Lucky Luciano, feeding her lies about his "connections" and showing her off at nightclubs he couldn't afford. By daylight he was just an ex-boxer who did favors, like the time I was eight and he went to prison for a deuce for one of the big boys. A mobster's lackey, she said. A nobody. The day they paroled him, she packed a suitcase and called a cab.

"Where we goin', Ma?"

I watched her at her makeup table, brushing mascara on her long eyelashes, framed in the mirror with me in the background, a dwarf stage-door johnny. When the taxi honked she kissed me on the cheek and walked out.

In my dream, I'm always sitting alone at the bare kitchen

table, trembling, waiting for him to come back from the big house with his forty dollars and his new suit. The doorknob turns. I have to tell him she's gone, and I don't know what he'll do. Maybe he'll kill me.

I can still feel her kiss on my cheek, still hear her voice echo. "I'm leaving your father, I'm not leaving you."

Watching from the window as the blue and white taxi drove off, I knew for the first time that I was completely alone. And that I always would be.

Ring.

Ring. Click. Tape rolling. "*This is Dan. Go ahead.*" Beep.

"*Hello, Sergeant Reles? This is Martha Nell from Dispatch.*" Her voice twanged with tour-guide cheer. "*Pick up, please.*"

I killed the machine and worked up the spit to speak. "Yeah."

"*Did we wake you?*" she said with a sympathy I save for widows and orphans. "*Have I told you how good it is to have you back? You know you're on call.*"

"No. Waller," I muttered. "I'm not even next."

"*Sergeant Waller got a call on Saturday, one o' those murder-suicides? Filled out the forms and got home by lunch. And I guess they changed the rotation with you back in action, because you're next on the list.*"

Miles must have rigged it so I'd come up soon and win some points fast, coming off suspension. I opened my eyes. Sunlight hit my retinas and burned back to my ears. "No."

"*New case today. City bus knocked down a boy and dragged him down East Twelfth.*"

"Vehicular deaths. Traffic Department."

"Isn't that funny? That's just what Lieutenant Niederwald said you'd say!"

I coughed something dead from the back of my throat. "Look, Martha Nell—"

"He said to tell you Capital Metro anticipates a lawsuit, so they're claiming it was suicide."

"Christ. Where is it?"

"The ravine that cuts under the 700 block of East Twelfth, just west of Casa Rosa Apartments."

"Any ID on the remains?" I sat up heavily and scratched.

She'd already hung up.

2

9:30 A.M. East Twelfth Street

Death approaches from the left, a medic once told me.

Its cold form moves up beside you from the left, touches you and takes you. In desperate situations, medics park themselves on a patient's left side to get in death's way.

I badged the patrolman on guard and parked in the commandeered lot at Casa Rosa Apartments, a two-story modern complex with a wrought-iron outside staircase and puke pink stucco. Fire Department, EMS and APD uniforms crowded the scene, crossing each other's paths like they were all chief surgeon at the Mayo Clinic. Ambulance lights flashed uselessly while techs blocked the street and held reporters and gawkers back with yellow crime-scene tape so they could measure the space between skid marks, chunks of broken headlight and detached extremities. Low-end lawyers who heard about the accident on the police band, scampered up to sniff for manslaughter charges or a juicy wrongful-death lawsuit. A ghostly white patrolman cornered me with a paper coffee cup.

"Sergeant Reles? I'm Flenniken, sir." Looking past Flenniken, I thought I saw Joey in the crowd and I blinked hard. It was a husky dark guy, but a decade younger and alive. Joey's body got pulled from his car, autopsied and buried six months ago, I reminded myself. But I never got to say goodbye and I still kept half-expecting him to sneak up, slap me on the back and yell, "Dañel! Let's get 'em!"

I gulped half the lukewarm coffee. "How'd ya know it was me?"

"Dispatch told me to look for someone who . . . who looked like he might want a cup of coffee," Flenniken said.

"Nice. What'd she really say?" A fire truck headed off to find a fire. I looked at the sky.

He coughed. "She said you were muscled and handsome in a busted-up boxer sort of way. You'd look like you got your clothes off the floor. And you'd need coffee. Sir."

"Jesus, nine-thirty A.M. and it's baking already. What month is it?"

"September."

The coffee kicked in. I swallowed the dregs and handed him the empty. "Good. Only five months left of summer. What happened here?"

According to Flenniken, Rick Schate left his girlfriend's house, paid for a breakfast taco at a stand on the south side of East Twelfth and shot across the street—the driver and four passengers confirmed this—to catch the number 6 westbound bus just as the number 6 eastbound bus slammed into him, threw him twenty feet, then hit him again and rolled over him as its brakes squealed, catching his rib cage on its axle and dragging him another fifty feet before it came to a full stop on the overpass above the creek, a bloody stripe of Schate mapping its path. The Fire Department, first on the scene, backed up the bus and dislodged his crushed torso from the axle. They respirated and CPR'd him, bunched up on his left, then watched his face turn a cyanotic blue and felt a cool presence move through them as his last heartbeat blipped across the tiny screen.

Flenniken led me to the area in front of the bus where the medics had already slipped what was left of Schate into a clear bodybag—head, crushed torso, left leg, detached right leg, left arm, separated section of left hand. "Where's his right arm?" I asked. Flenniken and the medics looked around like they forgot their homework. "Christ, Flenniken, go back to the point of impact. One of you go with him."

I climbed down the sandy slope into the ravine, muttering about sniffing for lost arms on a bullshit case that came down to protecting the city from a legitimate lawsuit. A tiny creek trickled south under East Twelfth Street. A paved footpath ran parallel to the creek, through the underpass. Someone thought to tape off the pass north and south, to keep the area clear of morning joggers and kids getting high before school. I scanned the underpass: gang graffiti splattered its walls alongside hieroglyphics of overturned champagne glasses and the declaration I LOVE BROOKLYN spray-painted in block letters, probably by an exile like me. Mosquitoes swarmed in the vapor. In the shadow against one wall, I saw something that made me blink. It looked like a woman lying near the wall but the head and arms were barely formed, as if they were melting, real but not real. I got closer and blinked again, tried to focus my eyes in the sudden shade. I saw it was a sculp-

ture, a sloppy sculpture of a woman made of sand and
dirt, the head a big formless clod of gravel, the arms
spread, one leg straight, another pile of dirt that was probably supposed to be the other leg bent at the knee. Something about it felt wrong. I stepped closer and bent over
her. She was fake, sand and gravel fake, not even a good
job of it, in the head, arms, and legs. But the rest of her,
from the collar down—breasts, midsection and pelvis—
was real, human, naked and very dead.

I stumbled toward the sunlight, wide awake now, and
yelled at the first tech I saw. "Send Flenniken down here
with a print kit and get the medical examiner. We have a
homicide!"

It was past eighty degrees in the shade of the underpass. I
stood watching Dr. Margaret Hay, a tall, slim woman of
about sixty, with white hair and the leathery skin of an
old farmgirl. Wearing a breathing filter, rubber gloves, a
lab coat over a T-shirt and jeans, and sneakers, she
crouched by the remains and gently brushed away sand.
The victim's head, arms and legs were neatly sliced off,
bones sawed away and sanded to keep us from matching
the saw. They'd cut the flesh away from her midsection,
revealing her ribs and internal organs, like a map of her
own anatomy, and left only the skin over her breasts and
pelvis. Someone was very thorough, and very neat. Hay
zipped the bag and ditched the mask. "Adult female," she
growled, facing the body. "Dead a few days I think, but
she landed here before dawn. She's still cold." Hay turned
to me. "Welcome back."

I glanced at the remains. I saw lots of victims: shot,
stabbed, mutilated, sexually assaulted before death and

after, the endless barrage of horrible sights and smells that follows every cop and medic home at night and keeps us company as we dream. But no one on my watch ever went to this kind of trouble. Until now. He might have tortured her on any of the body parts he cut away, but the cutting we could see was neat, methodical. A Satanist might take one or two parts. An inadequate personality might take a souvenir. This guy was organized. Kill site separate from the dump site. No face, no teeth and no fingerprints.

Once they called Hay in after a tornado. Countless livestock were picked up, gutted and tossed by the twisting wind. She had to go through mounds of rotting organs and tell the locals which were human. No one beat Hay for professional distance—she didn't cry and she didn't make grisly jokes—but today she pulled her jaw a little tighter than usual.

Hay said, "From the skin tone and body hair I'll tentatively say Caucasian. I'll know more after the examination."

"When's that?"

Hay looked under her eyebrows at me. "You can follow me back to my office. If you have no plans." She liked Joey better than she liked me, a common sentiment.

On the way to the car I decided to look for the guy I saw earlier in the crowd, the one who looked like Joey. But when I got closer, he was gone.

I mounted my brown '83 Impala Narcmobile, a vehicle with a command presence as subtle as a blue-and-white blaring its sirens in Harlem, and headed west along East Twelfth. Charlie Sector: Spanish East Austin. Low-cost housing built way east of the interstate, the way the city planned it in 1922, so that even if segregation was out-lawed, we'd never integrate. Little houses, some run-down, some painted bright colors like carnival booths. Mothers hustling kids off to school. On the side of the library, a mural of African masks and Aztec gods represented a multicultural America that exists only on the sides of libraries. Repo houses with boarded windows, bodegas advertising "WIC Vouchers Accepted," Planned Parenthood, the black college, storefront churches and mortuaries. Liquor stores and gun shops, white-owned.

Most of the cops here requested El Barrio detail, particularly this strip of East Twelfth where the action is, where junkies go to score, where hookers proposition you, shouting "Here it is, baby!" as you pass by at thirty miles an hour, where the graft is rich.

Public radio sang the blues: *"One in five Americans live in poverty, a twenty-nine percent increase over 1979. In Texas, ninety-two percent of the poor are African American and Latino."* Texas, from the Indian *Tejas*, meaning "friendly." *"Thirty-six percent—"* I switched to the oldies: *". . . all you wanna do is ride around, Sally—"* anything so long as it wasn't news. Through years of traveling Austin's daytime and nighttime worlds, I'd developed an intimacy with the town, a marriage of sorts, while the news reported the cursory assessment of a first date.

When I was in college in the seventies, pipe-dreaming about my future as a gang-busting G-man, Austin was still a sleepy town—no big employers besides the university and the state government, and by law, no polluting industries and no building tall enough to hide the Capitol. In the eighties, hi-tech industries came, changed the laws

and grew the town vertically. Houston yuppies broken by
the oil bust rolled in, begging for jobs they weren't quali-
fied for. A Hooverville of cars and shacks sprang up behind the offices of the daily paper. By the time the
aftershock of the oil bust made its way to Austin in '86,
the skyscrapers were complete, and mostly empty. Nou-
veau homeless from all over the state drifted into the
town famous for its beauty and its social programs; they
sat on the Capitol lawn and waited, just waited, their
grimy clothes cooking pungent in the broiling heat of the
six-month Texas summer.

My father's mob "connections" had landed us both
here in 1968 when I was fifteen and on my way to a
Golden Gloves boxing championship and for all I knew,
the Olympics. (*"Wake up, we're leaving the state. Now!"*)
Nine years later, the same connections would keep me out
of the FBI.

After high school I joined the service, two years as an
MP in Frankfurt, back to Austin for college on the GI Bill.
Dad drifted around the country, making friends with cab
drivers, pool hustlers and other late-night entrepreneurs,
so said the unsigned postcards he used to send, postmarked St. Louis, Kansas City, Vegas: "Met a guy, working
on an entertainment deal." A year later: "St. Louis didn't
work out. Got something you might want to get in on.
Will call with details. Someone said you got married." The
postcards trailed off around '83.

Spring of my senior year at UT, I warmed up to the receptionist at the local FBI and called her every few days
about my application. In June she greeted me with, "Dan,
I'm so sorry," and, "It's not you, it's your father." The FBI
didn't trust me to help them destroy the mob that destroyed my family. I sat by the river, watched the crew

practice. A college graduate with a spotless military record and as of that week, a new wife—Amy, my college sweetheart. Small and shapely, blond hair in a flip, Bambi eyes, cherub cheeks, peaches smell, everything in place. A pixie Donna Reed in a peasant blouse. She was my first "good" girl, and I'd resolved to be a good husband, whatever that was. Screw the Bureau. The police force would jump at me. I'd be in charge in no time. How hard could it be?

I patrolled like I meant it: if I couldn't stop the mob, I'd clean up the world one crook at a time. Amy left just shy of our third anniversary, the day I passed the sergeant's exam. She said she couldn't live with my anger.

"Have I ever hit you?" I said, barely holding it back. "Have I ever even *yelled* at you?"

But I could see her cringe. "I'm always afraid you're going to."

I celebrated my sergeanthood by punching the wall, yelling, "*Why? Why? Why?!*" and resolved to be a better cop, since I didn't have anything else. People always leave.

They sent me to Criminal Investigations, working robberies and petty thefts. Meanwhile, Homicide Sergeant Joey Velez was trying to convince the Fifth Floor that there was such a thing as organized crime outside of the movies, but no one wanted to hear the news.

Joey zeroed in on Bertrand Gautier, who ran a record label out of his famous blues club, Gautier's, Austin home of the greats: B.B. and Albert King, Arlo, Clapton, Stevie Ray—all Gautier's close friends. A rash of car thefts was blowing through town, and Joey was tracking a murder that happened near one of them when an owner caught the theft in action. "The witness said he never saw anything like it," he told me. "A dozen of 'em pulled the doors and windows, yanked the radio, hoisted the engine

and hauled ass all in about fifteen seconds. You gotta ad-
mire that!" Joey connected the killing to the thefts and the
club: they were selling the parts and turning the money
into coke they could have on the street the same day.

Joey put together a team with guys from Vice, Narco
and Surveillance. He said he needed somebody on CIB to
track the car thefts, somebody smart.

"Reles. Where's that from?" he asked as he drove us toward the club.

"My old man's family's from Galicia, but—"

He laughed. *"Pueth, ereth Gallego! No tuve ninguna idea!"*

I had to wait till he was done saying *Buenoth díath* and
Thí, thí, theñor before I could tell him it wasn't Galicia,
Spain, but Galicia that laid over part of Poland and the
Ukraine.

He chuckled. "So you're not—"

"Nah, I'm a Jew."

"Yeah, I didn't think so." He flashed a grin. "You could
be passing."

"If I was passing, would I tell you I was a Jew?"

"You might. Have to work on that Spanish, though,
mi'jo."

"I took it in school, but, y'know . . . I'm thinking about
taking a class . . ."

"You should." Long pause. "I never met a Jewish cop
before. You're my first."

I said, *"Bueno, mazel tov, amigo."*

He roared with laughter, a big booming laugh that
made me laugh with him. It occurred to me that I could
be friends with this guy. I didn't tend to make friends. But
for years afterward, long after I'd learned enough barrio
Spanish to rattle the homies, he'd find a reason once in a
blue moon to turn to me and say, *"Mazel tov, amigo."*

We'd sit at Magnolia Café and he'd jive with Paul the manager while scribbling crazy diagrams on napkins. A family tree: Big Bosses lead down to Gautier, leads down to car gangs and coke dealers. Or he'd draw a triangle: car theft to car sales to coke, like molasses to rum to slaves. Every time it was a new diagram—lineage, circles, 3-D scrawls that cut across time—but once in a while he'd point to a spot where a name was missing and say, "This is the guy we need."

We started hanging around Gautier's club. Joey "bumped into" Gautier a few times and they became pals. Gautier sold him grams of coke, like a pal. One weeknight we were in there and a local group was on the bandstand, five guys with short mohawks doing Rolling Stones covers for a small crowd of about fifty people. Gautier stood at the bar, shmoozing with customers in his signature cowboy hat, string tie and plaid jacket. Joey was holding court at a table with a guy and some women, doing kamikaze shots. I stood at a wall, scanning the room and pretending to watch the band.

So I was the first to see a heavyset, fiftyish white guy at the bar eyeball Joey and stagger across the room to him like a drunk with a mission. "I know you," the man said when he got within ten feet of Joey, with the unmistakable look of someone about to finger a narc. The comment caught Joey as he raised another shot to his lips and the smile froze on his face.

Later Joey told me he'd ID'd the guy as Rush Clayton, a child molester Joey had sent to Huntsville "for a little reverse therapy," transferred to county jail because of overcrowding and released after thirty months for the same reason. Joey didn't wait for details: he tossed his drink into Clayton's eyes and lunged for him, pops to the mouth too close together for Clayton to spit out the word "cop" in between. A bouncer the size of a truck grabbed Joey from behind and pinned his arms. The crowd tumbled away from them. Clayton climbed up on all fours, drooling blood, and spotted Gautier. I grabbed a wooden chair and flung it through the front window, alarm ringing a high C. The crowd rushed the doors so fast you could see the smoke swirling. Clayton made it toward Gautier, who flashed a look of horror back at him. I ran for Clayton and grabbed him, said, "Stay away from that motherfucker"—with a nod at Joey—"he's crazy," and pulled him toward the door, glancing back at a grateful Gautier. Joey was bloody in the mouth but just getting the better of the bouncer as Gautier made toward them to intervene.

Patrol cars rounded up the few drunks and stragglers who hadn't made it out of the parking lot. They hauled in Gautier, the bouncer, the bartenders, Clayton, Joey and me, the last three of us sitting silently in the back of the same patrol car. At Central Booking they split us up, let Gautier and his people go, and put Joey in a room alone with Clayton.

Joey went back to the club the next afternoon while they were caulking the new window in place. He brought a bottle of Chivas and an apology for starting a fight. Gautier, already three sheets to the wind, said, "S'okay, man, happens all the time. Wanna do some candy?" Rush Clayton left town that day and never came back. The next story Joey told a cluster of detectives was how I protected his cover by throwing a chair through a window and beating the crap out of a child molester, not half the true story but it made me out to be a team player. And out of a barroom brawl a partnership was born.

We piled the evidence. Joey wore a wire, witnessed the

deals and brought everyone in: car thieves, dealers, Gautier and—thanks to the RICO Act—everyone up to the hands-off guys on top, hiding their faces from the TV cameras as patrols marched them into Central Booking. Joey was a big hero: the press loved him, the Organized Crime Division was made permanent with Joey and me on regular staff, and the DA got reelected. When the DA was indicted for tax fraud eight months later, the Department decided OC needed to be "reorganized," and Joey and I got sent back down. Joey saved me from the scrap heap of a long-term assignment on CIB and mentored me onto Homicide—the squad's youngest member, first Yankee, first Jew, and, now with Joey gone, the designated outsider, the foreigner.

Mazel tov, amigo.

I cut under the interstate, a mortician's wet dream of fifteen-foot entrance ramps—zero to sixty in half a second or you're dead—separating East Austin from White Austin, headed south on the frontage road and parked under the highway at Eighth Street behind a minivan with a cute bumper sticker reading WHAT'S YOUR HURRY? YOU'RE ALREADY IN AUSTIN! The municipal parking lots served APD staff and visitors, the municipal courts, Central Booking and, quietly in back, the office of Margaret Hay, M.D., the Travis County Medical Examiner.

That's when I first met Aaron Gold.

3

As I walked in out of the sun, a hippie college boy, skinny, about five-foot-six with long hair, a scraggly beard, John Lennon glasses and an army knapsack, strode up to me holding a scrap of paper and followed me in. "Is this the Medical Examiner's?"

"Yeah." He trailed me past reception into the back hallway.

"I got a message at home about my roommate. They were looking for his parents but they're in Houston. His name is Rick Schate. Was he in an accident?"

I stopped dead outside the autopsy room as a gurney rolled toward us.

"Are you a cop?" the kid asked. "Is he under arrest?"

I couldn't say anything before the gurney holding the mashed remains of Rick Schate, globs of flesh placed near what was left of each arm, crossed our path and slowed long enough to push the autopsy room doors open. The long-haired kid turned white.

An assistant in green scrubs let me through the doors of the cutting room, a spare operation with fluorescent lights, concrete floor, metal sink and a butcher's scale— Drop the organs in, see the dial spin, Joey used to say. The faucet had a hose for spraying and a clear hose for suction, so you could watch it swallow.

Hay in scrubs and a clear plastic face shield stood over Schate. She clamped two vice grips on a lone fist and broke the fingers open with a crunch, a dozen tiny bones snapping in succession, and her mouth twisted into something like a smile. "Sergeant Reles?"

"Yeah?"

She didn't look up. "What's the current fare on Capital Metro?"

"I don't know. Fifty cents?"

"For students?"

I shrugged. "Twenty-five maybe? Yeah, why?"

Hay exchanged a look with Number One. "I don't know what I can say about the suicide theory. But you can tell Capital Metro they have twenty-five cents coming to 'em."

She took a student ID and a quarter from Schate's palm with her bloody glove and tossed the quarter onto the metal gurney. The bloody coin fell with a dull clink and stuck.

Assistant Number Two wheeled in the second gurney, slamming it through the double doors feet first if she'd had feet. No limbs, pallid breasts and crotch, a fleshless abdomen. I kept shifting my gaze. If there's a right way to look at half a naked dead woman, I never learned it.

Hay's other assistant had to leave with Schate's body and if Sergeant Reles wanted to stay, would he help out as scribe?

Hay cut down vertically between the breasts, peeled back the flaps, took something like a chain cutter and snipped open the ribs one by one. Then she stood over the remains in fresh gloves, dictating: "Liver somewhat enlarged . . ."

"Alcohol?" I asked.

"Just take this down." Number One tubed blood and bile. "Dead a few days. Refrigerated most of that time." I could have told her that but I kept my mouth shut. A three-day decomp leaves a stink you can't get out of your nostrils for days. Makes you want to smell some nice fresh shit for relief.

Hay cut a lung loose and weighed it. "Right lung three hundred eighty-five grams." Then, "Left lung three ninety grams. Petechial hemorrhages on surface of lungs." More cutting and weighing, liver, spleen and heart.

"What can you get from disecting the heart?"

She glared daggers. "It's *diss*-ect, with a short *i*. Not *di*-sect."

"Uh-huh."

"You can *bi*-sect, you can *dis*-assemble. You can't *di*-sect." She watched me for some sign of assent, didn't get it, and looked back at the table. The kidneys got a "Hmm" out of her and she sliced one open. "See that?" she asked. White specs freckled the cross-section of kidney. "Talc. Or whatever they're using to cut heroin nowadays. Probably heroin."

"Shit."

"Disappointed?" She cut open what she told me was the uterus. "Papilloma. Probably HPV. And chlamydia. For a while, too. The fallopian tubes are clogged with scar tissue. I'd say late teens, early twenties at the oldest."

"How . . . ?"

She prodded the tissue with her scalpel so I could see it bounce back. "The organs are full grown, but still plenty of elasticity, in spite of the damage. Ribs soft, not calcified. Iliac crest not fused yet. No more than twenty-two. Young adult, no question."

Hay cut open the stomach, flooded with a milky fluid. "Semen," she said. "More than one brand. Not much of an eater otherwise. Peptic ulcer, stomach cashing in on itself. And this." With tweezers, she lifted a small charm out of the stomach and held it up, a ghoulish little black skull, chipped white paint in the caverns of its cheekbones and marking its irregular front teeth. A loop on top for a string. The teeth made me flash on Joey at the bottom of 2222, in the white Chevy drenched with water from the fire trucks, body burned beyond recognition, head flung back at an impossible angle, chipped front tooth sticking out of the black crepe of his face.

I blinked and pulled myself back into the room. Why this charm? A cult killing? "Was it forced down her throat?"

"It'd be in her throat. I say she swallowed it."

I asked if I could have the charm. Hay raised an eyebrow.

"You want me to wash it off first?"

"Can you test her for other diseases?"

"What difference does it make? She's dead."

The fumes burned my eyes. "Would you just do it."

Hay to Number One: "Tell Serology to test her for everything—HIV, syphilis—Sergeant Reles is concerned about her health. While we're at it, see what you can find out about different drugs, opiates especially. Kidneys don't look so good. And do ABOs, genotypes, phenotypes, PGM, EAPs. Maybe we can match them to something."

I shoved my way out to the reception area to breathe, and think about this girl with the voodoo charm in her belly. The long-haired boy still sat in the chair where I'd parked him, pale and sweating in the cool room.

"I just talked to Rick this morning," he said when I dropped into the seat next to him. "He stayed at his girl-friend's. He was supposed to meet us."

"I'm sorry."

He looked at me, a lost kid. "What do I do?" I couldn't think of anything so I gave him my card and, like an idiot, wrote my home number on it. He read the card. "Homicide?"

"Rick was an accident. I'm here for something else." I was trying to think about how I could cross out my home number without it looking suspicious.

"You're the first decent cop I ever met."

"It takes all kinds."

Back in the autopsy room, Hay dropped the skull charm in a specimen cup of alcohol and handed it to me like a highball.

Joey winked at me from the autopsy table and vanished. "Cause of death?" I asked.

"Undetermined," she said. "The hemorrhages on her lungs, maybe asphyxiation. If we had the neck I could tell you if she'd been strangled. Figure strangled, maybe suffocated, maybe bludgeoned. I'm making casts of the flesh cuts in case you find something to match them to."

"Neat work," I said. "Think he had a medical background?"

"Or a butcher," she said.

"Can you test the semen?" I asked, glancing at the cavern where the girl's stomach had been.

Hay peeled off her mask and gloves as she walked to the sink. "Draw it," she told Number One. "See what Serology can figure out." She pumped red liquid soap into the palm of her hand, then turned to me. "And if nobody claims it in thirty days, it's yours."

4

Home Sweet Homicide

11:30 A.M. APD Homicide Squad Briefing Room

A newspaper story on police brutality prompted the Fifth Floor to bring in a conflict avoidance consultant who lectured us on the levels of force. He left his chart on the wall:

1. COMMAND PRESENCE: BEING THERE.
2. VERBAL DIRECTIVE: "PUT YOUR HANDS ON THE WALL."
3. PHYSICAL DIRECTIVE: PUSHING SUSPECT AGAINST WALL.

Jeffries added a final level in grease pencil:

4. *Beating suspect to death.*

Senior Sergeant Lloyd "Buck" Jeffries, lead cracker, waddled in, tossing a sneer in my direction, followed by sidekick Milsap, and sat opposite me. Both wore cowboy boots, their badges and guns cleverly concealed under Buddha-size guts. Jeffries slicked his reddish-brown hair back from his ruddy face with what could have been lard. He was the bigger and fatter of the two, but no bigger than our CO. "I weigh more, but Jeffries is fatter," Miles told me once. "He *thinks* fat. Jeffries has a fat soul."

I assaulted Jeffries a few weeks earlier for a comment he made during our last full-squad case, the ice cream killings. Somebody robbed an ice cream joint at closing, then covered his trail by torching the place and killing the staff, four teenage white girls, what the press likes to call "innocent victims."

In the months after Joey died I drank every night. When my number came up on the ice cream thing, I couldn't pull it together to take charge. Miles pulled me from the case, the first black mark on my record. The second came a week later when I found Jeffries in a taco joint, letting loose with some ideas about Mexicans. I told him to cool it. Jeffries jolted to see me, then grinned, oozing malice. "Didn't mean nothin' by it, Reles. I *like* Mexican barbecue!" Suddenly the image of Joey Velez's charred body flashed across my eyes. My skin ran hot, the fury bubbled up in my chest and it burst to the surface before I saw it coming.

Jeffries was out of commission for two days. "I didn't do *nothin'*," he told Miles. "Damn Jew walks in and goes psycho on me." Miles suspended me immediately. The rage I'd learned as a kid, that had cost me my marriage, now jeopardized my job. Jeffries always hated Joey Velez for being Mexican, marrying a white woman, making Senior Sergeant first, and God knows what else. He hated me from the day Joey mentored me onto the squad, a New

York Jew college boy. And now he hated me for knocking
the shit out of him in front of witnesses. And fresh back
from suspension, I had two strikes on my record—fucking
up on the case and assaulting Jeffries. He'd do anything to
help me get that third strike.

The secret about the rumor of my insanity was that it
was partly true. In the months after Joey's death there were
days I couldn't form a whole sentence, nights I woke up
screaming from my dreams. I'd see flashes of Joey everywhere. A moment's thought made me realize it was just
my imagination, but my imagination was as vivid as my
nightmares: I dreamed almost as much awake as I did
asleep. Sometimes it was hard to know the difference.

So after suspension I vowed to pull it together. I
couldn't make myself sane, so I decided to act sane. What
cop would know the difference? If it seemed like people
were laughing at me, I'd act like they weren't. No way of
knowing if I imagined it or not. And if I saw Joey I'd remind myself he wasn't there. But when acting crazy might
give me an advantage, I wouldn't pass it up.

Internal Affairs determined the squad had "internal ran-
cor" and bounced Jeffries's buddy, Marks, back to Vice.
Velez and Marks got replaced by Lonnie Waller from Vice
and James Torbett from Narcotics. Torbett was black—you
could hear jaws drop the first time he walked into the squad
room. No surprise he didn't laugh off the nigger jokes Jeffries liked to tell when he was feeling warm and friendly.

The squad settled into the Briefing Room. Torbett sat on
the left, solid build, five-ten, thirty-nine, gray suit and tie,
every muscle in his face clenched high-blood-pressure
tight. In interviews he put on this "don't mind me I'm just

a sleepy cop" face. But his silences during bullshitting sessions won him the suspicion of the squad and the nickname "Reverend" behind his back.

Between Torbett and me sat Lonnie Waller, a neat, goofy, low-key brownshoe with plastic-frame glasses, thinning sandy hair, forty or so; divorced, no kids, no accent. Born in Utah, Waller might have been considered suspect by the squad of Texans, but my New York accent and swarthy complexion took the heat off him so I think he was grateful. He was sharp and quick-witted in a way that no one else on Homicide was, and it made me want to see him as a co-conspirator, two immigrants on a squad of shitkickers.

Torbett and Waller got partnered together a lot since they joined Homicide at the same time, but nothing between them smelled like friendship. Partnerships on the force were unofficial: you could get teamed with someone for as little as a ten-minute interview if it suited the case. After Joey died I didn't stick with anyone for more than a day and I didn't plan on it. But if I did, Waller was first in line.

Jake Lund was a wiry computer information search specialist with a badge and a gun. A fresh haircut gave away the forceps marks in his skull—the outside world didn't interest him from the start—and he sat across from Torbett with a Dr Pepper and a box of Jujubes. He traded regular duties when he could for the privilege of chasing information on the computer or the phone. These trades were strictly *verboten* but he was worth more in the office so the brass let it slide.

Our CO sat down last, on my right. Lieutenant Miles Niederwald, head of Homicide, forty-six but could pass for sixty, two-hundred and fifty pounds under a stooped back and wisps of white hair flaked with dandruff specks the size of maggots. A professional drunk, Miles white-knuckled it until lunch, then painfully rationed enough drinks to get through the day without passing out or getting the shakes. Once I asked him if he ever drank water and he grimaced. "Fish fuck in it."

At Joey's memorial, Miles kept me from following Joey's wife, Rachel, when she walked out on the eulogy, delivered by newly appointed police chief Lucille Denton: ". . . years of service, shining example." Denton didn't say Joey was a credit to his race but I could tell she wanted to. When she got up to her friendship with Joey (they never met), Rachel made a good clip up the aisle and pushed out the double doors. Miles's fat hand grabbed me as I jumped up to follow. "Don't," he said. "Everyone'll think you're screwin' her."

Miles wore the look of defeat you see on older cops outranked by women, in this case Chief Lucille Denton, a fifty-something heel-clopping office-manager type from California. Her name brought a scowl to his face. She was at APD less than a year and her strong suit was looking good on TV: most of APD wanted to see how good she looked on pavement, outlined in chalk.

Miles Niederwald the CO, Jeffries and Milsap the crackers, Jake the geek, Torbett the reverend, Waller the joker and Reles the nut: all present and accounted for. Used to be Joey would lead the briefing and I'd toss in useful details. Not today. The room reeked of ammonia. Jake chewed Jujubes, Waller flicked the flint on his lucky Zippo lighter, Jeffries spit tobacco juice into a Coke bottle, all watching to see what crazy Reles would do. Waller leaned toward me with a grin and whispered, "I bet Jake twenty bucks you'd flip out before the end of the briefing.

Do it and we'll split the difference." I swigged coffee,
killed half the fluorescents and lit up a slide of the underpass. I said, "Case Number 88-09-12-H-0026."

"25," Jeffries said.

"Waller's murder-suicide was 25, this is 26. Victim
found in the ravine under the 700 block of East Twelfth,
arms, legs and head missing, neck missing, skinned
around the midriff." I lit up the autopsy slide, the mutilated torso on Hay's table, the strip around the middle
exposing a four-inch-high view of her stomach, intes-
tines, et cetera. Not a sound in the room. "All we got is
female, white or possibly light-skinned Latina, likely
brunette, late teens or early twenties, and blood typing
info. ABO: A-negative. PGM: one neg. Genotype: AH.
Phenotype: A. EAP: BA. Date of birth: say '65 to '71 at the
outside. Dead three or four days, refrigerated. Keep an
eye out for more parts we can match, similar actions in
the past."

Miles moved close to me, but not so close as to keep
anybody from hearing him. "Tell 'em the rest."

"Thanks, Miles. From the damage to her uterus," autopsy slide, "she had human papilloma virus and chlamydia, and she had 'em for a while." I could see them
mentally putting on rubber gloves.

"Tell 'em the rest."

I made a note to scratch Miles off my Christmas card
list. "Enlarged liver and kidney discoloration, likely alcohol and drug abuse." Their interest in the case was already slipping—cops want to think they're avenging an
innocent—but I couldn't let Miles prompt me again so I
gave them the works. "Multiple strains of semen in the
vagina, no violent penetration. And multiple strains of
semen in her stomach." Burst of laughter from the

squad. Belly full of spunk, just another whore killing. "We don't assume she was a whore," I said as the chuckles wound down. "And if she was, there's still a law against killing her."

We took turns being in charge, but most homicides were more straightforward and didn't warrant more than one or two officers. This was my first full-squad case without Joey, not counting the ice cream killings. If we didn't nail it fast, I'd be rotated off the squad before the file got closed—unsolved. I left the lights off, the projector humming and the autopsy slide on the screen. "Whoever left these remains in Shit Creek had no trouble getting rid of the rest of the body. Al's Corpse Disposal and Dog Food Factory wasn't gonna take the arms and legs and refuse the torso. And if they did, no one would drop it in a heavily trafficked area six blocks from HQ unless they wanted it to be found."

Torbett: "You saying he was trying to get caught?"

I shrugged.

Waller: "Maybe he's a psycho."

Jeffries: "Or just really stupid."

Me: "Who'd be smart enough to cut up the body that neat and stupid enough to leave it where he did?" No answers. "Think out loud. No points off for stupid ideas."

Jake: "Someone trying to send a message?"

Me: "To who? No one would know who the victim was."

Torbett: "Gang related?"

Everyone: "There are no gangs in Austin." Universal laughter, except Reverend Torbett.

Jake: "Sex crime?"

Me: "Maybe. She could have been kidnapped and used for a sex slave, but for how long? Factor in the advanced stages of multiple sexually transmitted diseases, absence of violent penetration." Jeffries chewed that thought, then spit a long stream of tobacco juice into his bottle.

"Jake, I want you all over the Missing Persons files." I slid him a folder. "See what you can find in the right age range, check blood types if you have them. Keep an A file of everything that looks possible, a B file of everything that's not impossible."

"Big fuckin' file," he said.

"You'll need those handy when we find more information."

Jeffries: "*If* we do."

"Homicide is the final act of aggression," I said, shooting Joey's words at Jeffries. "Final and irrevocable. You came to this squad so you'd never have to ask questions like right or wrong. Once a guy kills somebody, he's wrong. Enjoy it." Silence as I handed out copies of a map I'd drawn grids all over and slid a manila file to Jeffries. "Jeffries and Milsap, this is a printout of the butchers in the area. Ask questions and search the premises."

Jeffries snorted. "Got no warrant."

"Tell them if they volunteer you'll be out in ten minutes. If they don't, you'll have to close them down to do a thorough search when the warrant comes. Torbett and Waller, I want you to talk to Vice and get a list of pimps in Charlie Sector, names, photos, records, haunts. Divvy them up and start rousting. Start with anyone who has cases pending, especially possession or assault and battery. Make 'em rat out their friends. After that, Jeffries take area A, north of East Twelfth and west of the ravine. Milsap area B, including the methadone clinic; Torbett C, including Planned Parenthood; and Waller D. Start close to the dump site and work outward. The stores and bars listed at the bottom are places where I know people. I'll take those and the Casa Rosa complex. We'll meet back at Casa Rosa at five with whatever we got so far and regroup."

Jake asked, "What are we gonna call her?"

I'd given it some thought. "Sally."

Jake hummed, "Mustang Sally."

Waller suggested, "Long tall Sally."

Jeffries said, "Dirty Sally," the name of a university area bar with a penchant for vice.

I nodded. "Let's just call her 'Sally.'" Everybody seemed to go along with it. But I could tell which one would stick.

Jeffries: "Why Charlie Sector?"

"*If* she was a streetwalker it's fifty-fifty she worked there. If she was a junkie she probably scored dope there. We know that's where she landed."

Torbett: "What do we ask?"

"Talk it up. What kind of action is going on in the neighborhood? What's anybody heard? Any fights? Lovers' spats, angry pimps, whores looking to get out, cults . . ."

Waller with a sparkle in his eye: "Did anyone notice a girl they haven't seen lately?"

"With scabby knees," Jeffries said, and laughed.

No motive, no suspects, no ID on the victim. The best thing we had was a doer who didn't mind fucking with the cops, and cops glad for the excuse to roust some pimps. Small pieces of a big puzzle. And the black charm she swallowed. If it wasn't the perfect crime, it would do until something better came along.

But I'd been disciplined twice. Sally was my chance to become a rising young detective again—my last chance. Jeffries whispered something to Milsap loud enough for me or anyone else to hear, about "Tonto" not being much good without "the Lone Ranger." Or at least I thought he did.

Milsap said, "Hey, what's the matter with Reles?"

Jeffries said, "Some cops don't handle stress so good. Depends how you grew up."

I said, "Hey, Jeffries, did I tell you about my dream?"

He eyed me. "No."

I leaned into the light of the projector, Crazy Reles. "I dreamed we were in prison and you were my bitch."

The squad froze. Terror slammed Jeffries's huge face. *"Whut?!"*

"Yeah, there we are in Huntsville and I'm fuckin' your fat ass." I punched my palm. "Bam! Bam! Bam! I wonder what it means."

Miles covered his eyes. Another moment of dead silence before Waller broke it with a guffaw and flicked on the lights. The squad broke into laughs except for Jeffries himself, beet red and breathing heavily like a cornered animal, and Torbett, who never laughed, only listened.

I looked around the table. "The first seventy-two hours determine everything. Public Information is doing a good job of keeping a lid on this. Today the big story is a bus accident. No guarantees for tomorrow. When the press comes in, figure Jack the Ripper stories, mutilation pictures, Denton'll get curious. And we fuckin' well better have something to show her."

"I'll show her a luncher," Jeffries muttered.

"Have lunch on your own time," I said. "We're not eating this one. That goes for the rest of you. Before someone turned her out on the street she went to high school with your kid sister. This guy's good at cutting up girls. If he's done it before he'll do it again. So you can dick around till he finds a classier victim or you can do your fuckin' job and find out who hacked up Sally."

But before we could guess who killed her we had to find out who she was, this faceless girl who was so important that someone cut her up and left the rest for pickup. Who was she and who needed her this dead?

And how many more would be gone before we found out?

5

12:30 P.M. Casa Rosa Apartments, East Twelfth Street

Joey used to tell me 97 percent of a detective's work is re-search; the last 3 percent is outright terror. The problem is you never know when the terror's gonna come.

By the pink stucco walls of Casa Rosa: "Do you know any of the girls in the complex?"

"No."

"How long you been working here?"

"Two years."

"Twenty units in the building. You been the super two years and you don't know any of the girls?"

"Well, yeah there's this one girl works out of number 11 by the washing machine—"

"What do you mean 'works'?"

"Well . . ."

I was good on my own, but with two of us, Joey and me, shooting questions rapid-fire, no one stood a chance.

Joey: When did you start working for Bertrand Gautier?

Car thief: I didn't.

Me: So you know him?

Car thief: I didn't say that.

Joey: But you do know him. [No answer.]

Me [to Joey]: He doesn't know if he knows him.

Joey [ad-libbing]: You better know him. He owns that tow truck you were driving.

Car thief: Fuck.

Me: You been in on this since the beginning?

Car thief: No, just this month. . . .

Me on my own: Knock, knock. Door opens, number 11. Bodacious Latina, a familiar face from the Joey days, long red-tinted black hair and fiery green eyes, wearing not much of anything and bursting out of it. Gravity was someone else's problem. She went by the name Vita.

"Hey, Tonto! Come on in!"

"This is business."

"They all say that."

"You been holdin' your little ear to the ground?"

She breathed close to me. "Any position you want."

"We're trying to track down this hooker."

"What'd she do?"

"What she mostly did was got killed. Maybe some john killing hookers."

"Shit." She stepped back. "Who was she?"

"That's what we're trying to find out. Think hard. Who do you know who you haven't seen in a while? Skinny, white or light Latina."

"That's a joke, right?"

"No."

"What are you gonna give me?"

I sighed. "Vice is planning a big sweep."

"Big surprise."

I leaned in. "Stay away from the parks."

"Really?" She dropped back, thoughtful. "Okay. There's Missy. Ain't seen her for a while."

"White? Black? Latina?"

"Latina."

"Anybody else in this building besides you operating a home business?" No answer. "No busts. I just want to find out about this girl."

She sighed. "Fuck it. They'll get killed before you bust 'em. Two stupid white boys downstairs in number 5 wanna be dealers."

12:45 P.M. East Seventh Street

Sergeant Carl Milsap rode shotgun in Senior Sergeant Lloyd "Buck" Jeffries's Grand Prix, cruising along Seventh Street toward the first butcher shop. Milsap watched Buck chewing a fried chicken leg and thought what he'd been thinking since the ice cream thing, how maybe he and Buck had played too hard for too long. The near-misses were getting closer together. Buck was shaking down the owner of the taco place the day Reles clobbered him there. If the fight hadn't happened, Reles could have guessed what was up and blew the whistle. "We coulda lost our badges, even gone to Huntsville. We sent lots of guys to Huntsville. Some of them was innocent." If they got hold of Milsap . . . he didn't want to think about it.

Buck chuckled, tossed the chicken bone out the window. "They don't find nothin' they don't wanna find. Look at that." Buck pointed at a familiar figure, a skinny blond hooker, bouncing along the sidewalk. She spotted

the car and scampered up an alley between two stores.
Bad idea.

"You got your twenty, Buck. You could retire."

Buck pulled in and cornered her. "Hell no," he
grinned, climbing out of the car. "Havin' too much fun."

Milsap held her still while Buck Jeffries took her
money and slapped her. Milsap hated doing it but he
wouldn't cross Buck, not after all they'd been through together. He wouldn't dare. And Buck only slapped
women—he would never punch one. But he'd surprised
Milsap a few times before with what he *would* do, and Milsap hoped this wasn't one of those times. "I don't know.
Leave me alone!" she shrieked. And then finally, "Tula!"

"Tula?"

"Or Lula. Something like that. Mexican."

"Who'd she work for?" Jeffries roared.

"I don't know. I saw her here lots of times, and once on
the Strip." Buck signaled Milsap to let the woman go, and
she fell to her knees on the alley pavement.

"Anybody else?"

She held her hand up to protect her face. "That's all I
can think of. I swear."

Buck unpocketed the small roll of bills and handed it
back. Milsap thought, This wasn't so bad. The girl grabbed
the roll then looked up from the ground and noticed Buck
was waiting for something. "Thank you," she said.

Buck said, "Looks like I just saved you a bad beatin'
from your boyfriend."

"Yeah, I guess." She put the bills in her purse, pulled
out a tissue and a mirror.

"So I guess there's no hard feelings."

"No," she sniffled.

"You mean it?"

Buck stepped closer to where she knelt, hoisted his belly and unzipped his fly. Milsap looked away, thinking how it could have been worse. Much worse.

12:45 P.M. Casa Rosa Apartments, Number 5

Show of force, Joey would remind me. *Emphasis on show. Like you're saving something for the honeymoon. They're only a little shook up by what you did, twisted their arm a little, smashed a few bottles. They're scared shitless of what you're gonna do next.*

Close enough to the first-floor door of apartment 5 to hear two male voices. I gauged the door at about six ounces, kicked it open for show, waved my badge and .38 and yelled, "Freeze!" at two piss-scared white college boys frozen at a bridge table in front of a big steel scale and a teaspoon of white powder.

"You boys mind answering some questions?"

1:45 P.M. East Seventh Street

Sergeant James Torbett thought for the first time today about how the detective manual said not to flash your badge unless necessary—and how it didn't add "Unless you're black and nobody will believe you're a cop anyway." Waller's pimp list somehow got divvied up without Torbett, no surprise, and Torbett headed off into Charlie Sector alone. He flashed his badge at a massage parlor and got the half-answers he expected. He wasn't even surprised when the hints he dropped about a Jack the Ripper targeting neighborhood hookers didn't get him more than blank stares.

Keep the focus on what's right. It doesn't matter how you feel; it matters what you do. Torbett kept a hatful of slogans like these to take as he needed them, and he needed them: not just the day his baby sister made the mistake of going to the police after getting sterilized at an abortion clinic; not just the day nineteen years ago when Torbett was three days back in the world—a badass veteran at twenty—and had to bail out Alvin, his big brother, only brother, who'd been scooped up for being black after sundown and trounced for resisting arrest; not just the day two years later when he found Alvin dead, OD'd on the painkiller cocktails he'd been mixing himself ever since that truncheon crack on the spine; not just the day Nan begged him not to become a cop, and not just the day he graduated from the Academy, honor grad, when the commandant shook his hand and said, "You're a smart boy, Torbett. Don't be so smart, you'll live longer." But every day, every day and ten times a day. *If I don't do it, who's gonna do it? If it's not me, who's it gonna be? Who's gonna watch out for us?*

He braced himself, put on his sleepy look and walked up the steps of Planned Parenthood.

2:00 P.M. H-E-B Supermarket

I knocked on every door at the Casa Rosa Apartments and hit a dozen stores and bars around it. Then I pulled in at the H-E-B on East Seventh to grab a sandwich, pocketed my keys and felt the skull in my pocket, the little black skull with the chipped front tooth. *Joey,* I thought, *help me or get out of my face.*

The guy who left Dirty Sally in the ravine wanted more

attention. He had another show planned, maybe more than one. I could wait for the bodies to mount up as I tried to predict a pattern from pushpins on a map, or I could try to get ahead of him. But to do that I needed to be smarter than I was, at least smarter than I was alone.

I started to think about Joey's scrawls on napkins, the maps and diagrams he drew of cases. I never paid any attention to them. I never had to. If I could look at a few, maybe I could find a model for this case.

In the supermarket I grabbed a prewrapped sandwich and dialed Rachel's office from a pay phone.

"Capital Realtors."

"Rachel Velez, please."

"Excuse me?"

"Rachel Ve—"

"Oh, Rachel, she's on another call. Would you like to hold?"

A six-year-old girl in a pink party dress wandered from her mother's shopping cart and asked me for a dollar.

"Rachel Renier." Rachel's sultry voice. She pronounced it "Ruh-NEER." French name, Texas pronunciation.

"I thought it was Velez."

Pause, chuckle. *"Don't you have any friends you can play with?"* Cool tones, hot underneath.

"No, I'm all alone."

"It was Renier first. You try to sell houses with a Mexican name."

"I need something."

"Can't you get it from someone else?"

"Joey's stuff. Papers, notebooks. Crazy diagrams on napkins and paper scraps. He must have left it lying around."

"Oh, that. His papers are in a box. I redecorated."

"Can I see it?"

In the silence I wondered what she was wearing, and dug my thumbnail into my finger to shake off the thought.

"Call over the weekend," she said. *"I have a busy—"*

"How about tonight?"

"Why the rush, cowboy?"

"I'll grab the box and go. I swear."

She said, *"I'll call you when I'm free,"* waited a moment and hung up.

6

5:00 P.M. Casa Rosa Apartments

I met the squad at Casa Rosa and we pooled our info. From all our bush-beating we had a dozen hooker names; on follow-up, most of the girls were still alive. We couldn't find a Latina hooker named Tula or Lula, and another one named Vicki who was maybe white or maybe Latina or maybe not. Vice gave us mug shots of girls working under the same or similar nicknames, and I gave them to Torbett and Waller to track. We'd also attached names to two pimps Vice had no leads on: Ray, a white guy with dreadlocks, and Lyle, a black guy with a cut-up face and a gun-metal gray Cadillac. Jake had twenty missing females born in Texas between '65 and '71 with A-negative blood; the list was growing and he was making phone calls. Jeffries and Milsap didn't find anything at the supermarkets and butcher shops.

I sent them off and drove south, figuring I'd grab a bite on South Congress and work the Strip once it got dark. The local radio stations said something about Rick Schate getting flattened by that bus, left his name out, and not a word about the murder. Yet.

It would be the first time I ate at Magnolia Café since Joey died. I hated going there without him, but the case kicked something loose in me. I missed him. The closest I could get to seeing him was to hang where we had hung, be with someone else who missed him too.

Someone besides Rachel.

For the nice folks in Central Austin, students and ex-students who stayed in town for the atmosphere, the town is clean and pretty. Cappuccino shops and clubs and crunchy-granola hippie hangouts like Mag's. For cops and hoods, the town is pool halls, whorehouses, crack dens. Cops see the nicest houses only when there's a corpse on the rug. Even the same sights look different: that refurbished two-story number on Twenty-eighth Street is desirable real estate to someone—to me it's where that architect gutted his wife in front of their kids.

The crossover point between the nice Austin most nice folks see, and the bleak one I know, is Magnolia Café, thanks to the rare, magical words "Open All Night."

I walked into the chilled air of the restaurant past the unmanned host's desk and dropped down in a booth on a cracked vinyl seat, the table protected by clear plastic stapled over a batik tablecloth. Vapors of six varieties of coffee wafted between the mournful moans of Tom Waits over the speakers. Blackboards barked the day's hippie specials and mysterious desserts. Pictures hung for sale, huge pencil sketches of the staff: A long-haired waiter with a bandana, the fry cook in his huge knit hat, a waitress with multiple tattoos and nose rings and probably more piercings for the man lucky or unlucky enough to find them. And Paul, the manager.

Paul and Joey grew up in the same border town, across the street from each other. Paul was about ten years younger, an only child with a sickly mom and an absentee dad. Joey kept an eye on him, kept the tough kids off Paul's back. When Paul's mother died, Joey's mom took him in, raised him up, even helped him get to college.

Joey and I used to come in here a lot and Paul sat with us. In spite of his border-town origins, Joey had no accent unless he needed it or was drunk. Paul talked like a college boy. But when they got together their accents got thicker and thicker. In a few minutes, they'd be speaking a Spanish I couldn't make head or tail of on my best day. But Joey bringing me to hang with him and his oldest friend was a gesture I didn't miss. Paul and I didn't have much in common—just two orphans Joey took in.

Today Paul sauntered over in an Izod tennis shirt and khaki shorts with a cup of black coffee and a sad smile on his face, grinding his voice to a Bob Dylan tune.

"The cops don't need you and man they expect the same."

He put the coffee in front of me and slipped into the booth. "Asshole," I smirked, sipping.

"Two-skin!" A two-skin, by Paul's reasoning, would be half a foreskin, a reference to my mixed lineage. "How's it hangin'?"

We tossed it back and forth for a few minutes. We couldn't talk about Joey. What would we say? "He was doing really great. He was really focused at the end there. You think he was partying too much?" So the conversation rolled down to a sad halt, but he sat with me anyway until my burger came. I waved at him as I walked out the door.

At a pool hall down the Strip, I chatted up a hustler I knew and watched him lose five dollars to me like a master. He blew easy shots by millimeters and used them to set up ones I couldn't miss blindfolded. When he offered to double the bet I tried out some of the names I'd heard.

"No, I don't know no Lyle," he said. "Hey, you gonna give me a chance to win that fiver back?"

I caught the gaze of a pimp I knew, his head shaved bald except for inch-and-a-half sideburns, giving me the evil eye across the room, so I bummed a smoke and strolled out front. I was blowing out my first drag when he appeared by my side.

I said, "How's it goin', Rich?"

"Don't be fuckin' with me, you don't even smoke."

"What are you so rank about?"

He waved at the darkness and a skinny blonde in hot pants appeared out of nowhere, with one of her cheeks bruised and dried blood on her lower lip.

"Was a cop did this."

I shook my head, dropped the Marlboro. "Shit."

"I ain't shittin'!"

"I believe you. What cop?"

"That fat fucker."

"Right, the fat cop."

"No, man, them two fat fucks from Homicide. The big one and the little one."

Jeffries and Milsap.

"They was slappin' her around tryin' to find some ho' they don't even know. Then they gave the money back like they was doin' her a favor and made her suck they fat dicks and didn't even pay."

I peeled off a twenty and handed it to her. Then another. Rich nodded and took the money from her, then motioned her into the dark. I tried the names on him.

"Don't know no Vicki. Know a Niki. Scaggy white chick fucked up on horse. Hardly nothin' left of her."

"When'd you see her last?"

"Who knows, man. A month? Down by the Sands."

"It's boarded up."

"Them raggedy chicks don't care. What you want her for, anyway?"

"I'm trying to find out if she's still suckin' air."

"Give it up, man. Girl like that die of OD or starve. She ain't ate in six months I bet."

I asked him if he'd seen anything around her neck, maybe a Mexican charm or something.

"Never got that close. Who'd want to?"

I talked to some of the girls working the Strip and got more of nothing. After a few hours I headed home.

Hyde Park was an old neighborhood north of the university, dating back to when it was a suburb of Austin, a horse-and-buggy ride from the town proper. My block was strictly rentals; some of the houses, like mine, no more than three- or four-room shacks. My bedroom sat on the front right corner of the house, with the bathroom and kitchen behind it, and a screened-in porch we never got around to using. The living room on the front left had a couch, chair next to a phone on an end table, and a TV. Amy furnished on a shoestring when we moved in, Salvation Army couch, wicker chairs, trunk for a coffee table, all covered with cute little Indian throws, perfect for when I'd come home with a newspaper under my arm and say, "Hi, honey, I'm home!" I did that once as a gag and got a few extra kisses for it, in the early days when we were playing house, spending a lot of time in bed and a lot of time laughing. Everything was new. But the newspaper under the arm didn't take. You can't follow a question like "How was your day?" with "Pulled a dead baby out of an oven. And yours?" Amy replaced the furniture piece by piece, the overstuffed white couch and chair now gone gray, and big framed art prints, Matisse and Picasso, that she took when she left and I never replaced. The bare walls gave the house a half-furnished, empty feel that I got used to. An arch headed to what had been the dining room; that's where I set up my weights and drums.

The house baked sauna-hot when I walked in. I cranked the A/C and it revved like a train engine, spitting water. I stripped off my belt and holster and emptied my pockets: wallet, badge, keys, and the girl's charm, the shining black skull. I held it up to the light. How long since I'd played with anything so small, like a tiny plastic car or a fake tattoo, before I was ten and my childhood suddenly ended. *You weren't lucky for her,* I thought. *Be lucky for me. Tell me something, before the next body turns up.*

I peeled off my shirt and pants, pulled on shorts and sneakers. Fifteen minutes jumping rope, ten hard on the heavy bag, ten whapping the speed bag, push-ups and sit-ups. Going over the specs of the case in my head.

A girl got killed and diss-ected. Stories dead-ended on a Vicki or a Niki, and a Lula or a Tula; a black pimp named Lyle with a scarred face and a gun-metal gray Cadillac, and one called Ray who was white and had dreadlocks. Set up the weights and start pounding them.

There was no gym in town where I could work out like this except at HQ, and the last thing I wanted to do after spending twelve hours with cops was to sweat with them and hear what they had to say in a locker room when they relaxed. When I was done, I turned on the stereo and sat at the drums.

My vinyl collection, heavy with R&B and R&R from Memphis Minnie to the Rolling Stones to Stevie Ray Vaughan, was practically the only material thing that mat-

tered to me. Besides the drums and my mother's eight-by-
ten glamour shot hidden in a dresser drawer, those records
were all that marked the house as mine. Rock and roll is
about standing up to the man. Once I graduated from the
Academy, I *was* the man. My uniform got me dirty looks
almost everywhere I went. So I'd go out and fight crime
the best I could, then go home and bang on my drums
while blasting The Who.

You can't keep up with Keith Moon. He does the work
of three drummers—I tried to play along with one of
them. I cranked the speakers as high as they would go, listened to the first notes, then played along, one beat for
Keith's two, then sweating to catch up. I ran pictures of the
day's hookers across my eyes, trying to decide which one
Dirty Sally looked like. White with peroxide curls? Light-
skinned Latina with green eyes? I had no face for her at all,
just a charm, but my brain wanted to fill in the blanks.
What would Joey do?

In two weeks, the department would evaluate my sanity, a follow-up on my suspension. I couldn't go back to
Criminal Investigations again. And I sure as shit couldn't
go wherever I would have to go if they bounced me off
the force.

The music roared. I banged as hard and fast as I could,
spraying sweat in all directions.

Then I showered, dressed, and headed back to the
Strip, to the places no self-respecting whore or john would
ever go.

7

1:00 A.M. South Congress Avenue

I was too early for the pre-dawn rush of discount tricks at the abandoned Sands Motel, but I slipped out of the shadows of the palm trees and listened at the doors anyway. I heard some quiet talk behind one door ("Just a second . . . there ya go . . ."), pulled my .38 and shoved the rickety door open, shouting, "Freeze!"

I froze a naked redhead with a gap between her front teeth and a belt around her thigh, and a little nerd in a grimy blue seersucker suit and a few days' patchy beard, a hypo in his hand and fury in his tiny eyes. The room stank like a sewer. The nerd froze, still holding the rig.

"APD. Put the needle down."

"Get away from me!" He stepped forward.

"Put the needle down!"

"It's hers, she gave me it!" Another step. I don't think he knew he was moving.

"Sir, you are in violation of Texas State Penal Code Section 71.02, Possession of a Controlled Substance." He kept moving. *"You are also wielding a deadly weapon against a police officer! Put the needle down or I will fire!"*

He moved, I fired between his feet and he dropped the needle, screaming, "Are you trying to kill me?!"

He ran at me like a child. I tripped him and threw him on the floor, face down.

He was shouting, "You wanna go *mano a mano* right here?" scuffling until I managed to cuff him. I dragged him to the car, called for techs to sweep the room and a patrol to take the girl.

When I threw him in the back seat he said, "Who do you think you are?"

"Shut the fuck up! If you answered a few questions you'd be free by now."

At HQ I set the two of them up in separate interrogation rooms, Seersucker with his face down, twitching and barking. "I'll sue. You wait!"

I sweated the two of them for a couple of hours, watching procedure now that they were in custody. A patrol and a young goober from Criminal Investigations witnessed from behind the two-way mirror.

The girl: Didn't know no Niki, no Kiki, no Tula. She had the geek before. He liked to shoot up with the bad girls. He gives them speed or heroin and he thinks they like him.

Seersucker, twitching and bouncing in his chair: "You don't want to do this."

"Why?"

No answer. I tried the hooker names on him. Nothing. "She gave me the coke," he said. "You'll be sorry."

"I caught you shooting up with a prostitute. That's possession and soliciting and I'm not even trying."

He struggled with the cuffs, trying to rip the chair loose from the floor it was bolted to. I asked him when he'd been at the Sands last.

"When?" he asked.

"Yeah, when."

His eyes darted around the room, then found me. "What day is it?!"

"Monday, going into Tuesday."

"No!"

"Yeah."

"It's Friday!" he insisted.

I caught a whiff of his suit. "When'd you put that suit on?"

"Friday. Thursday. No, Friday."

"Is that when you were at the Sands last?"

He scowled into a sunset he saw over my shoulder in the darkened room. "I should sleep," he said.

On a hunch I said, "When you were there on Thursday or Friday. You shot up with a skinny girl, a girl with black hair." He nodded, then stopped to think about it. "The same needle? The one we got from you tonight?"

He started clenching and unclenching his teeth. "I . . . I . . ."

"What?"

"I wiped it on the rug," he said.

I ran out of the booth and phoned the techs about the rug, then I went back in.

I watched his eyes, tried a long shot. "What did you do with the body?"

Now he stopped twitching. "What body?"

"The girl you shot up with. The black-haired girl. What did you do with her?"

He looked at me uncomprehending. Then his face ran pale and he opened his mouth to yelp but nothing came out.

He didn't know anybody was dead.

2:00 A.M. 764 North Pleasant Valley Road

"P-please, no. I can't," Emmett Tejani said. The basement's single light bulb overhead shined in his eyes.

"Sure you can," he said. "You did it before."

"I don't want to. I can't sleep."

He grabbed Emmett's collar and pulled him close. "You think I *sleep?*"

"Please," Emmett begged. "I can't close my eyes. I keep thinking of her face. Her beautiful face . . ."

Emmett felt a blow to his neck and the cement floor against his shoulder as he gasped for air. The blow was nothing to what he was supposed to do.

"Pussy! Don't tell me." He kicked Emmett in the stomach. "Four years I ate shit in that hole while you went home to your *wife!*"

"I sent money, Armand," he slobbered. "I paid your lawyers. Don't make me do this. I have kids."

Armand smiled close to Emmett's face. "You do have kids."

Everything went quiet. "No. No, Armand, not my kids, don't."

Armand lifted Emmett's shoulders and laid the man across his lap, cradling his head and stroking it. "I love you. You know that."

"Sure, but . . ."

"You love me."

"Of of course I do . . ."

Armand's tone softened. "You have to do it, baby brother. You're the only one who knows how."

8

TUESDAY

Every morning and night I thought about Rachel, and when I did, I had to think about the life I had before, and the moment I crossed the bridge from that life to this one.

Joey and I were doing tequila shots with Jake Lund in a Tex-Mex restaurant. Joey slammed two shots for every one of mine. We used to be even. He'd made a subtle shift over the last months, though I didn't see it then. Once a guy who loved to party, now one who needed to. He was cracking us up with the story of how Buck Jeffries blew his first chance at Senior Sergeant, going out alone on a domestic disturbance. Joey at his happiest, telling a story and cracking up his friends. Arms waving, huge powerful hands grabbing the essence of the situation and holding it up for inspection. "Jeffries kicks through the glass door and swoops in like a fat Superman, slams the guy in the balls and busts his teeth with the butt of his Taurus. Then he cuffs him, throws him in the car and goes back to make a play for the wife. But Jeffries doesn't cuff him tight enough."

"No."

"Yeah. The drunk dislocates his own thumb, slips out of the cuff and drives off in Jeffries's Grand Prix."

The waiters flashed us dirty looks, three drunk cops laughing like idiots. Joey turned serious and said, "I gotta go."

We said, "No, stay."

"I promised her I'd be home early."

A shadow of sadness rolled over the evening as we staggered out to our cars, saluted each other. As I was getting into my car Joey called out "Mazel tov, amigo," across the empty parking lot. Congratulations, friend. Or, Good luck.

Before morning, he was gone.

Dispatch called and woke me out of a drunken half-sleep to tell me Joey was dead in his Chevy at the bottom of a cliff, that three fire trucks and a helicopter had just succeeded in putting out the flames. It took me twenty minutes to climb down the muddy slopes to see his drenched charcoal remains. Rachel wasn't home when I called, so I drove back to their house, still covered with mud. I parked in the driveway, sat on my hood and waited. She drove up around seven A.M. wearing big sunglasses and last night's dress, and stood inches in front of me, smiling drowsy like she'd been out all night screwing and I was next. Her full red lips were chapped, lipstick eaten away. She touched the bottom lip with her tongue. "Have you boys been playing in the mud?"

I leaned close enough to smell her breath. She didn't move away. "Joey's dead," I said, and her head snapped back. "Get in the fucking car."

At the Medical Examiner's office, Miles pulled me aside. "This is bullshit. Hay can ID him."

"Mrs. Velez can take it," I said, making sure she heard. "She's a rock."

I locked my hand onto Rachel's arm and steered her into the cutting room where Joey lay on the table, most of his heavy flesh burned, a skeleton in embers, its head arched back, mouth open in a terror scream, busted tooth jutting out between shriveled black lips. Rachel squirmed.

"That's him," she said, and turned to me, the sunglasses giving her face the effect of an Italian movie star. "Sergeant Reles could have told you that."

I snarled, "I'm not next of kin."

Absence of skid marks and the word that Joey was drunk led to an unwritten "passed out at the wheel." If that word became official, she could lose his pension and life insurance. Still, at the inquest she gave half-answers from behind those same big beach-going shades. Where was he going? "Northwest on Twenty-two twenty-two." What did he say before he left? "Nothing I recall." And as she crossed those smooth tanned legs a horrible voice I tried to crush down inside me, crept up between my grief and hatred for this cold hot woman, smug and superior, miles away and right here waiting for me, who had betrayed my only friend the last night of his life. The horrible voice of desire and rage crawled up and said, Now she's mine.

8:00 A.M. Sands Motel

I had the techs sweep the motel room at the Sands for prints, hair and fibers. They pulled bodily-fluid samples from the rug in droplets and larger than droplets, owing to the way bodies relax when they die. Serology made the match while I dozed in the squad room. Dirty Sally shot up with the guy in the seersucker suit in that room, maybe in the wee hours of Friday morning, and went home to Jesus. I was pretty sure Seersucker hadn't sent her there, at least not on purpose. I was sure he hadn't hauled out the

body and cut it up. We booked him for possession and soliciting. We let the redhead go.

I didn't have a lot but I had the kill site. I could plant
patrols nearby, question everyone who stepped near the
place. Not bad for starting with a sand sculpture, I
thought.

I was still busy congratulating myself when the phone
rang. The rest of Sally was starting to show up. Fast.

10:00 A.M. Law Offices of Anderson and Guerrin, West Satellite

The gears of the universe hummed in perfect pitch as Tina
LaMarque opened the morning mail. It was a ten-minute
job that never took less than forty minutes for all the
times the phone rang. Another receptionist would sweat
it. Tina was just biding time till the big score.

She answered the phone on the first ring, smiling. "Anderson and Guerrin. One moment, I'll connect you."
Hold, transfer, extension, transfer, hang up. "Anderson
and Guerrin. . . . He's not in right now, may I take a message? All right, then. Have a good day." Hang up. Smile.

Guerrin was difficult to manage these days, with all the
projects and all the tension, and on top of that, moving
half the operation to this crazy satellite on the edge of a
swamp—the new Barton Springs office. Guerrin kept hint-
ing about private dinners and neck rubs, commenting to
Tina how he liked women like her, tall, strong brunettes
who could take care of themselves. She made sure to do
her job perfectly so he wouldn't have to cover for her and
think she owed him something. Flirting was easy. The
hard part was making sure he wanted *her*, just her, and no

one else. Guerrin hot and bothered wasn't enough. Any woman could take care of that. He had to be *obsessed*. Then she could negotiate. First real estate, *then* cootchie.

Open the envelopes. Résumés, inquiries for Anderson. Yale Alumni newsletter for Guerrin. Payment for Anderson. Payment for Draper. Legal volume for Guerrin titled *Conflict of Interests*. Large manila envelope for Guerrin. Inside it another manila envelope, labeled "Trilateral Commission." She knew not to open that one. Box for Guerrin, cold to the touch, dropped downstairs. Sushi? They should have brought it up.

She took out the big letter opener and started to cut open the box when the phone rang.

"Anderson and Guerrin."

Attorney Royce Guerrin, his silver hair artfully combed and starched over a bald spot, stood at the window of his office looking out on a huge expanse of not much. Soon Barton Springs would be heaven—country clubs, luxury condos, golf courses. Now it was nothing. Trees.

When the Barton Springs deal was complete, he could retire. But until then, that meant hundreds of man-hours a week for the office with no income. He had to work double duty to keep the office going. It would all be over in a matter of weeks, if he didn't wind up dead or in prison first.

Stacks of documents on his desk that no one else could touch waited for him, fortunes to make and protect, and for no specific reason, a rising erection in his shorts. Over fifty, courting a coronary, his suits altered every year to accommodate expanding bulk, and he still had the libido of a teenager. It would be nice to take some time off to wrestle with his voluptuous receptionist. But disaster was always just around the corner. That he'd avoided prison for twenty-five years of high-risk legal practice was no guarantee he'd avoid it in the future. High-profile attorneys often wound up holding the bag. Every week he arranged payoffs, hid evidence, covered trails. There was work to be done, rules to be played by, and boning a twenty-two-year-old on company time fell into the category of "letting your guard down." The thought was rolling around in his head when he heard Tina scream.

The sound rippled in the air. Guerrin ran to the front desk and said, "Shh. It's okay," putting his arm around her shoulder as other lawyers and secretaries gathered around them. "Nothing to worry about," he told the others, scattering them. All Tina's muscles clenched: touching them was exquisite torture. "I'm here," he breathed into her ear, then followed her gaze to the box.

Vapor escaped as he lifted the cardboard flaps. Inside, fragments of ice stuck to the plastic wrapped on an orange Styrofoam tray displaying a slab of bloody meat, a cross-section of leg with the bone in the middle like a target, maybe bloody lamb or venison. On closer glance, he noticed that there was still skin on the meat, that the skin was blue-gray and hairless. Then he saw that it wasn't quite hairless, but had very short dark hair, like razor stubble.

Guerrin's lungs seized as it dawned on him. Like razor stubble on a woman's leg.

10:30 A.M. Homicide Squad Room

The phone calls came faster than I could answer them. Ten times in the first hours of the morning, people opened their front door and found a package of something cold. They opened it, saw a chunk of bloody meat with bluish-gray skin, and started screaming before they could think. Someone was swinging by homes and offices and dropping off human flesh.

11:00 A.M. Anderson and Guerrin

Guerrin watched the TV screen thinking of Tina's terrified face. She'd screamed once, then spent half an hour shaking in his office while he calmed her and convinced her not to call the police. He sent her home in a limo and scanned the channels for news flashes: half a dozen men with the same package. He called the police himself and answered their questions with shocked innocence, blank stares when they hit him with the names of the other recipients.

Guerrin spent fifty-plus hours a week in the office, keeping up with the never-ending demands of a wife who lived to shop and two children in private universities. He hated the work from the first day. Now on the cusp of triumph, he swam a half-stroke ahead of the sharks.

He dialed the mobile phone, a new expense the size of a cinderblock. Harrell answered on the third ring.

"Frederick Harrell."

"Remember you're speaking on an unsecure line."

"Y-yes. Yes, sir."

"Is there anything I should know about?"

"No. Why?"

Guerrin listened to Harrell's breathing. "Has anything unusual come up? Any developments?"

"No, Mr. Gue—"

"No names!" Using Harrell was a mistake. But he did

the business Guerrin wouldn't and had friends who could do the dirty work. Half a step up from bail bondsman, Harrell more than anyone straddled the fine line between attorney and thug. And still it was hard to think of the man as corrupt. Utterly without malice, Harrell always seemed to be doing his very best to get along in a world too large for him.

"No. What's wrong?"

"I'm just checking." Guerrin was certain the younger man hadn't deliberately sabotaged him: that kind of complexity was beyond Harrell. But this morning's disaster stank like Frederick A. Harrell, Esquire. Static crackled on the line. "Call me back at five."

"Yes, sir."

"From a pay phone."

Guerrin watched the muted TV screen. The phone shook his hand before he heard it ring. He clicked it back on and put on his calm voice. "Yes?"

"Did you get my gift?"

Guerrin jolted. The voice put him in mind of a horny weasel. He answered politely curious. "Who am I speaking with?"

The weasel cackled. *"You tell me."*

"This is a private line. State your—"

An unearthly high-pitched screech, nails on a blackboard, and Guerrin pulled away from the phone.

"How did you get this number?" Guerrin insisted.

"Call me from a pay phone."

"What?"

"Has anything unusual come up? Any developments?"

"What are you . . . ?" He'd been listening in.

"Don't be rude. We're in business together. You just said so."

"When?"

"When you didn't hang up."

The man couldn't have tapped Guerrin's phone. He must have tapped Harrell's. Who would know to do that? "What do you want?"

"What do I want? What does everybody want? MONEY! I want MONEY! Lots of it! And if I don't get it, I'm gonna FUCK A HOLE RIGHT THROUGH YOU!"

Guerrin felt his blood pressure shoot up. "Yes . . . of course. Why don't you just come up to the office and . . ."

"And what, turn myself in? I go down, I take you with me, and whoever paid you to get that little gash out of the way. Let's look at the list. Was it Mr. Keenan? Or maybe Mr. Grant?"

"No names! We're both businessmen. I'm sure if we stay calm and use our heads, we can come to an agree—"

"Bite me! An agreement? Bite ME! I have the cards. I talk. You listen." The line went dead.

9

11:30 A.M. Medical Examiner's Office

I spent the morning running between Forensics and the Medical Examiner's. Hay laid out the new parts on the autopsy table, four slices of one arm, five of the other, and one of leg. None of the parts duplicated the others, and the arm slices fit together. Pending tests, it was safe to say they were all from the same body, Dirty Sally's body. Her killer on the move.

"Find the head," Hay said.

"I'm working on it."

She gestured to the table. "Tell *her* that."

TV cameras hovered around APD. Greer in Public Information told us he'd be on the noontime news fielding questions and trying to look calm. Torbett and I split up the list of recipients for questioning. Waller went to match the Styrofoam packages and track the deliveries, maybe figure out how they were done. Jeffries and Milsap got a fresh printout of more butcher shops to check out. I kept a copy.

We had more pieces of the puzzle. Just as many pieces as somebody wanted us to have.

11:30 A.M. 3809 Peck Avenue

Rachel Renier, formerly Velez, finished showing a house to an artist couple with a one-bedroom income and five-bedroom tastes. She showed them one they stood a chance of getting a mortgage on, and when they turned it down she lit a cigarette and left them on the lawn. She had bigger fish.

Too many cigarettes, she thought as she drove. But she never denied herself a smoke. She had to stay thin, had to look good for business reasons, so eating every time she felt low was out of the question. And if she didn't have the cigarette she might have a drink, and then she'd be back where she started. She'd been to Hell and she wasn't going back. The worst smoking could do was kill her.

She stopped at home, flipped on the TV, called the office for messages and pulled off her gray skirt and jacket. From the hall closet she grabbed a white linen summer dress—less professional by half, but she needed to stand in hundred-degree sun and not look sweaty. On the floor of the closet sat the corrugated cardboard box of Joey's things.

Joey kept most of his old papers in the box—reports, certificates, commendations. "Receipts," he'd said when she suggested framing them. "Paid bills. Keep 'em in the closet." She'd tossed in everything she found while redecorating. His notebooks, phone numbers on scraps and matchbooks. She remembered meeting Joey that first horrible night in Houston, how he showed up with her cop friend Jack when she called, hysterical. How they helped her, kept her out of trouble, told her what to say when the other police arrived. And how Joey stayed on her couch that night after they hauled the body out, held her while she shook and screamed out as she saw the moment again and again, in all its horror. "Nothing's gonna happen to you," he said.

"Why?"

"Because I'm here." And she could see for the first time his broad shoulders and heavy brow and his bearlike paws, how he held her and didn't try anything, the first time a man had held her that way, any man, and she knew she was safe.

He held her the next days, through the shakes and the night frights, with the orange juice and honey and the purloined Librium. And the third night when she started to feel better, stood frail on her pins and invited him into her bedroom. How he'd kissed her on the cheek and held her in his arms and said, "I'll wait till you grow up." And how he brought her home to Austin with him and protected her ever since. But not from her nightmares.

She knelt down and pulled out papers by the handful. Case notes, glowing evaluation reports. It was with Joey's help that she stopped drinking and getting high, turned her life around, married and played house and got a job where all you needed was fire in your belly to make money. But once the shine was off their new romance, once he saw that she could be strong and independent, once she got some flesh and muscle back on her bones and stopped looking like a punked-out waif he could rescue, he started asking questions about her old life.

"Where'd you meet him? Did you go to that club a lot?"
He grew suspicious about the first night, and the dead
man in her apartment in Houston. To this day she wasn't
sure how much Joey knew. Or what he'd told Dan.

She pulled out a letter-size brochure, *Buying Rental
Property*. It was a sucker book from the agency. She gave it
to people with great credit ratings and land-ownership
dreams. If you meticulously followed its instructions you
could wind up with mortgaged rental property your income would never cover. But your real estate broker would
have her commission long before you figured it out. She
must have thrown it in by mistake. She tossed it on the
floor face down.

On the back she saw notes Joey had scrawled in pencil. She picked it up again: *Seized property on Ulit: 150G.
Less 80 is 70G. Ten units at $200/mo.*

Joey had real estate dreams. It was her own doing, talking about it all the time, how property was the only thing
you could count on. Joey wanted property, maybe even
got as far as buying it. He never told her. But at the end he
didn't tell her anything, she had to figure out what he was
up to for herself. Alcohol. Whores. Cocaine. She knew the
signs.

And cocaine means money, coming and going. And
desperation.

She'd put the brochure aside and show it to Dan another time, maybe. She looked again at Joey's scrawl. *Less
80?* Does that mean someone was going to knock eighty
thousand off the price to be sporting? Or did Joey have
eighty thousand dollars?

And if he did, where did it come from?

11:30 A.M. Clarksville, West Austin

"Boy, you get away from the house or I'll call the police!"

Torbett had to push past a small cluster of reporters—notepads, tape recorders and a video camera, about the same at each of the ten houses—to get to the front door. He held his badge up to the peephole when he knocked again, but he learned long ago it wasn't foolproof. You can get shot at just reaching for it. Wearing a suit was better protection. And he hated going to Clarksville. Hated? He felt however you feel when the neighborhood you grew up in gets discovered by whites who decide to "renew" it, squeezing you and yours out in the process.

Edward Keenan opened the door when he saw the badge, blushing to the satin collar. He apologized, admitted Torbett, pushing the door closed against the intruders, and led Torbett to his den. Keenan's wife found the meat pack at 8:30 A.M., still cold. Keenan and the other nine men who got the packages—two surgeons, three lawyers, a bank president, a broker, a building contractor and a psychiatrist, a *Who's Who* of Austin professionals—claimed they'd never heard of one another. All receiving parts of the same young woman, infected with every venereal disease known to man, and according to Reles, meeting her end in a boarded-up motel.

They were each questioned twice and told not to talk to the press. No one saw anything get dropped. No human and no security camera on any of the residential blocks or at any of the offices. The packages were suddenly just "there." Torbett asked Keenan the same questions and recited the names for him just to watch his eyes. Nothing. Then he tried the big question.

"Whatever you say will be held in the strictest confidence."

"Of course."

"I need to know about any interactions you may have had over the last two or three years with prostitutes."

Keenan erupted. "What? How . . . how dare you!"

Torbett kept his voice sleepy, like he was reading from a script. "Ten well-off men including yourself got flesh samples delivered anonymously today and I'd like to know why you were targeted. Maybe you were involved in a business venture, or some secret club."

"I don't have time . . ."

"Neither do I." Torbett, suddenly wide awake, leaned forward enough that Keenan backed away, a vein twitching on his forehead. "I don't give a damn about your whoring parties. But if you've been holding out, I'll bust you at your office and leak the story to the papers. I'll leave my number with your *wife.*"

Torbett stepped into the hall when Keenan grabbed his arm and said, "Don't!" Mrs. Keenan saw them and froze. Keenan smiled a guilty red-faced grin. "We're almost done, honey." He pulled Torbett back into the den and plucked out a bottle and two glasses. "Drink?"

"Knock yourself out."

Keenan nodded and sipped and finally talked. "June, July maybe. I was working hard on a deal and I was all wound up. I picked her up on South Congress. We went to a motel there."

"Which motel?"

"That place with the lights. The Austex?"

"What did she look like?"

"Redhead. N-natural red," he said, like that would help

the search. "Big hips. Space between her teeth. She was always rolling the tip of her tongue on it like this."

"How tall was she?"

He held a level hand about at his nose. "I don't know. Five-six?"

"Is that barefoot or in heels?"

"Yeah. Yes."

Torbett took a breath. "Which one?"

"Heels. Definitely."

"Okay. Anyone else?"

Keenan shook his head.

"Mr. Keenan, I don't mean to be rude, but you've been married a long time. The one time you cheated on your wife was three months ago?"

His shoulders curved over. "And a ... a ..." He glanced up at Torbett and then away.

"A black one?" Torbett offered. Keenan nodded. Torbett handed the man his card. One meat catcher connected to two hookers.

Only how did anyone find Keenan's address?

11:45 A.M. Clarksville, West Austin

I buzzed my Impala between interviews on the blocks so thick with trees you could barely see the palaces behind them, the kind of block I never saw until I came to Texas as a brooding fifteen-year-old, and then I only wanted to break their windows. Ten meat packs, ten receivers' names leaked to the press, all hounded by their own personal reporters and paparazzi.

The radio crackled. *"Homicide 8."*

I picked up the mike. "Homicide 8, go ahead."

"*You got a call from Mrs. Velez. Call her at home on a land line.*"

I pulled up at a pay phone and dialed. "It's me," I said when she answered.

"*I found your souvenirs. I came home to shower. If you're here before I leave, they're yours.*"

"Can I get them later, like tonight?"

"*I'm busy later. I'll call you over the weekend.*"

"No, wait. I'll be right over." I hung up the phone, cursing with the feeling I was being played like a fish. And that I was asking for it.

12:00 P.M. Old Austin Club

A thick stripe of light from the twelve-foot-high southern window fell across Royce Guerrin's face and made him squint as he squirmed in the huge leather chair, briefcase beside him, and tried to discern the old man's thoughts through the glare. At best he could make out his silhouette in front of the antique guns on the wall. It was Guerrin who finally broke the silence. "Of course we don't really know for sure."

"Have you spoken with your man yet, your 'Mr. *Payne*,' or whatever you call him?"

"No. Not at length. It wasn't him."

"Payne didn't do it?"

Guerrin cleared his throat. "No," and didn't elaborate.

The old man's calm voice jarred Guerrin, considering the threat underneath. "Are you saying you won't tell me who you hired? Or that you don't know who you hired."

Guerrin wiped sweat from his lip, passing off the action as a thoughtful gesture. "For your protection as well as mine, I made sure to stay one remove from the . . . proceedings." A few more body parts on a few more doorsteps—teeth, hands—and the police would know who the girl was. The old man was dead silent. Guerrin couldn't hear him breathe.

Finally the old man stood, took a deep breath and began. "The Romans were far ahead of their time," he said, rounding the huge oak desk. "Technology. Political structure. The construction of the known world didn't live up to its potential, so they *re*invented it, Royce. Two thousand years ago. They restructured the world, and in that sense, created modern history."

Guerrin filled the pause. "Yes, sir."

The old man stood before him, his imposing six feet and white hair casting a shadow over Guerrin's bulk. "One poorly placed Jew threatened all that."

"Sir, please, I'm meeting with my operative this evening. I can fix this."

He nodded, reached out a small booklet from his breast pocket. "You'll have help."

"That's not necessary—"

"What do you make in a year, Royce? Eighty thousand? Ninety?"

"Something like that . . ."

"Would you know what to do with eighty million?" he asked with a distinct calmness. "Don't answer. Do you know what eighty million would cost you, or where it would come from? What the court of public opinion could do if it turned on you? The potential for disaster here is greater than you know. I didn't want to call in outsiders, Royce." His voice rumbled. "You made it necessary.

I'm hosting many valuable guests on Saturday. I want this long resolved by then."

Guerrin caved. "Yes, sir."

He leaned his face forward just enough that Guerrin could make out his solid features. "I simply asked you to tie up a loose end. What could be simpler than that?"

10

12:10 P.M. 3809 Peck Avenue

I don't know how other Jews think about Anglo women
because I don't know any other Jews. To this Jew, they're
everything he desires and hates: blue eyes never quite
looking at him, always far away. Smooth white skin that
makes his own swarthiness look dirty. Untouchable even
in his embrace. Even at her most passionate she's far off, a
thousand miles across the divide between the olive-
skinned Yids huddled around the stove for warmth and
the Aryan storm troopers who might bust in any second
and haul them away.

My father saw my mother that way. Me, I had half my
mother's blood and still, somehow, I was a Jew and she
was something far away. I could see my mother in Rachel,
and it gave me the willies. But there I was knocking at her
door trying to borrow a box of Joey while meat packs were
getting dropped and my case was blowing wide open.

I pulled up outside Joey and Rachel's house and killed

the engine. I didn't want to look at Joey's home, his coffee table, his TV. I knew I'd see him sitting in the empty easy chair, bellowing, "Beer's in the fridge, man. The game's starting!" No time for this shit. Get in, get the notes and go. There was a new car in the driveway, a sporty white Celica I guessed she'd bought with Joey's life insurance check.

I rang the bell. Rachel shouted, "Come in!"

Rachel wore a white silk robe and was towel-drying her wet hair, Anglo brown, not Jew brown, brushed back from her low forehead, big dark blue eyes turned up a little at the corner like her grandmother was a geisha, over high, wideset cheekbones and full lips. Water beaded on her smooth skin and the robe clung to the curves of her chest and hips. Barefoot, she stood five-eight or so. A flat white opal on a silver chain hung between full round breasts, and if it was supposed to make me look there, she didn't need it.

She glanced at me. "Sergeant," she said, thick, pouty lips in a half-smile. "I haven't seen you since the inquest."

"You're not counting the memorial."

"No I'm not."

"I like your car," I said.

"I sold a five-bedroom in Clarksville."

A white sofa faced the window. A white leather chair against the wall. Well-fed plants everywhere. Chrome-framed black-and-white art photos, American landscapes and French couples kissing. The stereo played some modern jazz instrumental, too modern. Glass coffee table on an off-white carpet, TV cabinet, no easy chair. Not a thing was the same, not the furniture, not the pictures on the walls, not even the lights. Only the arrangement of the windows and the stink of cigarette smoke told me I was in the right house. It wasn't Joey's home, but it wasn't Rachel's either.

I said, "The cigarette smell is pretty bad in here."

"Yes, but think how good I *look*."

"Where's his chair?"

"Did you want it?"

"No, I just—"

"Drink?"

"I can't. Where's the box."

"You look like you need a—"

"Beer."

"I don't keep it in the house anymore."

"No, you wouldn't. Not a drinker."

Her eyes glimmered. "Why don't you rustle up some franks and beans. That's your specialty, right?"

"I can boil eggs now. I took a class."

"Look in the hall closet."

The robe stretched around her behind as it swayed toward her bedroom. The cardboard box sat on the floor of the hall closet, under an assortment of women's jackets that looked new. I pulled the box out and flipped through papers, reports, pocket notebooks. Enough to keep me busy for a while, but not what I was looking for. There was a copy of an old department newsletter with Joey's obit.

APD NEWSLETTER, MARCH 15, 1988

THE ULTIMATE SACRIFICE

It is with deepest regret that we report the passing of one of our most beloved and respected soldiers, Senior Sergeant José Rodrigo ("Joey") Velez, in a car accident early in the morning of March 9 while re-

sponding to a call. Velez joined the Austin Police
Department in 1974. He maintained a model
record and was twice commended, the second for
his work on the Gautier case, an interdivisional operation organized by SSG Velez resulting in the department's first organized crime prosecutions
under the RICO Act. He was rotated to Homicide
five years ago from the Vice Squad, where he had
served with distinction for seven years. In addition
to his duties, he was active in public service as well
as playing on and coaching the APD softball team,
the Capital City Blues. He is survived by his wife
Rahcel.

SSG Velez was unmatched in his service, as he
was in the esteem he was held by his peers. He will
be sorely missed.

Memorial service is this Saturday, March 19 at
Civic Center, the eulogy to be delivered by Chief
Lucille Denton. It is requested that all off-duty offi-
cers are in attendance in full dress uniforms.

"Rachel," she said, standing close enough to read over
my shoulder, and I could smell her perfume. Sandalwood.
Pretty earthy for the glass and chrome furnishings, but I
liked it fine. "R-A-C-H-E-L. Is that so hard?"

"Cops can't spell."

"Misspelling the widow's name is the final insult. It
says, 'Screw you, he was ours, not yours.' "

She'd put on a white sundress, thin straps, full cover-
age on top, pulled close at the waist and loose to the
knees. A skinny woman would have looked virginal in it;
Rachel may as well have worn crimson. "Is there anything
else? Papers, documents, pictures?"

"Not in the house. How about the car?" she asked.

"Burnt to a crisp."

"Safe deposit box?"

"Why?"

She looked away. "I don't know. Sometimes people hide important papers in safe deposit boxes."

"Did he have a key to one?"

"Not on his keyring."

"Why would he hide it?"

"Search me," she said, and brushed the hair back off her face to let me know it wasn't a real offer. "Drink?"

"I gotta get back. You don't drink."

"I keep it for guests."

I didn't know why he'd have a safe deposit box or hide the key if he did. I wondered why she'd ask about it, the same way I always wondered why she wasn't home when he died. "I gotta run."

"Let me know what you find. I'm curious," she said, with a warmer tone than I expected, drawing my attention back to that thin dress and the opal between her breasts. Almost like she was saying, *Stay in touch.* It was all I could do to grab the box and run.

2:00 P.M. Austex Motel, South Congress

"You're the civilized sleepy black guy," I told Torbett outside the Austex. "I'm the psycho Jew."

"You're *playing* the psycho Jew," Torbett said. "There's a difference."

Torbett had radioed me about a meat receiver named Keenan, two hookers and the Austex Motel. One of the hookers turned out to be Seersucker's redhead from last night. Torbett and I decided to converge and do a Mutt and Jeff on the motel clerk for better leverage, what I used to have with Joey.

The desk clerk stood about six-five, nearly a half-foot taller than either of us and fifty pounds heavier, some of it muscle. He could have hurt me if someone dropped him from a building. His shaved head made me think of Baby Huey, whining and fighting for his dignity at the same time, a loser's bet.

"What are you hassling me for? I'm just the clerk."

Torbett talked like his nap was being interrupted. "Just check the register for the last few nights. See if it jogs your memory."

"I don't know their names!"

"We know they sign in," I said. "One name or another. It's policy."

"Fuck you, asshole! I don't have to show you anything without a warrant. That's my rights."

There was the counter between us but I leaned forward until my face was close enough for him to hit me without reaching. "We're not having a problem here. Are we?"

"I don't got a problem. You're the problem!"

"I don't have a problem either. I'd hate to think what would happen," I stared him down, "if we had a *problem*."

The clerk broke, pulled a three-ring binder from under the counter and flipped pages.

Torbett said, "Try these. Niki. Kiki. Lula. Tula. Anybody else you see a lot, but not lately. Maybe not the last week."

"Yeah, we got a Niki. I ain't seen her in a couple of weeks."

I locked eyes with Torbett, then turned to the clerk. "Do you usually see her?"

"No, only sometimes. She don't work the Strip."

Torbett asked, "What do you mean?"

"The other chicks got it staked out."

"So why was she here?"

"Oh, you know, they drift around. If she can pick up a trick without getting into a fight, she's okay."

I knew the fights got pretty rough. A guy'll cut your throat or smash your skull with a brick, but he won't scratch your face open with his bare hands. Women have no rules. But if someone killed Dirty Sally in a catfight, that wouldn't explain the parts. I saw the name Nikki. "Is that her handwriting?"

"No, mine."

"So she was a regular."

"Like I told you, once in a while. That's the last time I seen her."

I made him go back to an early page that had her own handwriting, Nikki with two *k*'s, wrapped it in paper on the off chance we could get a partial print off it, and tore it out. "Hey!" he said.

"Who's her pimp?"

"I never talk to no one but her."

Torbett. "What'd she look like?"

"Kinda worn out, but not too bad. Well, pretty bad."

"What color?"

"White, but kinda dark, black hair."

"Dyed black?"

"I wouldn't know." A new thought. "Skin hangs loose on her."

"Heroin?"

"Maybe. Yeah. She was something once."

"How do you know?" I watched him for twitches.

"Ah, you can tell."

"How can you tell?"

"You can just tell. You know."

"No, I don't know," I said. "Tell me!"

The clerk jolted, then searched his memory for details. "Her eyes."

"What about them?"

"They were . . . blue. Not just blue. Real blue, like . . . glass. No, not glass. Just blue, really blue, like sky. What'd she do, anyway?"

"I don't know if she did anything. Maybe she got killed."

"Shit, why didn't you say so? You got a mean streak in you, anybody ever tell you that?"

In the parking lot with Torbett, my head roasting, half-blind in the sun. "Nikki. Caucasian. Black hair. Sky blue eyes."

Torbett shook his head. "Or Tula. Or Lula. Or none of the above."

Nikki, I thought. *Dirty Sally was Nikki.* I'd put Nikki to rest, and she'd save me. That's what I thought.

5:00 P.M. Anderson and Guerrin

Guerrin sat in his black glove-leather chair, gripping a cut-crystal tumbler of iced bourbon when the huge mobile phone rang.

"Yes."

"*Sir, it's me.*" Harrell.

"How are you?" He spoke in a deliberately calm voice, like the old man's, but squeezing the tumbler so hard the imprint cut into his fingers.

"*Uh, fine, sir. And you?*"

"Just fine. Well, no, not fine." The weasel-voiced man

who called him must have tapped Harrell's phone. A wild renegade couldn't have the machinery to tap Guerrin's. And he knew about the girl. And he wanted money, lots of it.

"Son. I used to give you only small jobs. I hoped you'd work your way up, come work for me someday, get out of that little office."

"Yes, sir. Of course."

"I need a favor. A big one. Can I count on you?" He sipped through the ice.

He could almost hear Harrell salute. *"I won't let you down, sir."*

"We have a problem. Something may have surfaced around that last errand I had you take care of. The big one."

Harrell's breath caught.

"Just listen. Go through your files. Pull anything that associates you with me or any of my friends. Take anything that connects you with your operative or any others. Do the same thing at home. Put it all in a box."

"Sir?" Harrell's voice started to quiver.

"It's for your protection, Fred. Some of our recent ventures might be seen in a negative light." Harrell didn't answer. "I don't think you want to do time for this."

Harrell's throat made a soft version of the noise cats make just before vomiting. *"You mean prison?"*

"I'm trying to save you. Now, put everything in that box, copies and all. Don't miss a scrap! The authorities can be very thorough. Stand fifty feet west of the entrance to your apartment complex at ten o'clock tonight. I'll come with a car and pick you up. And, son?"

"Sir?"

"Don't talk to anyone. Stay calm. Everything will be fine." Guerrin clicked the phone off, laid it in the drawer and looked at the man across from him.

The old man's operative, in a charcoal gray suit and sunglasses, nodded almost imperceptibly but made no move to leave Guerrin's office.

5:15 P.M. South Congress

After Torbett and I split at the Austex Motel, I phoned Dispatch, spreading the message to the squad to sniff around for word of a run-down brunette streetwalker named Nikki with loose skin and sky blue eyes. A shopkeeper I questioned slipped me a fifty "for good luck" he said, laying some suspicion on the beat cops. I slipped it back. A cop is the first line of judgment, long before the judge. Once he's compromised, he isn't a cop anymore. Like Joey used to say, A cop who does well doesn't do *good*.

No one I spoke to over the next few hours knew Nikki, or was in the mood to say so. No one on Vice, no one on the street. I swung by HQ to check the messages and found an interoffice memo from the Fifth Floor as the phone rang.

"Homicide, Reles."

"Uh, hi. This is Aaron Gold."

"Who?"

"Rick Schate's roommate." It was the long-haired kid. He sounded pretty shaken, the kind of shaken you get after you accidentally see your roommate in pieces and then have to spend the night in the empty apartment.

"Oh, yeah."

"Can I, like . . . talk to you."

"Go ahead."

"No, I mean . . ."

"In person? I'm kinda busy . . ."

"I know. I know that."

I thought about all I had going on over the next few days. And I thought about this kid coming to bail his roommate out and finding him dead, and me trying to identify Joey's charred remains in the same office six months earlier. "Meet me at Magnolia Café around nine-thirty. You know it?"

"It's the only all-night place."

I clicked off and opened the memo.

From: Chief Lucille Denton
  To: Detective Sergeant Daniel Reles, Homicide
       Division
 Date: Tuesday, September 13, 1988
   Re: Evaluation Hearing
   Cc: Lt. Miles Niederwald, Sr. Sgt. Lloyd Jeffries,
       J. Killacky, MD

Be informed that your evaluation hearing has been rescheduled for Friday September 16 at 7:00 A.M., Fifth Floor Conference Room.

They moved the hearing ten days up and to the dawn hour, just to catch me off guard. As the wronged party, Jeffries would testify to my sanity and performance. If Denton thought it would help her image she'd have news cameras and a marching band.

I had three days to perform well enough that anything he said wouldn't count, that anything crazy he could prove I'd said or done over the last six months wouldn't land me back on Criminal Investigations or as a security guard at the mall. I had three days to bring in the killer.

5:30 P.M. 2823 East Oltorf, Apartment 1918

Tina LaMarque unlocked the apartment door, dropped the four shopping bags, closed the door, flipped on the TV and poured a glass of red wine. Nothing happened at work that shopping and wine couldn't cure, she kept telling herself. Anchorwoman Lyda Collins blabbed about a bus accident, her New England features giving sharp contrast to her unearthly brown contact lenses, an Anglo passing for Latin. Tina saw right through her.

Lyda Collins talked about the meat packs. They didn't mention names but said packs went to ten prominent Austin businessmen. She used words like "dangerous psychopath" and "killing rampage." The phone rang.

"Tina, it's me." It was Guerrin, in his nighttime voice.

She put a timid quiver in her voice. "Yes, sir."

"You don't have to call me 'sir,' especially after hours."

"Oh. Right." She sniffled.

"You're not afraid? You know I wouldn't let anything happen to you."

"I'm just a little shook up, that's all. I don't think I could handle another shock like that."

"Would you like me to come over?"

"That's very sweet of you. I think I'm better alone right now."

"You were very professional today."

"I try to be. You know that, Mr. Guerrin."

"I spoke to a detective at the police department. He came over very discreetly and made a complete report. There were nine others just like it. Some lunatic targeting successful businessmen. Nothing personal at all."

"I know."

"You don't have to come in tomorrow. Take as long as you like."

"No, I'm much better. I'd rather be at work."

"I'm glad. Is there anything I can do? Anything at all?"

"No. Not *now*." She let a little warmth out in the words. It worked. *"How about later?"* he joked.

"Oh, Mr. Guerrin," she giggled. "You're a married man!"

"Is that all you're worried about?"

"Yes," she said with significance. "It is."

He thought for a moment. *"Be patient, Tina."*

She hung up without another word.

Soon, soon.

9:30 P.M. HQ

Looking for Nikki, I ran through hooker mug shots like a fiend until they all looked alike, all nineteen years old or twenty-nine and doped and jaded, all with a shade of a scared ten-year-old girl underneath, cornered by her stepfather. Everything I ate at lunch balled up in the middle of my stomach like a rock. The rest of my stomach felt empty. I left and rolled back toward Mag's thinking about the first night Joey brought me to his house, sitting with Joey in his kitchen as Rachel served up chili from his mother's recipe. My head has a picture of her, wavy brown hair swept back, round breasts bursting out of a navy blue silk office dress Joey couldn't have paid for and her full lips pursed to a half-smile, like a former model still half-amused with playing the dutiful wife. When I first saw her my body jolted at the sight of this tall brunette bombshell, nobody's victim, no one's waif, who could take me two falls out of three. She caught my look, my dilating pupils, and looked back right into me. No smile, no performance, no pretense, just us, you and me, eye to eye. Her eyes showed a hard, dark past, like the one she saw in my own, I thought. She couldn't have missed the way I looked at her. And maybe that was all she was reacting to, a woman who likes attention. But maybe, just maybe . . .

Now Joey was gone and Rachel wasn't about to stand in the kitchen serving me chili, not after the way I treated her the night he died. And she betrayed Joey and I had no business dreaming about her.

But somehow I needed to see her.

The first marriage I got in the middle of was my parents', a complicated situation from the start, made more complicated by the wife and kids he already had when he met her. Whether he divorced his first wife, or never really married my mother, or was married to both of them simultaneously, was added to the list of items my parents never bothered explaining. Maybe they never thought I'd wonder about it, or never considered that I had the capacity to wonder.

The question of their marriage came to a head one sunny day when I was about seven. Isolated images of the day fade in and out of my memory: My parents in the front of Dad's huge '51 Ford. Me in a bridge chair in the back. Someone had tossed a cigarette into the moving car years before, torching the seats, and Dad had never got around to replacing them. My mother had the barber clip my hair close to the skull in expectation of the big day. I wore a blue plaid jacket and bow tie. "You're gonna see your grandma and grandpa, and your big brother and sister and all your cousins," my mother went on, through the half-day drive from Elmira all the way past the spectacular Manhattan skyline, across the island itself to a mystical land, the only place I knew that started with "The." Dad had worked things out, cleared our entrance to the family reunion in the Bronx, or that's what my mother thought.

Chatter rattled out from inside, through the wooden-frame screen door, and we entered without knocking, announcing, "We're here!"

Memory plays tricks on me. There's no way I could have sorted out the mass of humanity into a specific number—one dozen or two dozen relatives, how many men versus women, how many kids, which of the kids might have been my half-brother and -sister—as they stopped their chatter dead and stared at us like we'd busted in to rob the joint. Everything broke into frenzy. Shouts at my dad, "How could you bring them here?" words I didn't understand and one phrase that landed hard, "the little bastard." In the midst of all this an old lady who could have been my grandmother, cupped my cheeks in her wrinkled hands, turned me side to side like she was evaluating my bone structure. Then she walked off.

Dad said, "Wait in the car." I remember sitting in the car a long time, watching the screen door, until my parents finally came out of the house, my mother crying, "You said! You said!" something, something. And then the long drive home in silence. And hunger.

Something I think about on long drives, or every time I show up at a place where I might not be welcome.

I was tapping my fingers in a booth at Magnolia Café, wondering what the killer had planned next as a follow-up. All the parts he dropped were from the same girl, so as far as we knew, she was the only victim. But he'd surprised us before.

Paul the manager was giving some kind of instructions

to the fry cook, something that didn't involve exchanging his knit cap for a standard-issue chef's hat, shaving his ratty beard or removing the hand-rolled cigarette that hung from his lower lip. Aaron Gold strode in with his army knapsack and talked to Paul, who put a hand on Aaron's shoulder and brought him over to me. "You know this kid?" Paul asked me. "He's a friend of mine, student radical from a good family."

"Small town," I said. "Sooner or later, everybody knows everybody." Aaron slid into the booth as Paul walked off.

"Paul says you're an honest cop. He trusts you."

"He said that?"

A thin young waitress with a navel ring slid an oval-shaped plate and a mug in front of me. A burger on a wheat bun, overdone, with avocado, sprouts, burned home fries, homemade ketchup and black coffee. She gave Aaron a menu and he put it aside. He didn't mention his dead friend so I didn't either. I chomped on the burger hoping I could finish off the conversation before my meal was done.

"Where you from?" I asked, my mouth full.

"Houston."

"Born and raised? No accent. Smells like money." I tried to smile but it didn't take. Vegetable oil slithered down my throat.

"We had some once." I kept eating. "I need to talk to somebody," he said. "I know some things and I need to tell somebody who'll listen and do something."

I nodded.

"I have a police record," he dared me.

"So do I."

"Yeah?" He thought for a second, then pulled a stack of photocopies from his knapsack and began:

"Did you know that TriMondo Developing was one of the greatest corporate polluters in the world, that their mining destroyed a section of South Africa and killed most of the local population?"

I was expecting some sob story about how Rick Schate was like a brother to him. But I figured he was just trying to stay busy and I let him. "No, I didn't know that."

"Before they started mining in South Africa, they contracted a team of geologists from our own university to do the testing they needed. Did you know that the university has a rule that its president must personally approve every research contract?" He showed me photocopies of the rule from the university's administration book, and the contract between the university and TriMondo, dated three years ago, 1985, and signed by university president Bill Oliver.

"Okay."

He flushed like the speech wasn't going right. "Before the contract, the university was deep in the red. Six months later, they're in the black and everyone's praising Oliver for being such a tough negotiator with TriMondo. But by 1986 when the university pushed through the development of the Blacklands in spite of protests, the university is partnered with TriMondo. A clear conflict of interests. Now Oliver's on the board of the proposed Barton Springs Country Club, another TriMondo development."

I remembered the Blacklands as a section of black East Austin just east of the university. They pushed the squatters out of it to make way for luxury housing and a new sports facility, dubbed "Gym Crow" by the locals. All the same, this private-school kid from Houston was grating on me.

I looked over the documents that backed up all his research. "Okay, but I'm Homicide. Why tell me this?"

"Because Rick Schate was murdered."

10:00 P.M. Barton Springs Road

Fred Harrell loaded the white file box holding every last scrap of evidence of his relationship with Guerrin and Guerrin's clients into the back of the limousine, and slid in after it. The limo rolled away from the curb.

"I'm sorry, Mr. Gue—" Harrell's words were stopped by the sight of three men sitting on jump seats opposite himself and Guerrin, their faces in darkness.

"Don't—don't say anything just now, Fred." Guerrin looked straight ahead, past the men. Headlights of moving cars flashed across Guerrin's profile, enough to show that he was shaking. "I'm going to ask you some questions, Fred, just a few," Guerrin said. "I need you to think carefully and not leave anything out. Do you understand?"

"Yes, sir."

"Good. Short, clear answers. Now . . . who is this fellow you hired?"

10:00 P.M. Magnolia Café

I put my burger down. "Oh, jeez. Now I feel sorry for you."

"Rick was my friend . . ." He busted a tear, but he looked more scared than sad.

"I'm sorry."

"We were both going after TriMondo and the university. Oliver knows me."

"No. No."

"We were gonna make a big stink at the city council meeting yesterday morning. Rick didn't show up. Then I found out he was dead."

"He got hit by a bus."

He barked, "How do you know that?! How do you know somebody didn't just shove him at the right moment? My friends keep dying in freak accidents. Rob gets jolted jump-starting a car that came from nowhere. Rick slips under a bus. Everyone I know disappears—"

Past his hair and glasses, Aaron Gold wasn't a bad-looking kid, skinny as he was. With a shave and a haircut, he'd have girls all over him, provided he didn't open his mouth.

"Why didn't they get you?"

"That's the point! I'm the last big radical on campus. I'm next!"

I wiped my hands on a napkin. "No. Conspiracy theories don't work. You can't get that many people to agree on something."

"They wouldn't have to agree," he blurted. "It's just the way they do business. I was at the Blacklands!" he said. "I know!"

"You're not that important."

"I'm onto something . . ." He hushed to a whisper. "Something very big is happening. Things are shifting. I can't prove it yet. You're the only cop I know. You have to take me in."

I almost laughed. "Protective custody?"

"People track information. If I know something, someone knows I know it. I can't do this unless you take me in."

I felt sorry for him losing his buddy. They were out trying to get the bad guys together, like Joey and me. I didn't want to leave Aaron Gold out in whatever crazy place he was in. But I sure as hell wasn't going to take him in.

"You have my number," I said, standing. "Call me when you come up with evidence of a crime."

"You mean something street level," he said, angrily. "Pimps and hookers. Not the big corporate crimes that kill thousands."

"All right, yeah, street level—something you can prove that has a law against it!"

I walked away steaming. Street level, that's me. Tri-Mondo takes over the world and I'm busting jaywalkers. But Aaron Gold was earnest about something. I hadn't seen much of that before. I didn't expect to see much of it again.

11

10:15 P.M. Eric's Billiards, Airport Boulevard

Armand Tejani lined up a bumper shot. If he hit that exact spot . . . He slid the cue back and forth and shot. The seven ball hit the mark and missed the side pocket by a quarter inch.

"*FUCK!*" he hollered, drawing stares. People would leave him alone, he knew that. It was the old rule about not interrupting a screaming crazy man alone at a pool table.

He scratched the tiny round scar on the back of his neck, thinking how good he looked in baggy pants and suspenders, his broad black silk tie hanging over the table, when he spotted Harrell at the front entrance in a cheesy gray suit from Sears, looking like he was selling life insurance on the way to his own funeral. Harrell crossed the poolroom in short steps and neared the table, pale and sweating in spite of the heavy A/C. Tejani was wound like a spring and liking it—he just had to make sure not to pop too soon.

"How could you do this?" Harrell hissed.

Tejani chuckled, eyes on the table, and continued playing.

"Do you know how much trouble I'm in?" Harrell went on. "Are you trying to get us killed?!"

"I thought about that. See, now nobody knows anything. A whore died, if they even got that much. If I didn't leave my calling card, they'd never have even looked for her. Believe me, I know cops. Here's the way I see it: I get caught, big deal. Armand Tejani, half-breed ex-cop from Atlanta, kills whore. Who gives a fuck? I can do time again. But a big lawyer like Guerrin hiring her killer? They'll crucify him and you, indictments for all his clients. Me, I got nothing to lose. How long would you guys last in prison?"

Harrell looked around the room, talked low. "You were supposed to do this clean. We had a *deal*."

Line up, shoot to the right . . . *sink!* "Yes!" He moved around the table. "Yeah, I feel bad about that. Thirty K, that's a lot of money."

"Too much," Harrell fumed.

"Much too much. That's what got me thinking. Move." Harrell moved and Tejani lined up the next shot.

"Thirty K, that's a lot of money to you and me, more than the lease on your crappy little office for a year. Way too much for a hit on a street whore. This ain't Vegas. So I figured, some big cheese wants a girl out of the way, but he wants to keep a step away. So he hires you to hire somebody. Or maybe he has someone else hire you. Maybe they give you more to do this, a lot more, figured you'd keep a little for yourself, hire some good out-of-town fixer. But you wanted a bigger piece. So you kept your bigger piece, and you hired me."

"It's bigger than that."

He laughed like a tickled rat. "Don't get me wrong, I'm flattered. Problem is, now you got me all excited. I want more."

"You got more than you deserved."

"That's the beauty of it, Fred! So did you. Man, you can't even keep your files straight. Took me half the night to go through them. Truth is, Fred—okay if I call you Fred?—I didn't even know it was Royce Guerrin. But I figured that money had to come from somewhere, and it sure wasn't none of your bikers. So I dropped my calling cards. I slipped the meat to everyone in your files with a fancy address and waited to see who called you. Now it all makes sense. Guerrin was the one hiring you to do errands for everyone else."

"You tapped my phone?!"

"I'll never do it again. Move." He glided around the table, aimed for the eight ball.

"You left her torso for the police!" Harrell hissed.

"I had to light a fire under your ass. And now you're here." He sank the eight ball and racked them up again.

"How much?"

"HAH!" Tejani barked. "That's right. How much! How much is a million five. I don't want to be greedy. I just want to retire. I have debts," he said, scratching his nose. "I want out. A million five well invested would keep me away from lawyers for a long time."

"You're crazy. You're not worth it."

"How many more meat deliveries before the local cops ID her?"

"Five hundred!" Harrell said suddenly.

Tejani stopped dead. "What."

"Five hundred thousand."

Tejani looked up from the table and beamed. "Kiss my ass."

Harrell glanced at the back door. "We can't talk about this here."

Tejani snorted something into the back of his throat and swallowed. He blinked and opened his eyes wide. "Ha-HAH! Yes!" He glanced at Harrell and snapped his fingers twice. "Gimme a twenty."

"What?"

"For the table." Harrell fished out a twenty and handed it over slowly. Tejani went to the cash register and announced, "Carlo, this is for the table, and shoot the change. I'm gone for the night. Let's go, Fred!" He headed toward the front door. Harrell stopped him.

"I'm parked around back."

Tejani straightened his broad silk tie and followed Harrell up the back hallway, ready to spring. Harrell held the door. "After you."

"No, after you, Fred," Tejani said, gripping his belt buckle.

10:30 P.M. Eric's Billiards

Harrell was supposed to send Tejani out first, but figured he was lucky to get him out the back door at all. They'd destroy all the evidence. As long as he delivered Tejani, he'd be all right. He'd have to dodge as the limo rolled around. He pushed the steel exit door open and led Tejani out into the dark parking lot—a few scattered cars, trash cans and a fence—as the limo pulled near them, headlights dark, windows sliding down.

"What's this?" Tejani asked.

"My car. Come on." Harrell turned to Tejani to move him ahead but Tejani grabbed him by the collar and pulled him close enough to smell Tejani's rotten teeth.

"Don't you know who you're dealing with, Freddy boy?" he grinned.

Something sharp sliced across Harrell's chest and burned.

"Tag," Tejani said. "You're it." Tejani threw Harrell into the limo's path and the car screeched to a halt. Harrell doubled over on the concrete, clutching his chest as blood soaked his hands. The blast of a gunshot from nearby cracked the dark sky and rattled Harrell's body. Then two more shots exploded from far away. Harrell recognized Guerrin's voice.

"Oh my God! His head, his head!" Guerrin yelled. Harrell grit his teeth against the searing pain in his chest.

A car door opened and someone got out. "Where is he?"

"There!" One of the men fired, the sound jolting Harrell. The pain seized his ribs and his legs kicked out on their own.

"Was that him?"

The headlights flashed over Harrell. At the far end of their light something dark rolled and lay still. "It's a dog. Kill the lights—" A shot from the distance shattered one headlight. The other light went out.

Tears rolled down Harrell's cheeks. He rocked his head against the cold pavement, muttering, "Help me, help me . . ."

Someone said, "There, on the fence."

"Well, shoot him, for God's sake!" Guerrin said.

"No shot," the man said. "He's gone. This is on you, Guerrin."

"Oh God!"

"Get this one into the car."

Harrell started to shake from the cold as hands lifted him into the limousine. At least, he thought, the hospital was only a mile away.

11:00 P.M. 4612 Avenue F

At home I peeled off my clothes and showered, letting the water wash over my head, and I hoped, my brain. I felt dirty, inside and out. I'd questioned everyone the patrols picked up near the Sands without getting any closer to Dirty Sally. With a little luck I could identify the victim . . . then I heard Joey say, *Before the perp dies of natural causes* and laugh hard. Dead guys kill me.

I checked the fridge: three eggs, some vintage cold cuts, hot dogs, coffee, half a pot of beans, two beers. Nothing worth the trouble of eating. I flipped through Joey's notebooks looking for some clues into the patterns of his thoughts, something I didn't get from him directly. *Gautier's, Guad./29th. Two back exits. Bartender Gus, coked* and so on. Details. I looked at big pictures and focused down. Joey started on details and expanded. I lay in bed and stared at the ceiling, too tired to sleep, hungry in a way food couldn't solve, letting my mind go blank to see if something came to me.

I closed my eyes and saw Rachel. Distant, mysterious Rachel glancing from a doorway, leaning over a table. Looking into my eyes, reaching to me. Rachel walking out on Denton's eulogy to Joey. Rachel pissed that they spelled her name wrong. Rachel alone in Joey's house. If she was alone.

11:30 P.M. **Route 2222**

The limousine sped along the mountain stretch of 2222 toward the lake. Inside, the engine hummed. Harrell leaned against the window, a hundred foot drop to his left, two of the large men on his right, Guerrin on the jump seat facing him. The other large man sat on a jump seat, leaning against the window, eyes wide, a bloody rupture denting his forehead. They'd wrapped Harrell in a blanket but he was shaking hard.

"Fred," Guerrin broke the silence, a forced air of calmness giving way to a quiver in his voice. "This Tejani," Guerrin continued. "How exactly did you choose him?"

Harrell blushed painfully. He chose him wrong.

"I hired you for your low connections, Fred. You never failed me before. I almost don't under*stand* it." Guerrin leaned forward, a sheen of sweat coating his face, hysteria in his voice. "Just how much of that fifty thousand did you keep for yourself?" Harrell squeezed his eyes shut. "I'm on the right track, right? What was it? Ten thousand? Twenty?" Guerrin leaned back. "Doesn't seem like much now, does it? I wouldn't mind if you took the money and still hired someone competent. A level of larceny is necessary for the movement of the machine." Suddenly Guerrin bellowed, *"But you cheapen it, Fred!"* Then he sat back. "You think I'd bring you into my firm? You're a disgrace to your profession."

Suddenly the large man next to him grabbed Harrell's right arm in a paralyzing hold and jabbed a hypodermic needle into his wrist. Harrell winced with pain.

"W-what was that for?"

The man said. "High-grade uncut Afghan heroin. The best."

Harrell felt his dinner come up and land in his lap.

Guerrin's jaw dropped. The large man said, "Did I mention it was a triple dose?"

Harrell slumped against the window thinking that the car smelled like throw-up and wondering why he hadn't noticed it before. For the first time in ages he felt calm; things were going to be all right. The last thing he heard was the large man saying, "Now you know how it's done."

12

WEDNESDAY

The day my mother left, I sat alone, tapping my feet, staring in the hall mirror at my growing nose, Mama's little Jew, waiting for Dad to come home. When he did, he tore up the house, flipping between tears and fury. "The one beautiful thing I had in my life. How could she do this to me?" Then, "I rotted in that shithole two years for her!" When he finally collapsed in a chair, he turned to me, surprised. His face said, What are you still doing here?

For the first ten years of my life, she was with me all the time. Making breakfast, helping me off to school, telling me funny stories about the neighbors, taking me to the movies, singing to me, kissing me goodnight. My dad was an occasional scowling presence, standing at a distance, barking, "You treat him better than you treat me." Then she left me alone with him, with my enemy.

Years later the Academy taught me the secrets of Social Security numbers and I tried to track her. She'd held a few secretarial jobs in New York City briefly in '65 and '66, and after that nothing, no driver's license, no death certificate. I had a *few more avenues to search when I realized that she knew where I was until I was fifteen. She could have found me if she wanted to. I fought the urge to keep looking.*

After she left, Dad was always at the gym so there was nothing to go home for after school but an empty apartment. I hung around the gym. Dad gave me lame tips on boxing and smart tips on the boxers and their owners. "That's Sam Zelig. His brother used to own me."

The gym was a huge dark cave with cigar-smoking managers, ugly goons pumping iron free-weights and sparring matches that occasionally ended with a mug getting knocked out and not waking up. When I was eleven, my father put me in the ring against a blubbery twelve-year-old monster named Ferber.

"Don't watch his hands," Pop said, "watch his eyes. That'll tell you where his hands are going. Work his midsection and keep your feet apart. Keep your feet apart!" The bell rang just as a truck hit the middle of my face.

Nothing beats the pain of getting your nose busted for the first time. The pressure's so intense you think it's going to explode and when it does, when blood rushes out, the pressure isn't any less. Some hatchet-faced old hood named "Doc" sets it with his bare hands. Mugs crack wise about how it gives your face "character," then rib your father for your performance in the ring. Your father doesn't say a word to you for weeks. You lie in bed at night missing your mother and if you cry you cover up the sound by snorting blood.

When I came to on the canvas, Pop was staring down at me, disappointment in his eyes.

"You shoulda kept your feet apart."

I promised myself I'd never be in that position again. I'd learn to be strong, fast and smart. And I'd get big. I spent all my free time at the gym, working out and taking pointers from anyone who'd give them, anyone except Pop.

One day Sam Zelig himself, in a polyester suit, gold rings around his fat scarred fingers, saw me sparring no-contact with some other kid half a foot taller than me. Zelig blew cigar smoke in my face, said he'd seen me in the ring, and cackled. "I ain't seen no one take a punch like that since your old man here got clobbered by Mortellaro!" Bellows of laughter burst out of his huge mouth. "Ya motherless chump!"

Blood rushed to my head, my face burned, my heart pounded and tears welled behind my eyes. I saw the kid I was sparring with, laughing along with Zelig. I pounded the kid in the mouth, then hit him with a right-left-right combination I just learned. When he didn't fight back I went wild, arms swinging, hooks, jabs, roaring as I hammered away, the grin long gone from his bloody face. I didn't let up when he hit the floor.

I could barely hear for the ringing in my ears when they hauled me off of him. But I looked around, grimacing at everyone, boys and men. They'd stopped what they were doing and watched me in awed silence. Zelig slipped what turned out to be a fiver into my glove and said, "You're all right, kid. You're a tough Jew."

That was the first time I felt that burning rage. No technique but enough fire to flatten every kid in my weight class and a bunch of kids above. I stopped thinking about my mother all the time, and I never cried again. I ran with the gym kids, a circle jerk of pockmarked, motherless porn thieves, sons of the boxers and wheel men and cops who frequented the place. We'd steal cigarettes and beer and, eventually, condoms, razzing the good kids from our station outside the school's west entrance, the bad entrance, with our roughly used girlfriends in tow, girls who hadn't been warned away from broken-nosed hoods like us. But I kept up my workout schedule, and I was smart enough to get good grades without studying, a fact I kept to myself. All part of my "tough" program.

*There were two kinds of Jews, tough ones and ones on the
canvas. I was a tough Jew, like Sam Zelig said. But in my mind,
every punch I threw cracked Zelig's rotten teeth.*

10:00 A.M. Anthropology Building,
West Campus

None of the ten meat recipients blinked when Torbett and
I swung by again to ask them about a skinny hooker
named Nikki with black hair and sky blue eyes. By ten A.M.
I was sitting across from my old anthropology professor, a
floppy-eared eccentric in a vintage tweed suit, hair parted
barely above the ear, in his sun-drenched cubicle of an office on the Central Austin campus where I was a GI Bill
student fourteen years before, making good grades and
dreaming of the FBI.

The professor held Dirty Sally's black skull charm and
furrowed his brow like a jeweler. "What do *you* think?" he
asked.

"Doc, I'm not a student."

"You pop up every year or two trying to learn something." He held it up to the light. "*Día de los muertos*
maybe? Day of the Dead."

"This skull, specifically, doesn't mean anything?" I
asked, tapping my feet. The tiny skull glimmered in the
sunlight.

With a nicotine yellow-toothed smile he said, "It
meant something to somebody."

The car radio crackled. "*Homicide 8.*"

"This is Homicide 8, go ahead."

"Package delivery at KTBX. Meet Sergeant Greer from Public Information when you get there."

"Greer? What's he doing there?"

The radio crackled as I drove under an overpass and pulled off the interstate onto Tenth Street.

11:00 A.M. KTBX-TV Studios, West Tenth Street

I saw a dozen TV monitors light Sergeant Greer's puffy face a dull green as he dropped the meat package onto the counter in front of me. An orange Styrofoam tray displayed the boneless, toothless, green-blue face of a young woman under plastic wrap, her lips arranged in a grotesque *O*-shape. Condensation made the half-thawed package wet and sticky. The cheeks lay flat, the nose bent to one side. Someone who knew what he was doing carried out the complex maneuver of skimming her face from her skull in one piece like the shell of an Easter egg. But he kept her eyes for himself.

"They dropped it in a bag near the entrance, just out of the range of security cameras," Greer said, wiping his brow. "The station got camera shots of it from every angle before anybody thought to call us. I've been keeping the heat off you guys all week. I'm sorry."

"Fingerprints?"

"You got the whole staff of Channel 2 right there."

Video monitors showed the pack from different angles. One camera panned across a row of porn videos, then zoomed in on the flat cupie-doll face of an inflatable sex doll in its package. Another screen showed the ravine where I first saw parts.

A handsome dark-haired woman by the console gave directions to a fat guy spinning knobs. I recognized her from the evening news, the new woman on Channel 2. Lyda Collins, the Latina's white woman, the white woman's Latina.

"*Are you shocked at the nature of these vicious, brutal killings?*" Collins on video asked a woman with an arm-load of groceries.

The woman on the screen looked confused. "*It's shocking . . . shocking.*"

Collins talking to a cab driver at roadside. "*Do you think the police are doing a good enough job?*"

"*I don't know what the police are doing.*"

"Good," she told the engineer. "Now cut out my questions."

Reels clicked and whirred, and in a few minutes, the cab driver showed up on the screen again. "*I don't know what the police are doing,*" followed by the housewife, who added, "*It's shocking . . . shocking.*"

I approached her. "Dan Reles, APD Homicide."

Collins didn't look up. "I spoke to your friend and the answer is no."

"You don't know the question."

"I won't cut the story and I won't put it off a day or two, not even if you promise me an exclusive that'll have me in Tom Brokaw's chair in a month. If this goes national I'll be there anyway."

"I can charge you with obstruction of justice."

She glanced at me, then stood straight and looked me up and down. Her fake brown eyes sparkled. "Reles?" she asked. "Are you a Chicano?"

"No, a Jew. Do you need a Chicano?"

Her smile dropped and she turned back to the screen.

"Obstruction of justice. A First Amendment battle would do great things for my career."

"Let me guess. The public has a right to know."

The screen showed her holding a microphone in front of APD, surrounded by a handful of locals gawking at the camera. One sign showed a cutout photo of the disembodied head with the caption FACE WITHOUT A NAME; another read STOP THE BUTCHER KILLINGS! It was a tight shot, suggesting they might be in the middle of a larger crowd. They weren't.

Just then the tiny crowd was joined by Chief Denton, wearing a plain dress and a look of deep concern she pulled from her closet.

"*Chief Denton, do you still deny the possibility of serial killings?*"

"*I'm glad you asked that, Lyda. This crowd out here today, especially the mothers, are evidence of what we, the public, won't accept.*"

Collins took the microphone back, but it was too late, the tiny crowd was clapping. Lyda shouted over the applause. "*But Chief Denton . . .*"

"*And another thing, Lyda . . .*" Denton boomed, wrapping her hand around the microphone and addressing the camera.

"*Lyda, I'm a mother myself. We have reason to believe this is a drug-related killing. I implore all you mothers out there, and anyone else, if you have any information that may be related to this event, please call us and make that information known. This is a war on crime and we can't afford to lose one battle. We're fighting for our children.*"

A contact name and phone number flashed on the screen. The phone number was the Homicide squad room's direct line. The name was Dan Reles.

The face stared eyeless at me from the package. Just what a detective needs most: fame. Forty-eight hours before his evaluation hearing and counting.

"When does this sideshow go on the air?" I asked.

Lyda Collins looked at her watch.

12:45 P.M. Homicide Squad Room

The squad cheered when I walked in on them eyeing the TV and taking messages from seven ringing phone lines.

"Dude's on the tube," Jake cheered. "Check it out! Captain Action's on the teevee!"

Waller slapped me on the back. "He's a hero."

"Gon' be a star! Here's some fan mail, good buddy." Jeffries handed me a stack of messages, his ruddy cheeks bouncing with evil cheer under dark expressionless eyes. A scrap of toilet paper marked a fresh shaving injury on his second chin. Jeffries's fat little sidekick Milsap turned down the volume. The messages named dozens of perpetrators, ID'd the face as fifty lost daughters, sixty runaway girlfriends. Two different men confessed to the crime, getting every detail wrong. Women turned in their husbands. One crank asked if the meat would be sold when the cops were done; another offered recipes. One message read, "Why does anyone care so much about some whore getting killed anyway?"

Jeffries showed his teeth. "That was from me."

On the small black-and-white screen, a tall white-haired man flanked by Girl Scouts spoke before a booming crowd, jet planes flying overhead. He spoke about the rash of crimes as a symptom of the soft-on-crime policies of the state's current administration. The anchorman wrapped up. *"And in a related story, police say Sixth Street crowd control is hard; they want time and a half. After this."* I pulled the plug.

"Damn right they want time and a half," Milsap kicked in. "Like to see *him* keep order out there on a Saturday night."

Miles sat with his feet up on my desk, chunks of dandruff flaking his stooped shoulders. He reeked of the deodorant he sprayed in the armpits of his shirt so he could wear it an extra day. "Where the hell you been?"

"Signing autographs."

I dropped a stack of packets on the desk. "Well I'll be damned," someone said. Everyone grabbed one.

They were sketches of the face. The police artist padded it to fill out the missing bone and eyes, then sketched it with a few variations on shape, long and short hair, straight and curly, black hair and light eyes if it was Nikki, light hair and dark eyes, and so on. The black-haired one seemed right, but maybe not. I couldn't help but think I'd seen her before.

"What the hell," Jeffries said. "He tryin' to get caught?"

Miles waved me into the hallway.

"Fifth Floor's pissed about this case gettin' so out of hand."

"I didn't tell her to broadcast my freaking phone number."

"Coverin' her ass. Instead of blamin' her, the whole town feels like they're on the case. You're lookin' at sex-killer frenzy. Mass paranoia, lynch mobs, women afraid to go out. You gotta upshift before the FBI comes in and screws things up for everybody."

I spent my college and army years prepping to apply to the Bureau, then got turned down for my father's mob affiliations. If I had a chance to look good in front of the Bureau, I wouldn't pass it up. We went back in, kicking up smoke.

"Waller, what'd you get?"

He adjusted his glasses. "The Styrofoam trays are all from the same manufacturer. They could have been lifted from one of fifty stores in town in the last two weeks. None of the legit couriers did the delivery. Nobody saw the packs dropped. Pretty impressive with all the doormen and security cameras, but possible. This guy's good."

"Possible for one guy to deliver all of them?"

"We didn't pinpoint all the times. A few of them would have been close. Sure, yeah. He'd have to be good."

"You just said he was. Jake?"

"NCIC in Washington is sending me files on all the missing girls born '65 to '71 with A-negative blood. There's more of them than you'd think, but we'll have pictures. Also, couple of unsolved hooker killings in Austin over the last five years, Velez on one, Marks on another," Jake said. "Both with different MOs. Serial rapist in Dallas."

"Check the new face against missing persons and mug shots."

"I can send it out on the Net."

"What do you mean?"

"I can do an FTP of the sketches, scan in the picture and see if any of the geeks have seen her."

A quick look around the table told me no one else knew what he was talking about either. "Sure, whatever. Keep on top of the phone calls. Anything that sounds real, send a team out fast. The rest of you check in with Jake whenever you have a free minute. In the meantime, everyone take the sketches and retrace your old steps." Big groan from the squad. "Life bites. Show 'em the sketches and see what their eyes do. I don't know if you guys read the autopsy report I gave you, but Hay says possible strangling, asphyxiation, even bludgeoning. I say even a street whore deserved better than that. Any arguments?" No response.

Tacked to the wall was a photocopy of a skull and crossbones. At the top read the words AUSTIN POLICE, HOMICIDE, inked in red, white and blue. At the bottom, a flowing ribbon reading, WE WORK FOR GOD. I turned back to the room.

"On North Lamar, across from Pease Park, there's a massage parlor next to a gun shop. Y'all know it?" They knew it. "Park on the side streets and meet me in the gun shop parking lot at five-thirty."

"What for?" Jeffries asked, almost drooling.

"I'll tell you at five-thirty."

13

    STP: Service!

                          Tolerance!

                                        Pride!

The billboard greeted me from high over the interstate a hundred feet from APD, the STP logo over a smiling white patrolman about my age shaking hands with a smiling Latino.

Back at the Austex Motel, I was serving and tolerating Baby Huey, the big clerk Torbett and I met yesterday. The clerk flipped through the sketches and found one with dark straight hair and light eyes, blue or gray.

"That's her."

"You're sure?"

"That's her. That's Nikki. She was skinnier, her hair was straight and black, her eyes were lighter, but that's her."

Nikki started to appear out of the flood of mug shots, chopped up legs and arms, as a human, someone with a name and an identity. Now I knew her. And if I could find her, I could find her killer.

There was a change in the clerk's expression and he looked up. "She dead?"

"Yeah."

He stared deeper into the picture. I asked again if he knew her.

"I told you, she came in once in a while. Nikki. That's all I know." He sat on his orange plastic chair and rubbed his face. "The girls come and go. I figured she was gone. I just don't usually hear about it."

"You know anything else about her? Her real name, where she was from, a pimp or other girls she hung out with?"

He shook his head, then thought for a few seconds. "I know one thing, though. It's not important."

"What is it?"

"She used to be a stripper. Not at the end. Before. Before she lost her looks, I guess."

"Where? Here in Austin?"

He shrugged. "I don't know. Maybe?"

I dropped my card on the way out.

I hit three strip clubs before I found a dancer who owned up to recognizing the sketch. A muscular blonde in a breakaway bikini and a lacy robe, a twenty-two-year-old body with a forty-year-old face, thought she recognized Nikki from Kansas City about a year and a half ago.

Sitting with me in a booth at the back of the club, she said, "I don't know. Karen or Kathy. Nikki on stage. She wasn't any good, but she was so pretty. That one, the one with the eyes."

"Do you know where she came from? Or where she went after Kansas City?"

She made a little ironic laugh. "Huh. After K.C.? Anywhere. You said she was here, but I don't know if that was right after. I guess she just raised what she needed to move on and left. Same as everybody. Same as me."

"Do you remember anything else about her, maybe some guy she was attached to? A boyfriend, or . . . ?"

"Or a pimp? Who knows. Girls see the money coming in and they go through it, sometimes real fast, and they want more. Or they need more, you know what I mean?" She made a show of rubbing her nose. "Maybe they turn a trick sometimes or if the guy is nice. Sorry, handsome, I don't remember no one. I remember one thing, though, but you know that already."

"What's that?"

"She was so pretty. Tough for me to say, 'cause we was sort of in competition. She didn't put on no airs neither, didn't think she was better than nobody. One time I came into the dressing room and she was all by herself crying. I asked her if it was a boy. She said no, and then she said, "I'm all alone," just like that, like a little girl. Her tits stood up like mine, you noticed, but she didn't spend all day at the gym. It was just natural. You could tell it wouldn't last, she'd lose it and then she'd be done. But she was just so pretty, like . . . I don't know. Like an angel with them eyes." Her eyes reddened and she grabbed at a cocktail napkin. "I'm not *that way*, you understand." She lowered her voice. "But I woulda done it with her. In a heartbeat."

3:30 P.M. Days Motor Inn, Interstate 35 Frontage Road

Tejani called the AAA Escort Service and asked for a girl with class. She visited him in one of the nicer motels, in a back room set off near the trees. He held himself back as she sashayed into the room past him; then he bolted the door.

"I don't usually do this," she said in a Lauren Bacall alto, ringing a lock of golden hair around one ear. "Gentlemen usually meet me for a drink first. But you seem okay."

She slipped off the light beige jacket that went with her skirt and held still as he walked up behind her and pressed his pelvis against her behind.

"My," she said. "You're a big boy!"

He slapped duct tape across her mouth, then punched her hard in the right kidney. When she fell, he wrapped her wrists in nylon cord and tied them to the bed frame, hissing into her ear as she moaned.

"You're lucky. Lucky bitch."

She shook her head wildly, mascara tears running down her cheeks as she moaned something that probably went with the words "No!" and "Please!"

This would do the trick, he thought. For sure, this would take the edge off. Tejani lit a cigarette, then ripped her skirt up the seam and pulled down his pants, spitting on himself.

"You'll love it, baby. You'll love it."

Her moan turned to a shriek as he started to force his way in and leaned forward, letting his cigarette sizzle through her golden hair into the back of her neck.

Lucky bitch.

4:00 P.M. **Parked on South Congress**

If I had the right girl, Dirty Sally/Nikki was a stripper a year and a half ago and a street junkie-prostitute last month, a cool slide down the sex industry. Maybe she started as a call girl with an escort service and worked her way down to the alleys and ravines. But alleys weren't in the phone book I kept in the car and escort services were. The phone book listed the AAA Escort Service first, for alphabetical reasons, making it my first stop.

The hostess was a smooth dark woman who talked like a college girl. She looked at the sketch and said she wasn't here if and when Nikki was. "But she reminds me of a girl I knew in Houston a couple of years ago."

"What was her name?"

"Who knows. We made them up anyway."

"Where were you working?"

She gave me a look. "What are you after?"

"We got a guy maybe chopping up professional girls."

"From television, right? I didn't know it was real." She thought for a minute. "Okay, you won't bust me for anything I say."

"My honor."

She chewed on that and looked back at the sketch.

"We weren't selling, we were party girls. They liked to have us on their arms. They said we were models and I guess we were. We'd toss in a tumble at the end of the evening as a friendly gesture. A man shows a woman around, buys her gifts and she puts out. Sort of like marriage. No money changed hands, but the gifts. You could return them."

"What about her?"

"All we really had was looks. But she was *too* beautiful. Her eyes I guess."

"What about them?"

"Who was that actress with the eyes, Lee something? Gray-blue, sky blue—like that only with black hair. Most of the men wouldn't go near her, like she was a goddess. She learned to work the goddess thing, but you could tell it took its toll on her. She didn't talk much. As if she wasn't allowed. I don't know who her friends were."

So Nikki was a knockout party girl two years ago in Houston. Six months later, a stripper in Kansas City, showing signs of wear. Last month she bottomed out on South Congress in Austin, hopped to the gills. She could have hit a dozen cities in between.

And that was the second comment I heard about how alone she was. I was rubbing the face off the little black charm she swallowed. I heard stories like this every day. But I hadn't seen their faces. I rubbed the charm. Nikki was all alone.

I needed Nikki to keep my job. But now I had her face, now she was a person.

And *she* needed something from me.

5:00 P.M. Public Records, West Eleventh Street

Aaron Gold was sitting at a table in the shadowed stacks of Public Records.

He couldn't work at home anymore with Rick's clothes, books, waterpipe, buzzing white noise at him from around the tiny apartment, Rick's Ché Guevara poster glaring down at him. The noise buzzed louder since Aaron made the phone call to Rick's mother, then heard her wild scream and sobbing. But he'd make the buzzing stop.

"Crazy conspiracy theory" my ass, he thought. How many deaths make a conspiracy? JFK, RFK, MLK. For Aaron it was Rob first, a freakish electrocution from jumper cables and a car no one knew he had. Now Rick. Two of the loudest student radicals on campus. Aaron was the third.

Aaron pored over TriMondo's contracts for hours before he noticed a footnote about the Securities and Exchange Commission. He looked it up. All shareholders of over 5 percent had to be named in a corporation's annual and quarterly reports to the SEC, all public information. Hallelujah.

Aaron tracked the reports without asking the librarian. *Cover your trail*, Rick warned him once. A stack of bound blue volumes before him, he burrowed backward through the Annuals, starting with 1987. Unfamiliar names back to '80. Finally, in '79, the first line leaped from the page.

CEO William Henry Oliver III: 51 percent. Three years before he became university president.

In '78 he had only 6 percent, and in '77 he wasn't even listed. But by '79 he somehow nailed 51 percent, enough to make him CEO, if that was how those things worked.

Nine years ago, Aaron was the kid next door, an occasional playmate to Oliver's now-motherless son John, the last of the guarded friendships between the Golds and the Platinums. "Mr. Oliver helps people in Africa," Aaron's mother said, not long before Oliver and his reassuring, fatherly smile guided the Golds' savings and Aaron's college fund into the vacuum of the stock market.

Oliver, you son of a bitch, I've got you. And I have evidence.

Aaron scratched out some notes frantically. A bass line pounded in his head as he hauled the crucial volumes over to the copier. He could only remember one line of the song:

"Hope I die before I get old."

14

5:15 P.M. Al's Guns Parking Lot

Opposite the soccer fields at Pease Park, a long green stretch of Lamar Boulevard, in a small parking lot sat a one-story building divided into two stores, Al's Guns and Exotic Massage. I made sure to be the first there, before the squad. Jeffries showed next, looking smug.

"We gon' have a party?"

"I hear you been having one," I said.

"What's that?"

"Got a call from a friend, you and Speedy been smacking hookers around for street skinny, then taking services."

His smile turned sour and he stepped toward me. "Who's your friend?"

I started feeling the rage flare up, and thought of Joey saying, *Show of force. Be smart.* A distant memory tells me to act sane.

Milsap and Torbett appeared from different directions.

Torbett: "What's going on?"

I glared at Jeffries. "We were discussing procedure."

Jeffries snorted and pulled Milsap aside. Torbett tilted his head in their direction. "Why."

When the whole squad showed I passed out the new sketches of Nikki I'd ordered, with long black hair and lighter eyes. I told them the plan, the kind of big shake-up we do once in a while when we need a lot of high-yield interviews at once, and when we need to make the squad work like a team. "I'm on point, Waller follows in fifteen seconds, then the rest. No unnecessary noise. I guarantee we walk out with something."

Jeffries said, "If we don't?"

"Squad outing to the Yellow Rose when we nail the fucker."

"If we do?" Waller asked with a half-grin.

"Same. Let's go." Grins and glances around the circle. A frat boy in a Volkswagen pulled into the lot, saw us and pulled back out.

I walked into the red-carpeted reception room first and let the door swing shut, smiled bashfully at the hostess behind the podium and mumbled until I got close enough to see her hands and the warning button.

"Hi, I'm Dan."

"Hi, Dan," she said. "What can we do for you?"

I showed her my badge. "Step away from the podium and don't make a sound." She froze. "I'm gonna say it again. Step away from the podium. Do not touch those buttons and don't make a sound." I led her away from the podium. Waller stuck his head in and I gave him the nod.

The squad slid in and moved up the hall until each of us was outside a door—no shortage of full rooms at rush hour. We each put an ear up to a door and waited for the big moment.

Torbett was the first to go. He slipped into the room, opening and closing the door silently. Whatever he said didn't carry out to the hall, but I guessed the guy in the room heard it.

I was closest to the lobby, so when one of the girls wandered out from the back room, I showed her my badge, motioned her to stay quiet. The customer in Room A was at a turning point. When he got to full moan I slipped in, shut the door and badged him.

"APD." He gaped at me. I held up the sketch. "This girl look familiar to you?"

The guy drew a blank. I heard Jeffries yell, "Live one!" and I ran to find him. A woman was standing behind the table in a black leotard, half-paralyzed. Jeffries had the customer, a scrawny little guy of about fifty, against a wall, crying and wearing the beginnings of a black eye he didn't get from the girl.

Jeffries hulked over him, fists clenched. "Where?! Where'd you see her?"

"I s-s-s—"

"What!" Jeffries punched the same eye again.

I pulled Jeffries off and threw him at the table. "Cool it!" I said. He picked up his two-hundred-something pounds and slammed me against the wall with them. I head-butted him over the eyebrow and he pulled back and got his bearings, yelling, "Kike bastard! Come and get me."

"No, come get me. Come get me Friday morning with your impartial testimony. You nail me, I'll fuckin' *crucify* you!"

Torbett yelled, "Hey!" and stopped me dead. "Jeffries, whatcha got?"

Jeffries checked his head for blood and turned back to the customer doubled up in the corner. "Tell him!"

"I saw her!"

I said, "What's her name?"

He shook his head.

"How do you know it was her?"

He pointed to the picture. "Eyes. Her eyes." It was her.

"Where?"

He sniffed and snorted. "L-live Models. Fifth Street."

It was a whorehouse, closed down six months ago. Men paid to watch models walk around in their underwear. The management said what they did in the back room on their own time was their own business. The Attorney General didn't buy it.

"When?"

He looked confused, like he never thought of keeping track.

"When did you see her?"

"I don't know. A year?"

"You askin' or tellin'?" Jeffries cut in and slapped him. The customer winced. "A year. Last year."

"Summertime?" I asked.

"Yes."

"You had sex with this pretty girl at Live Models on Fifth Street last summer?"

We got a few more specifics plus his driver's license and office phone before letting him put his underwear on. Jeffries handed the girl a towel and dropped his card. Then he made a show of letting me leave the room first, and I made a show of not worrying about turning my back on him.

I sent the squad off again with the sketches and the new dirt on Dirty Sally, and called Logan at the Attorney General's office. Logan likes cops. He wants to be one when he grows up.

"Dan the man! What can I do for you?"

"I'm gonna send you a sketch of this girl. All we know is she might have done Houston two years ago, stripped in K.C. a year and a half ago, Austin a year ago working at Live Models on Fifth, and Austin again a month or so ago, on the skids. See what you can get. Oh. She went by Nikki, two *k*'s."

I gave him her dates and blood numbers and called my answering machine.

"Don't hang up." It was Aaron Gold. *"I'm gonna stay by my phone. Call me anytime all night. I want to meet you tomorrow morning if you have five minutes. Concrete evidence. I know you're gonna laugh, but I think I'm onto something hot."* I heard him rustling paper. *"No, scratch that. I KNOW I am."*

15

The Big W.H.O.

8:30 P.M. President's Mansion, West Campus

University president William Henry Oliver the Third surveyed the ballroom with controlled pleasure. Champagne flowed. Captains of industry hobnobbed with captains of politics. Beautiful young women chatted up older men, took business cards, promised to send their résumés. Big-haired wives looked the other way. Men and women both beamed back at Oliver's warm, confident smile, then almost bowed away.

A few clusters away Oliver saw his son and heir John Oliver, twenty-five, fresh out of law school, a young, slim, fair-haired version of Oliver himself, chatting with two doting old dowagers. But John's smirk gave away his sense of superiority and entitlement. It would be his undoing.

The chatter hushed as Franklin Pollard took the podium, a white silk banner across it reading MISSION: SUC-

CESS! and adjusted the microphone down to his height. "Can ya see me?" They chuckled politely at the comforting contrast to Oliver's appearance, Oliver's six feet and full white hair versus the bald elf.

"Austin is the *oasis* of Texas," Pollard began in the studied East Texas medicine-show drawl that made words like "oasis" a challenge. "An oasis of cultural *re*sources as well as natural ones, beautiful hills, lakes, the evenin' sky, the bluebonnets. The early city planners saw all this and created well-intentioned but short-sighted policies affecting the *quality* of life of Austin's *citizens.*

"Your participation tonight celebrates the prosperity of the university and the resurgence in economic growth for the state, the future of Texas, and ultimately, the nation. *You* make that possible.

"Now, Ah'd like to talk to you tonight about a certain public figure, whose administration is notorious for waste and fraud." Gray-haired men shook their heads. "Who has been known to support higher taxes, even once suggested a state income tax!" The crowd grumbled. "A man who is *soft on crime.*" Someone started to boo. "But Ah don't wanna spoil your dinner." Laughter. "So Ah'm gonna go with a topic that Ah *know* is a crowd-pleaser—Dr. Bill Oliver, university president and patriot of the great state of Texas.

"Bill Oliver has spearheaded the anti-camping law which will discourage vagrancy and improve the quality of life of Austin's *citizens,* and for their children. Bill Oliver single-handedly turned the university around, brought in record amounts of research money, has supported ongoing construction and raised the university's national standing each year. His work has made the university the only branch of the state government to operate at a profit."

Hums of admiration. Oliver radiated his calming presence through the room, each guest almost blushing at his glance, as if Oliver were winking at him invisibly, as if he were Oliver's favorite, the subject and object of each declaration.

"Bill Oliver is tough on crime," Pollard went on. "He will lower your taxes, and he will root out waste and fraud and send 'em packin'!" Champagne glasses went around as Oliver moved toward the podium. "Bill Oliver will support development in Austin—development of technology for your homes and leisure, of a better quality of life, of freedom from waste and fraud and crime and taxes, of social services off the backs of the taxpayers like you and into the hands of private business, of high technology that will make unemployment a thing of the past." Applause as the crowd squeezed closer to him. "Bill Oliver has turned the university around and he'll do the same with the state." Pollard lifted a glass jubilantly. "Ah give you William Henry Oliver the Third!" He raised his pitch and volume on each word: *"The next—governor—of TEXAS!"*

9:00 P.M. HQ

I reached the squad room and lunged for the ringing phone. "Homicide."

"Detective Reles?" It was Aaron Gold, way hyped up and out of breath.

"Jesus. Look, I'm busy."

"Y-you said evidence, right? Concrete evidence of a crime. I've got it."

"I don't suppose you could tell me over the phone."

"Can't. Security issue."

"Give me a hint or I hang up."

"Do you guys still have an Organized Crime Division?"

"For TriMondo? You're talking white-collar crime. It's not the same."

"They'd never listen to me, but they'd listen to you, right?"

"Yeah, maybe, if I could prove something."

"I can prove it. I'm gonna meet with an old friend tonight. Tomorrow I'll tell you more than you want to know."

He was getting on my nerves, this spoiled middle-class kid playing spy. "I got a dead girl here. Can't it wait?"

He didn't say anything for a second, then blurted out, *"I got a dead guy HERE, remember?!"*

"All right, that's it. Don't call me again. I'll call you when I have time."

"By then it could be too late!" He sounded desperate, a big melodrama.

I hung up saying, "I'll risk it."

And I did.

9:30 P.M. The Outhouse

Tejani was shooting pool.

Not his regular place, you understand. Needed to stay out of the regular joints. Needed to stay one jump ahead of Guerrin, this close to the finale.

Tejani had the table closest to the dance floor, alongside the pinball and bowling machines. Some band was playing jungle music; tattooed, pierced young shitheads slamming around the floor. He didn't care. He had a cold beer, a noseful of candy and his own pool table. He lined up the shot.

He still felt raw and angry from the afternoon with the

chick from the escort service. He couldn't finish on account of the coke, untied her and left her boo-hooing in the room. "Why were you in the motel with him?" the cops would ask. "So you were whoring and you're charging this man with rape?" She'd never call the cops. She knew what to expect. She'd cover the scar and bruises and go back to work.

It flashed through his head again. *Il faut que le père ne sache jamais.* "Your father must never know."

The cue ball went into the pocket.

"Motherfuckin' shit!" he screamed.

Higher-ups who did worse than he did on their days off, stripped his badge and sent him up the river for four years in the Fed. He'd sent guys to the Fed, and they remembered him, branded him, laughed every time they saw his scar. Four years of pain made him hungrier for everything. Food, booze, dope, pussy. More, more, more. He scratched the scar on the back of his neck.

"Fuckin' Guerrin." He ground his teeth. "You're mine. While you're deep in sleep I'll be crawling through your house. You'll wake up looking into my eyes. *Then* we'll make a deal!" The crowd swung closer to the table and jarred his cue stick as he lined up a shot. He swung around.

A punk chick was slamming her body around. Not looking at anything, just slamming. Twists of hair in crayon red and green, a half inch of black at her roots, chubby cheeks and black eye makeup running with the sweat. She had on a baby blue tank top and jeans, and tits that stood straight out when they weren't bouncing. She was young, maybe twenty, but she knew how to have a good time.

She caught him looking at her and jumped up and

down harder. Finally she turned away, and he went back to his game.

As he lined up the next shot, someone bumped into him. The girl, dripping sweat. He looked down. "You got nice tits," he said.

She took the silk handkerchief from his jacket pocket, wiped her face and chest, and stuffed it back in place.

He watched her move back into the crowd, not looking at anyone. She slammed into a few people, got pushed back. Some guy told her to cool it. She screamed, "Fuck off, cocksucker!"

Tejani couldn't take his eyes off her. He made his way through the crowd and started dancing near her, then tapped her. She turned to him.

10:00 P.M. HQ

I spent the rest of the night hitting strip joints and massage parlors with Nikki's sketch and chasing down the least crazy phone calls we got from Denton's TV commercial. I met a lonely guy who watched a lot of television and called every number it gave him. A woman fingered a neighbor whose house stank, she said, from dead bodies. He turned out to be a depressed fat guy who couldn't get it together to do his dishes. They piled high in his kitchen, caked with rotting black sludge.

One woman showed me a picture and cried when I told her that the victim wasn't her long-missing daughter. She'd suffered so much, knowing the girl was dead would have been a relief. Then she said she wasn't sure what relief would feel like. I told her I understood.

•

10:00 P.M. Magnolia Café

Aaron Gold sat in his booth at Mag's sipping iced hibiscus tea and watching the entrance. The "old friend" chuckled when he heard Aaron's voice calling from the pay phone and agreed to get together. They hadn't seen each other in nearly two years. Aaron pasted a smile on his face as his old buddy stepped into the restaurant in a tailored suit, surveying the place as if he'd just bought it.

Aaron waved at him and he strode over, saying, "I can't believe you still eat here!"

There had been plenty of bad blood between their two families. Aaron didn't hold him responsible, but it was harder after John came back from law school, a young version of his world-dominating father. Aaron could put his feelings aside for an hour or so, or at least pretend to, while he pumped him for information about the old man.

He only hoped his old pal John Oliver was sucker enough to go for it.

10:30 P.M. 307 Barton Creek Boulevard

Tejani and the girl stumbled from his Buick into the darkened house. She peeled his jacket off him, then jerked on his tie a few times before untying it. He squeezed her breasts hard. Instead of whining, she kissed him harder, sucking his tongue till he tasted his own blood.

She slid to her knees, unzipped his fly and slid him into her mouth.

Tejani's back slammed against the wall. She liked cock, she liked the blood from his tongue. She let him feel her up in the back of the bar. He wasn't sure how he'd gotten here. "Ow!" he yelled. "Easy!"

She pulled him out of her mouth and ripped open his shirt, sending buttons flying. Then she pulled down his pants and shorts, toppling him onto a couch. She kicked off her shoes and peeled off her jeans, her black pubic hair wet and matted. She moved toward him wearing only the tank top, then straddled Tejani and slid him inside of her.

She rode like pure silk. Smooth, smooth, rolling wet up and down.

Il faut que le père ne sache jamais.

Your father must never know.

Armand Tejani, fourteen, cuts school and tails his mother. She's been dressing up and going out nights. Then the outings drop off to telephone arguments and finally, muffled sobs Armand and Emmett pretend not to hear from their bedroom. Their father's been on the other side of the planet tending his ailing parents for six months. One night Armand hears her make an appointment, agree to bring the money in cash and to come alone. He finds the address in her bag. The next afternoon he goes there half an hour early, scopes a cracked glass door opposite the bus station and waits.

He sees her walking short, clipped steps toward the cracked door, check the address and go in. He waits five minutes and follows, through the glass door, up the steep stairway, into the unmarked door at the first landing. Seedy waiting room, like a doctor's office only not quite, marked by a huge two-hundred-pound bulldagger in nurse's whites going yellow. "What?" she says. Past the dyke he hears muffled moaning behind a door and he engines for it. The dyke blocks his way and he thinks, That's my mother in there, and pounds the dyke with his fists, raining her with blows until he can shove her out of the way and open the door.

The iron smell of blood makes Armand recoil. A man in surgical gown spins around on a stool, his chest and arms dripping blood, to gape at the intruder. Armand sees a pair of legs, feet in stirrups, steel machinery spreading and intruding in a large bloody hole. Over that, the pale, weak face of his mother. "Il faut que le père ne sache jamais," she says. "Your father must never know," and in that moment makes him complicit in her dirty, dirty secret, her crime.

Tejani opened his eyes wide, shook off the image, reached the coke vial out of his pants and snorted.

He was on top of the world. He was high, he shot pool, he was a killer, a player. He had bigwigs running scared. He fucked up classy escort service chicks in motels. And now this sleazy gash who didn't know him from Adam only wanted to ride up and down on his cock. Life was smooth, smooth, from here on in.

The girl leaned way forward and started bouncing, slowly, then faster, then faster still. Tejani felt himself well up as she began a low moan.

"Oh, oh, my big man," she wailed. "I'm gonna come."

Tejani grabbed her buttocks and slid her up and down. She moaned louder.

Every bounce knocked the breath out of her.

"Petite mort." The words rolled out of Tejani's mouth as he heard her moan. The French words for coming. "Little death."

"Oui," she puffed between breaths. She spoke French.

He could feel her clamp down on him, her insides buzzing as the world welled up inside of him. He grabbed her tighter, tried to roll her over and couldn't.

"Me too! I'm gonna come too!" He kept pumping as he felt the tide break.

"*Petite mort!*" she said between breaths. "*Non! C'est magnifique! La grande mort!* You like?"

"*Oui,*" he said, losing his breath, grabbing onto her for one big final thrust. "*Oui.*"

"Good."

He squeezed his eyes shut, then opened them for an instant, just long enough to see the blur of the ice pick as she plunged it down into his heart.

10:45 P.M. 6009 Mount Bonnell Road

Royce Guerrin sat in his den, the large window overlooking Mount Bonnell, sipping a fresh martini as a brief sense of relief rolled warmly through him.

PART TWO

JIGSAW

16
THURSDAY

Round two.

I heard the story so many times I can see it. Big smoky night at the fights. Opening featherweight bout between Lefty Mortellaro and Ben "Kid Twist" Reles, a hundred and twenty-six pounds of solid muscle with a nickname he copped from his namesake Abe Reles, a badass New York gangster out of the thirties. Five hundred dollar purse, winner take all. Big guys at ringside chewing cigars or spitting tobacco juice. Ben Reles's young career was 6 and 0, 4 by knockout. Tonight he was a 3-to-2 favorite over Mortellaro. Half the goons in upstate New York were there, a big night.

Before the second round, Pop's manager came to him in the corner. "You go down this round."

Pop choked up. "What are you talkin' about?"

"You heard me. Stall about thirty seconds. Then he gets you with his famous left hook."

"His famous left hook blows dogs."

"Ike says so."

Sitting on the stool in his corner, Ben felt the blow in his guts. Ike Zelig said so. Kid Twist takes a dive against a bum. The gods decided.

"Round two!"

He danced around and made a couple of jabs to make it look good. Then he slowed down. He figured it might make sense if he looked tired. Lefty Mortellaro wound up for his famous left hook. Pop could've escaped on a bus. Instead he leaned into it and went down.

The crowd booed and threw beer bottles into the ring. Pop rolled over and got up on his hands and knees. They hated him. A voice pounded in his head, told him to get up, get up and fight! His manager shouted from ringside.

"Stay down, ya dumb fuck. It's a KO!"

Kid Twist dropped onto the canvas on his shoulder. A beer bottle knocked him on the head.

It was the first in a long series of favors my father would do for the mob, followed fast by numbers runner, delivery man, and finally the thing he swore he'd never do, shakedown man. He had a grudging respect for mom-and-pop storeowners and their honest day's work, even though he never put in a day like that himself. That second phase of his career ended suddenly the famous night he woke me up and drove us to Texas with no explanation except that "certain parties" were no longer crazy about him. I see him running out the door like a scared mouse, his career, his wife and now his home gone because of what the gods wanted. And me grabbing my mother's picture and wondering how she would find us when she came back.

The big boys needed something and little lives got crushed under their feet. That was in Elmira. In Austin, someone hacked up a girl and was sending pieces to the local gentry. But something felt familiar.

9:00 A.M. Medical Examiner's Office

By the time I got to Hay's office she'd run the bloodwork and confirmed that all the parts, including the face, were from the same girl. Hay was buzzing around the autopsy room, moving jars and signing forms. "It would be easier if I got a whole body," she said.

"I'm working on it." I gave her the sketch and told what I knew. Nikki, ex-party girl, ex-stripper, prostitute, a few brief contacts over a few years, no Known Associates. And not a hit on the doer.

"You'll like this, then," she said. "Partial print inside the plastic wrap on the face package. Forensics sent it up for tracking."

In the squad room, Jake Lund tapped at the computer. "Oh, hey!" he said. "There's some messages for you." He pointed to a mountain of message slips by the phone. "And this." He handed me an overnight package from the NCIC in Washington. I tore it open, a stack of Missing Person reports, A-negative females—white, brown, Asian—who would be seventeen to twenty-three, starting with the most recent and going back: pictures from college graduations, high school yearbooks, sweet sixteens, bat mitzvahs, first communions.

I flipped through the phone messages looking for anything legit and found a callback from Logan.

"Check this out," Jake said. He unfolded a tabloid newspaper on the desk. The headline screamed TEXAS JIGSAW MASSACRE!!!

"No."

"Dude, you're famous!"

They had cut up photos of three beautiful women—black, white and Latina—and patched them together as one multicolored one. Sex, violence and mystery—everything you need to build mass panic. I dialed Logan at the AG.

"*Logan here.*"

"Reles. Whattaya got?"

"*Just a second. . . . Okay, nothing on the name Nikki, not at Live Models when we closed them or anything. Slippery chick. I got a Vicki, born Anselma Markus, Dallas, 4/28/68, looked something like the sketch but brown eyes—*"

"No."

"*Maybe they know her with contact lenses.*"

"No."

"*Okay, 'Precious,' born Francine Kohl, Pepper Pike, Ohio, 8/4/70, light green eyes, and . . . Natalie Podell, born Abilene, 7/17/69. All type A-negative, all in and out of Austin in the last three years. I'll send you the files.*"

"That's it?"

"*The Live Models parlor was owned on paper by a guy named Fred Harrell.*"

The phone book had two Fred Harrell residences and one office. I called and hung up on three answering machines, shuffled through my notes and found something about the methadone clinic that made me think. The phone rang and Jake picked up.

"Homicide, Lund." He was writing notes and groaning about something.

Denton's press package made things hard, but I knew what I was after: one beautiful party girl/stripper/streetwalker named Nikki, Caucasian, black hair, glassy blue or gray eyes, born probably around '67, who once maybe worked at a massage parlor that closed six months ago. What I still didn't know was who she was and why someone chose her to send his message.

Jake hung up the phone. "Aw, man!"

"What?"

"911 call, jumper from University Tower, and I'm doing *this*."

"Tough break," I said.

"Dude, you think this is easy? It takes forever just to put it in, and I have to make sure it goes out to the right places."

"Info exchange between geeks."

"That's what they said about radio."

There was nothing to say to that except "I surrender," so I headed to University Tower. I figured I'd run through the suicide in half an hour, give Jake the paperwork and head up to the methadone clinic, then maybe swing by one of the Fred Harrells.

I drove up Red River to the university with my lights flashing, badged the security booth and followed the service roads to the main building and the tower that shot up, four windows wide and twenty-eight stories straight up in the middle of campus—the rest of town could kneel down and worship. I got out by two parked University Police cars and an ambulance and walked around to the north side of the building. Ambulance workers waited while a couple of officers in chalk blue uniforms held back a crowd of knapsacked students, and a fat white-haired geezer in a tunic and captain's bars took notes over what looked like a twisted, bloody duffel bag.

The duffel bag had long brown hair, a scraggly beard and John Lennon glasses. Aaron Gold would never waste my time again.

17

10:00 A.M. Chuy's Mexican Restaurant, Rear

Royce Guerrin steered his Mercedes into the narrow alley separating the restaurant from a chain-link fence at the grassy border of Zilker Park, checked his mirrors to see if he'd been followed and stepped out into the heat and the stench of rotten taco meat. He saw her winking from behind the Dumpster and he followed, looking behind him, recoiling from the stink and chafing in his silk suit.

She leaned against the red brick looking satisfied, a round-faced teenager bursting out of a black T-shirt, tight black miniskirt and army boots, black roots in her red and green hair and excess mascara for daytime, like an overgrown baby playing grown-up. "Well?" he asked.

She handed him a card, Armand Tejani's driver's license.

"You could have lifted his wallet."

She handed him a Polaroid, the same man flat on his back, eyes wide in a terror scream, red-handled ice pick plunged into his chest, nude, fully erect. Guerrin's empty stomach rushed up. He bent over and retched, coughing up bitter spit. When he got his breath he reached out an envelope and watched her count the four thousands. "Is this the only photo?" he asked. She nodded. "What about the . . . body?"

"Rat food. I mulched him. Teeth and all."

"How did you do that?" She nodded to the restaurant's kitchen door. "Don't tell me, don't tell me."

"I get to keep the car," she said.

"Make sure they can't trace it."

"You think I'm stupid?" she asked. He had no way of knowing. He'd found her number on a scrap of paper in Harrell's box under the word *"Anything."*

"Anything else?" she asked, her chubby hands now palming his crotch.

"No, please." He pulled away and found himself backed against the Dumpster. To protect his suit he stepped forward and deeper into Anything's clutch, now squeezing his genitals as he sweated through his suit, vomit taste in his mouth and the photo of the dead man in his hand. "No. Please," he begged helplessly, his heart pounding pre-coronary as she reached into his shorts and pressed her body against his.

10:00 A.M. University Tower

I gaped at Aaron, his right arm twisted behind him where he lay on the concrete, upper-right quarter of skull crushed down to the temple of his blackened face. His head soaked in a pool of blood and brain fluid.

A uniform appeared standing over me. Ruddy face

and white hair under his captain's hat made him look ex-Navy.

"I'm . . . Reles, APD Homicide." I realized I was kneeling.

"Ace Knippa, University Police. Looks like we got a jumper."

My voice rang hoarse. "The tower has restricted access."

"He didn't fall from the ground."

"Go on."

"Look at his eyes."

Aaron's eyes stared from his blackened skin. I thought of charred Joey at the bottom of that hill. Aaron's right pupil was blown, fully expanded, standard reaction from a crushing blow to that side. But the left pupil was a pinpoint.

"Look at his arm," Knippa said.

In the crook of his left elbow I found a bruise the size of a quarter.

"Heroin," I said to myself.

"Looks like."

I squinted up toward the crow's nest at the top of the tower. I couldn't see it for the glaring sunlight. "So he shot up and jumped off the tower?"

"Maybe he shot up before he went upstairs," Knippa offered.

"And high as a kite on heroin, he broke through security and climbed twenty-seven flights to the top of the tower, just to jump? It's not that kind of drug."

"What difference does it make when he shot it?" Knippa said. "He jumped!"

In 1966 a bank teller named Charles Whitman climbed those stairs and took target practice from the top of the tower. That and a dozen suicides and they only open the tower to trustees they're hitting up for money and only under strict supervision. "How'd he get in?"

"There's ways!"

"It's your job to see there aren't."

Knippa eyed his two flunkies, now gawking at the confrontation, and probably figured he couldn't afford to lose. He raised himself up to his full height. "This suicide is under the jurisdiction of the University Police," he fumed. "If you don't believe me, take the matter up with your own department."

It was horseshit but I needed outside authority to take over. I found a pay phone and called Miles.

"Niederwald."

"I'm on campus. A kid, Aaron Gold, was found at the bottom of the tower. University Police say he jumped, I say he was thrown. Who has authority?"

"Shit, Reles. This town only gets forty murders a year. How many you want for yourself?"

"He was my informant and now he's dead."

Miles thought it over. *"Doesn't matter. If it's suicide, it's theirs."*

"Nobody asks for protective custody and then jumps off a building!"

"Why, 'cause you say so?! Who's in charge, you?"

"Look—"

"No, goddammit, you look! I got Denton up my ass, the mayor calling . . . forget this shit and get back on the case!" He hung up.

I found a campus directory and tore out the page with Aaron's listing: Gold, Aaron Moses. CAS 703 W. 24th, Union 14E. Some kids use student organization offices as their campus address. I ran over to Aaron's office at the Student Union, the door labeled DEMOCRACY IN ACADEMIA, slid the latch open with a flat shim from my wallet and went inside.

Snapshots of Aaron and his friends were tacked all over a corkboard. Arms linked in front of the Capitol Building, Aaron yelling through a bullhorn. Aaron grinning into the camera, next to a fully-intact Rick Schate I recognized from his ID photo, and two other longhairs in Jamaican Rasta knit hats, all passing a pipe around a coffee table. Under that snapshot the name "Rob" cut out in paper over a cluster of Polaroids. A boy younger than Aaron, shorter dark hair, clean shaven if he had anything to shave. Rob was pictured with his nose in a book, then reading a speech before a crowd. Rob, Aaron, Rick and others marching with their arms around each other's shoulders. At the bottom was a laminated card. On one side it had a portrait of Rob. On the back it had the Lord's prayer and the name of a funeral home.

Next to the pictures of Rob hung a single snapshot of Rick Schate. Aaron believed Rick Schate had also been "disappeared."

I rifled through the desk drawers: paper clips, markers, condoms, rolling paper. Nothing about his pet project, Tri-Mondo Developing. I headed back to my car by the tower, my head spinning around the idea of a second murder in my lap, grunting, "I *should* have listened, I *should* have listened. . . ."

The university's motto thundered across the building's arch like the eleventh commandment, huge block letters carved in the stone: YE SHALL KNOW THE TRUTH, AND THE TRUTH SHALL MAKE YOU FREE.

I radioed Dispatch and told them to find Waller.

"He's not answering. He must've stepped out."

"All right," I said, and thought a moment. "Get me Torbett."

18

2:00 P.M. 703 West Twenty-fourth Street

James Torbett got the word on his car radio, call Reles on a land line, and a campus number. When Reles answered, Torbett couldn't help but think how the man sounded spooked. Reles said he would stay on Dirty Sally, that Torbett should take over Aaron Gold, the unofficial suicide of one of Reles's informants. Then Reles gave Torbett the specifics on Gold and told him to find out if they added up.

"Why don't I stay on Sally," Torbett asked him. "You take care of Gold. You knew him."

"*I can't,*" Reles said, his voice giving away strain.

"Why?"

"*I just can't, Torbett! Just do it. Please.*"

In a hostile system, Torbett thought, where half your job was staying alive, you needed an ally. Your best shot might be someone in the machine but not part of the machine, not a Texan or a Southerner. A Yankee and a Jew.

The building where Gold lived cropped up two blocks west of campus, a hippie enclave in an area heavy with frozen margarita bars catering to the fraternity system. The first floor housed a hair salon and a head shop. The second a tutoring service run by a pair of middle-aged brothers who walked around in their stocking feet, tutoring rich white kids for a feeble price. The third floor was apartments and squatters. On the front steps two stoned white boys in tie-dyed shirts jabbered.

"I had responsibilities."

"You didn't have responsibilities. You played your Walkman all the time and got high!"

"I was the guy—I had responsibilities! I had the keys . . ."

They finally noticed Torbett standing before them and blinked.

"You guys live here?" he asked

"Maybe."

Torbett stepped between them and went inside. There was a set of mailboxes, the names "Gold/Schate" written on number 31 in pencil. He took the stairs two at a time.

Three young people sat on bedrolls in the hall. The balsa wood door to 31 had been kicked open, not even jimmied.

Someone had ransacked the small, sunny apartment. Drawers pulled out and overturned, bookshelves standing empty. Besides the furniture, nothing marked the presence of two young men except clothes, a phone, a waterpipe and a poster of Ché Guevara.

"Pigs were here, man."

Torbett turned to see the less stoned of the two boys from the steps, standing in the doorway. "Which pigs?"

"I don't know," he chuckled. "They were dressed better than you."

"Did you see a badge?"

He shook his head. "They said they were police. Picked the place clean, I guess. Said they were looking for dope." The boy chuckled bitterly. "Dope, right."

Torbett dusted every smooth surface for prints and found they'd wiped the room clean. He picked up the phone and dialed a number at Southwestern Bell.

"Operator."

"This is Sergeant James Torbett, APD, clearance Alpha 7583. I need to know all the incoming and outgoing calls from this phone over the last forty-eight hours."

3:10 P.M. Anderson and Guerrin

Still shell-shocked, I ran down the list of meat recipients again, visiting them each with Nikki's latest sketch. Keenan, Grant . . . I greeted Royce Guerrin's receptionist, an athletic-looking young brunette, and had her ring him. "Mr. Guerrin? Sergeant Reles from Austin Police Homicide to see you again. . . . Mr. Guerrin? There's a Sergeant—oh, sorry, I didn't hear you. Yes." She gave me a smile I'd remember. "He'll be right with you."

I looked out a window onto a stretch of greenery. "Are you guys in on that Barton Springs thing?"

The receptionist smiled. "That's us!"

Some of the glass and steel furniture in the corner was probably made for sitting on but I couldn't figure out which, before Guerrin buzzed back with what was probably a commanding "Send him in!"

Royce Guerrin, fiftyish, pale and pasty, gestured to a chair. "Have you learned anything?"

I flashed him the sketch. He blinked. I might have missed it. "You know this girl."

"No."

"I thought you might have recognized her."

He squinted at the picture. "That's the murdered girl, right?"

"Have you met her?"

"Not that I recall."

"Ever see eyes like that?" He looked. Nothing. "Maybe at a party, or . . ."

He smiled weakly. "I don't get out much."

"I hate to keep taking your time, you and the other nine guys." I walked around the room, stealing glances at him. "But there has to be some reason you were targeted. Some misdemeanor, maybe something you don't want your wife knowing about. . . ." Nothing. "Thanks for your time," I said. He walked me toward the door.

"I'm afraid I haven't been any help."

"Call me if you think of anything." I stopped at the door. "We just want to find out what we can. We're not arresting johns." No reaction. "Later, of course," I half-smiled, "if I find out you were holding back, it would be withholding evidence, interfering with an investigation, maybe accessory after the fact." He stared blank, then laughed it off. I was operating on about two cylinders.

So the interview wouldn't be a total loss, I took a long look at his receptionist on the way out. "Thanks . . ." I said.

"Tina," she offered, smiling.

"Right. Thanks, Tina."

3:20 P.M. Anderson and Guerrin

Guerrin choked down a Valium and breathed hard. He couldn't get enough oxygen, five minutes on the witness stand with that police thug, trying to monitor his own breathing and his eyes, make himself look disinterested. Each interview got harder. They had to be onto him. He hauled out the mobile phone and dialed Payne.

"Yes."

"He was here. The . . . the one in charge," Guerrin gasped.

"So?"

"You have to do something . . . about him."

"Like what?"

"Something."

"You know what you're asking? He could get sucked up by space aliens. It wouldn't change anything."

Guerrin hissed in a frantic whisper. "I'm not going to prison. If there's a paper trail, it leads to me."

"All they can prove is you're a pimp."

Guerrin felt veins pop out in his forehead. "I don't want to be connected to those brothels and neither do you!"

"How long are you gonna throw that in my face?!"

"How long do you want me to keep cutting those checks?"

"Don't you have anything on him? I thought you had something on everybody."

Guerrin eyed the glossies in the drawer. "Just some old candid shots of his . . . Mexican friend."

Payne didn't say anything. Finally, *"Hold onto them. I'll think of something."*

"When—"

"*Don't push me, Guerrin!*" Payne shouted. "*I don't have much left to lose.*" The man hung up.

Guerrin breathed deep. He had to remember what kind of man he was dealing with. They could have a civilized conversation, that always threw him off. But he knew too well what Payne was capable of.

3:50 P.M. East Twelfth Street

The sun sizzled its daily peak at Fahrenheit 103 and with barely two brain cells to rub together I stopped at a methadone clinic famous for short-tempered counselors and sexual misconduct with clients. Milsap had been there Monday and today, or said he had, and got nothing, but I had a hunch. The clerk I saw thought she recognized the sketch and pulled a bunch of files, narrowing it to "Keeley Smith," DOB 2/14/67—Valentine's Day—Blood Type A-neg, SSN 989-00-8745, visited 7/15/87. The double zeroes indicated a dummy Social Security number, probably from a card that came with the wallet. They took her blood type when they tested her but didn't take any other numbers or keep a sample. They never saw her after that.

"I don't know if this is important," the clerk said, pulling a list of phone numbers from a drawer, "but we try to hook them up with other social services. They don't usually go. Suicide hotlines, food stamps, dental clinic—"

"Dental clinic?"

"Mostly their teeth are pretty bad."

The staff at the dental clinic remembered the face but not the name. I tried a few—Keeley Smith, Nikki Smith,

Nikki Kelly—finally, bingo on Kelly Valentine, DOB 1/1/67. Visited 7/16/87, the day after her visit to the methadone hut. Big bingo: full set of dental X-rays. I bounced them back to Jake to send to Forensics, Missing Persons and Washington. Now we had a face, teeth, full blood workup and a handwriting sample (but no finger-prints) from the motel register. It was only a matter of time before we matched them to a name, but how *much* time? Whenever I blinked I saw Aaron Gold with his skull smashed or Nikki's carved remains on the autopsy table. And I had a hearing at seven the next morning to establish my psychiatric fitness.

7:00 P.M. Public Records, West Eleventh Street

Torbett contacted every department at APD that might have had an interest in Aaron Gold. He also called the Sheriff's Office, Department of Public Safety, University Police and the FBI. Officially, no one had anything on him beyond disturbing the peace. No one had visited his house. Officially. Torbett tracked all Gold's contacts from his home phone for the last forty-eight hours. No one knew who he'd seen, where he'd been or who might want him dead. But everyone knew Aaron's target: TriMondo. Torbett decided to do some research.

He walked up to the clerk, a chunky white woman with a long gray ponytail, and asked softly, "Miss, what can I find on TriMondo Developing?"

"Oh, that again."

"Excuse me?"

"Nothing," she said.

"Are they popular?"

"Well. There's this young boy who's always looking them up."

Torbett forced a chuckle. "Really?"

"He sneaks around here like Sherlock Holmes, figures no one will notice him. Long hair and a tie-dyed T-shirt. And he puts everything back in the wrong place."

"When was he here last?"

"Last night, by the SEC records. I'll show you." Torbett followed her to a shelf of blue binders. "I haven't been here yet today. Hmm." She scanned the binders. "There we go. '77, '78, '80, '82 . . . he started with '79, I'm sure of it. He's a sweet boy but a terrible spy."

Torbett took the first few binders and began flipping for TriMondo information. In 1979 he found: "CEO William Henry Oliver III: 51 percent." Next to that, the faint impression of handwriting. Torbett found a sharp pencil, held it at an angle and brushed the page. Words emerged.

$$WHO^3 = TriM \quad WHO^3 = UT \quad \therefore TriM = UT$$

WHO^3—William Henry Oliver the Third—equals TriMondo. WHO^3 equals UT. Oliver, the same Oliver, Torbett remembered, was the university president. Therefore TriMondo equals UT. The SEC might not care. The courts might not even care. But Aaron Gold thought it was a connection worth making.

Torbett moved to the newspapers. TriMondo Developing, incorporated 1970. Major offices in New York, London, Johannesburg. Outposts everywhere else. Sixth-largest U.S. corporate toxic chemical discharger. Locally, current planned development on Barton Creek amid protests. Who didn't know that? Torbett scanned microfilm after microfilm, old newspaper articles on the projection screen shining into his eyes. TriMondo this week at City Council hearing: the Barton Creek Planned Urban Development (PUD) bill would allow unrestricted construction around Barton Springs, a popular local swimming spot known for its natural source and its bracing fifty-degree water. Development expected to make the Springs permanently unswimmable. TriMondo two years back developing the Blacklands in East Austin, moving the old tenants by force. The hairs on the back of Torbett's neck crawled. TriMondo in the seventies, clearing Clarksville the same way, Torbett's old neighborhood, to make way for a rich white development. Something felt very wrong. He abandoned the daily paper and moved to the weekly paper, then finally to the radical papers, the ones that appeared for an issue or two, mostly in the sixties and seventies, and vanished.

The Austin Alternative Times, Spring 1979, an article called "TOWER TOPPLES": *"A state pilot program, touted as the first effective collaboratively run program between the State of Texas and private industry, closed this week amid major scandal and allegations of fiscal abuse."* New paragraph. *"TriMondo Developing, backer of the program . . ."*

Torbett didn't have to finish reading. He knew how the story ended, knew it firsthand.

8:00 P.M. 4612 Avenue F

The sun finally set and my leather holster was cutting into my side and the image of Aaron Gold at the bottom of the tower haunting me every time I blinked, when I pulled up in front of my house.

I flipped on the A/C, popped a beer and sat on the floor by the cardboard box of Joey's stuff. Along with the notebooks: the obit, evaluations, certificates that should have been framed, instead stuffed into a manila envelope. No maps or diagrams scribbled on napkins. At the bottom a snapshot of a younger, thinner Joey in some restaurant I didn't know, sitting at a table with a flushed smile and a cocaine-skinny party girl with wild makeup and bright red hair sticking in three directions. Rachel.

Without thinking, I called the Department of Public Safety and identified myself. "I need a Social Security number for Rachel Velez, maiden name Renier, 3809 Peck Avenue." If they asked why I needed it I couldn't have answered. I had a clue about Rachel's secret past and I needed to follow it up. I needed to know. I needed something to think about, something besides how I let Aaron Gold get killed.

Finally, the clerk said, *"Got it. 092-58-"*

"092?" I cut in. "That's New York State."

"Beats me. Just says her last license was in Houston. She moved here in '81."

I got the number and called Houston DPS, waited ten minutes flipping through Joey's old notebooks while they looked up her records. *"Okay, Rachel Renier, DOB March 25, 1958. Passed road test September 15, 1979, third attempt. You wanna hear all these traffic violations? Mostly speeding tickets, a few red lights, a drunk driving arrest—"*

"What?"

"Yeah, two noise complaints. On the second one she attacked the investigating officer. He brought her in but nothing about charges filed. Guess it was one of those 'cute drunk chick takes a swipe at a cop' things. And I have something weird about a domestic disturbance in November of '81 but no details."

"Can you find the report?"

"*Sorry, Ace, no time. I can have the arresting officer get back to you. Jack O'Connor.*"

I signed off trying to figure what made wild young Rachel turn into straight-edge Rachel, and dumped a manila envelope with some scraps. A single-edge razor blade wrapped in cardboard slipped out, just as there was a knock at my front door. What was Joey doing with a razor blade?

It was Torbett at the door. "What'd you get?" he asked as I let him in.

"Dental records. You?" He didn't answer. "You want a beer?" He sat on the couch. I got him a beer, then sat by the phone, opposite him in the darkening room. He stared over my shoulder out the front window. "What's going on?" I asked.

He sipped his beer and cooled his forehead with the bottle. "Tell me again," he said without looking at me, "what you know about Aaron Gold."

"His roommate got flattened by the number 6 bus Monday morning, Aaron thought it was a conspiracy." Aaron had told me that two days ago. It seemed like two years.

"What did he say about TriMondo?"

The question jolted my brain like a spark plug. "Barton Creek development. The Blacklands. Gold thought something big was happening. Why?"

Torbett rubbed his face. "You don't know what these people are capable of. A bunch of black people getting tossed out of their houses, that's what they do to warm up!" He looked away, fury in his bloodshot eyes. "I have a baby sister, twelve years younger than me. Ten years ago she got pregnant and her boyfriend took off. She didn't tell me, didn't tell anybody till later. That's when TOWER opened up, the women's health center. Read about it?" I shook my head. " 'Course you didn't. They put all those things way east of the interstate. Texas Office of Women's Health and Reproductive Services. TOWER. Shit."

He took a long swig. "She figured she was in luck, a public, safe, free clinic. She didn't know anything. TOWER was a joint venture between the state and Tri-Mondo Developing. So why is a developing corporation investing in a women's health clinic? How the hell do I know! But I do know that if the funding's private it means a bunch of board members make the decisions. And they hire the doctors."

The last of the sunlight disappeared while he was thinking, and I could see him only by the lamp from the drum room.

He said, "She got her abortion, all right. Came home late so my mother wouldn't see her sneak into the house looking sick. In the morning she said she had the flu, stayed in bed for days. Third day my mother tries to change the sheets, sees they're soaked with blood. My sister's hemorrhaging." He looked at me for the first time. "Perforated uterus. Another day and she'd have been dead."

"You sue them?" I said.

He turned on me, snarling. "Sue them?! That's some white folks' bullshit. You know a different Austin than I do. She can't have babies. *Ever!* Her and five other black girls. Word got out and they closed up shop. Doctor disappeared without a trace. Who pays?"

Then he said, "Someone killed Aaron Gold. Two guys in suits cleaned out his apartment, took his books, papers, everything, left no prints."

He took a long drink from his bottle, finished it.

"Wait," I said as the full meaning of what he said dawned on me. "Took his papers?"

Torbett said, "They wanted to know what he knew and they wanted to make sure no one else found out."

"TriMondo?"

He handed me a piece of paper he'd torn from a binder, the highlighted words, "CEO William Henry Oliver III: 51 percent" next to a mess of brushed pencil marks, a few letters half-emerged in white:

$$WHO^3 = TriM \quad WHO^3 = UT \quad \therefore TriM = UT$$

"Bill Oliver ran TriMondo before he ran the university," Torbett said. "Anybody could have known that, it was in Public Records. But Aaron was gonna make something of it."

"He told me something about that before. I didn't think it was important."

"Somebody did." He looked out the window again. "You know what the largest creature in the world is?" I didn't. "It's a network of cypress trees. The roots are attached, tree to tree, over a span of hundreds of miles. You can cut down one tree but you can't kill the roots. You don't beat evil, Dan." He'd never called me that before. "You think you win, and it draws back and pops up somewhere else. But it didn't move. It's here, it's there, it has a network that stretches across the world. It only chooses to show its face sometimes, and if that doesn't work, next time it pops up with a different face. And it is always way bigger than you."

"So what do you do? Quit?"

"No. You keep slugging." He stood. "I gotta go follow up on some of these things."

"No, go home."

"I'm not your errand boy. You're on Sally, I'm on Aaron Gold."

"I got him killed—"

"Get a grip, Reles—"

"Go home, Torbett. Go home to your family."

"What do you know about family?" That hung in the air. Torbett said, "I'm—"

I cut him off fast. "I meant give it a break. Sleep on it."

He walked out without another word.

19

9:30 P.M. Homicide Squad Room

Buck Jeffries tossed back a few drinks after dinner and now stood in the squad room, taping a copy of the STP poster to the wall. He liked it because the cop in the picture looked like him, when he was younger and had his waist. He had two copies but someone at Denny's wrote "Stop The Pigs!" across one of them in grease pencil while he was in the toilet. Jeffries liked to make an appearance at HQ now and then on his off shift. Showing yourself when you're not collecting on bets is good politics for a growing bookmaking operation.

Tomorrow morning at seven he'd be at Reles's hearing, and he had to have something hot. "We thought he'd be okay, but he keeps losing his temper." Not good enough. If he could find something on Reles, something to knock him off the force, or at least off Homicide . . .

A couple of freckle-faced baby dicks from CIB swung by and Jeffries waylaid them, chatting them up and offering odds on Saturday's Texas-Oklahoma game when the phone rang. "Hang on." The voice on the other end asked something about Reles—another crank. The boys were slipping toward the door.

"Take it easy, Buck. We gotta go."

"You boys be good now, y'hear?" Jeffries put the phone back to his ear.

". . . *from University Police.*" Jeffries didn't catch who was calling, but he was pretty sure he caught the name "Reles." The caller thought he was the Jew. The voice was distorted, like through a car radio. Dispatch must have patched him through. "*You running the case on that girl they cut up?*"

"Mm-hm."

"*We busted this girl blowing some guy by the tower. On the way to Central Booking she wants to get out, starts blabbing about her pimp slashing some girl, cutting a strip across her belly and dumping her in a ditch. Anything to it?*"

Jeffries felt something good in his stomach. None of the press knew about the girl being skinned across the middle. No one made that up. He mumbled, "Address?"

"*2204 Santa Rita.*"

Jeffries hung up the phone and ran.

9:30 P.M. 4612 Avenue F

I'd spent the day trying not to think about Aaron Gold's "suicide," to focus instead on Nikki. Aaron wasn't suicidal. He was afraid of getting killed, believed it happened to his friends. He even wanted to be taken in for his own protection.

Evil draws back, changes form and pops up somewhere else.

I put on my shorts and stood in front of the A/C. Aaron lay at the bottom of University Tower, his face blackened, his skull smashed. Aaron Gold should have been taken in. I should've taken him in.

Once toward the end I caught Joey in a sad stare, the kind where someone's eyes drop out of focus as he looks at the wreckage of his life. It was my father's standard look, and on Joey it scared the shit out of me. I jumped in with some crazy argument about what he was worth as a cop. "You could be a chief, a commissioner."

He broke out of the daze and forced a laugh, tapping the skin on his arm. "Too dark. But you could."

"No, you—"

"Ethnic name, white features. You could rise up. *El hijo surpase el padre.*" The son surpasses the father. He'd be disappointed today.

If I got really quiet, I could see Joey's burly smile in the shadows outside the darkened window. I tried to think what he would say.

Don't worry, homey. You'll be all right.

I didn't save him, Joey. I didn't even listen.

Can't listen to everybody. Ain't enough time in the day.

I was a selfish fuck. I was so busy mooching guidance off Joey that I never stopped to think about what he needed, what was going on inside of him, behind that mournful gaze. And I didn't help Aaron Gold. A raccoon scampered across the yard. I'd laid the razor blade from the envelope on the window sill. I wondered what that blade was doing in Joey's stuff.

I put on a record, cranked it and sat at the drums. The song's first notes, an electronic doodle, mocked me.

Drumming was the gift of a high school music teacher who saw something in me besides a discipline problem.

The segue from boxing to pounding the drums was seamless. You'd think after all that punching and slamming I'd have worked off more steam by now.

I tried to remember saying goodbye to Joey, that last night he was alive. I knew he was drinking more in those days. What about cocaine? All I could think was saluting him, then him roasting in a ditch while Rachel was off with some guy.

Then the cymbals whispered.

chee, tutuchee, tutuchee, tutuchee, tutu . . .

The drum part started simple. Heavy bass twice and then a crash, repeat, repeat, then four on the high toms and four on the low.

BOOM BOOM chee, BOOM BOOM chee

Something started rising inside me and I pounded harder, slamming my whole weight into the drums. I doubled the beat, rolling down the tom-toms. Aaron's face at the bottom of the tower. And Nikki's, then Joey and my mother, long gone, popped up in my mind. Amy who left me for being too angry. And Rachel off with some other guy, instead of with me. Sweat flew from my head.

I punched the drums harder, growling. My arms felt too strong, and the drums weren't fighting back. Then the drums on the record stopped, the music tiny, almost silent. No one asks for police protection then kills himself.

The bass kicked in again top volume as the singer wailed:

"Whooooo are You-ooooooooo?"

The snare drum went first. It split open and I pounded harder, watching the crack spread across the head, then punching my fist through and pulling it out bloody. I went on to the toms, pounded harder on each head as it stretched and stretched and finally snapped. By the time I got to the third tom, I was roaring and stabbing at it with the stick till it popped and fell over. I tossed it at the wall over the chair, knocking over the living room phone. I flung the ride cymbal across the room like a Frisbee. It bit into the front wall and stuck. I punched through the bass, ripping my skin again when I tried to pull my hand free. Then I tore the phone out of the wall, dragged the trashed drums out the front door and flung them one by one toward the curb, the final notes echoing in my head.

Then I got into the car and drove to Rachel's.

10:00 P.M. Santa Rita Street

Buck Jeffries cruised down Santa Rita in his white Grand Prix, spotted number 2204, then parked around the corner. He checked his flashlight and his gun, a Taurus Model 83 with full clip, took a long pull from the pint bottle of J&B he kept under the seat, slipped the bottle into his jacket pocket and hefted himself out of the car.

The house was a narrow A-frame with a rusted tin roof, a single window in front and a porch with an awning, no screens. Two metal chairs rusted behind a row of plants. Not much of a place for a pimp, but who knew how many girls he had or what he spent his money on. Animals.

The paint on the back of the house was badly chipped. Three wooden steps led up to the back door with its big glass window. No lights, no music, not a sound. And since when did pimps stay home on Thursday nights anyway?

He'd get comfortable and stake the place out all night if he had to. When the pimp rolled in around dawn, Jeffries would beat a confession out of him and wrap up the case right out from under Reles, then bury him at the evaluation.

Jeffries looked around to see if he was being watched, then picked the lock.

10:00 P.M. 3809 Peck Avenue

Rachel opened the door and stood in the doorway in a short blue and white kimono and probably nothing else, her legs stretching up to heaven. She was holding a glass of seltzer and a cigarette, surveying my sweaty shirt and my bloody hands. "I have to get up early for work," she said. "The kit's in the bathroom." I followed her inside. "I should get rid of it. It attracts the wrong element."

Blood from my knuckles swirled down the bathroom sink, and I wrapped gauze around my hands and fingers boxer-style as Rachel watched from the doorway and smoked.

She said, "Does this mean you've found a suspect?"

"You smoke more now."

"Job stress."

"Why'd you marry Joey?"

"Is this a formal interrogation? We can use a kitchen chair." She lifted an eyebrow. "I'll get the ropes."

"This is a new sink. I keep wondering how far that insurance money is gonna go."

She grinned, looked upward. "What's that expression? Oh. Fuck you."

"No. No suspect, just another victim."

"A girl?"

"Aaron Gold. College kid, after the big bad guys. He was feeding me information on TriMondo Developing, and I didn't believe him. Someone threw him out of the tower this morning." I finished wrapping my hands and walked out to the living room. She followed, close.

"Jesus."

"Where were you that night?"

That stopped her. She took a deep drag and held it, with those lips. "I was nowhere near the tower, officer."

"Don't fuck with me on this. I think you were out fucking some other guy while Joey was getting barbecued."

"Is this your party trick? Every time we start talking you throw me in the interrogation room?"

"He was dead. You should've been there."

"He was dead a year ago! It took him six months to lie down."

I heard Joey's voice, something he used to say. *Three people can keep a secret if two of them are dead.*

I said, "Look—"

"You think you can bully everybody? I'm not afraid of you." She walked up to me like she was spoiling for a fight, and stood facing off. I smelled her perfume. "I wasn't afraid of him and I'm not afraid of you!" My brain had a twelve-car pile-up of conflicting thoughts and impulses, with a monster truck on top saying, *Now! Take her! Now!*

"I'm sorry—"

"What do you want from me? Do you even know? You got your bandages. Now get out of my house or I'll call a *real* cop." She pushed me out the screen door and slammed it shut behind me. I blinked in the dark and looked down to see a hard-on bowing out the front of my shorts. I hoped it wasn't there while I was in the house. Forget about her.

He was dead a year ago, Rachel said. She knew something about Joey's last days, maybe something to do with drugs. It might not mean anything to anyone else, but it might add up to a good night's sleep for me. I headed home with nothing. But I kept spinning around the only idea that made sense.

Three people can keep a secret if two of them are dead.

10:15 P.M. 2204 Santa Rita

Buck Jeffries held his weapon at port arms—close to chest, barrel up—as he stepped into the darkened house.

Suddenly something crawled on his neck. He grabbed it and tossed it with a grunt, a wood roach fallen from the ceiling. If anyone *was* in the tiny house they'd have heard him.

Light through a side window showed the sink and stove, putrid from rotten food. He stalked through the house and made sure he was alone, and checked the fridge to see if there was anything to eat. Hot damn, he thought, two of those little glazed apple pies just like he liked them! He tore open the wrapper and settled in on a chair by the wall.

Chewing on the pie, he thought about the Mexican neighborhood, the Mexicans moving into his own home town when he was in high school, the one smooth talker, Mercado, who almost talked his way into Buck's sister's bloomers, her just sitting there and giggling. Buck got his friends together and knocked Mercado bloody, cracked his front tooth with a baseball bat then pissed on him. A few weeks later, the beaner got his own gang and put Buck in the hospital. The law had something to say about that. On account of he was the only one Buck could identify and he wouldn't turn in his *amigos,* Mercado did a year in the reformatory, the first Mex Buck sent up. Then fifteen years later, there were Mexicans on the force like regular Americans. And all chasing white women, and all with their own gangs. Even dead, Velez had that half-a-Jew Reles, whatever kind of Jew-Mex name that was. No way in hell old Buck Jeffries would let Reles get the glory for this. Buck unscrewed the pint bottle from his pocket and took a long drink.

By morning, Buck would be a hero. By morning he'd be on television. By morning he'd be on Lyda Collins.

20

Rachel's body presses against me as we dance slow. I look at her face, and she's my mother. I can't believe she's back. But her hair is flat and black like Nikki's. I touch her breast and it comes off in my hand, cold and white. She stares at me from under Saran Wrap.

Then I'm at the bottom of 2222, looking into Joey Velez's white Chevy. His burned skin wrinkles around his bones. His blackened eyelids open and he smiles at me. I reach for him and put my hand in the puddle of blood and brains near Aaron Gold's crushed head. I'm looking from the top of the tower to the pavement, and the pavement is rising up, faster, faster.

My eyes jerked open. I was in bed, bandaged and sweaty. I thought of Rachel, angry, disciplined, passionate. I wished I'd met her when we were younger, before she met my only friend, before he died. Before my dreams got filled with death and mutilation.

I grabbed the phone and dialed Hay's office.

"Medical Examiner."

"Detective Sergeant Reles, APD Homicide. You got an Aaron Gold in today, a jumper from the University Tower. White male, about twenty, with long brown hair and a beard."

"Just a minute. I'll check."

The office wasn't big enough for anybody to be "uncertain"—the body was there or it wasn't. While I waited for her to clear my question with whatever assistant ME was on duty, I looked through the blinds onto the ratty lawn where I'd thrown the drums; scroungers had grabbed them before I got back from Rachel's.

"Sergeant Reles? It didn't come today. We don't have any paperwork on it."

I called the morgue and asked the same questions.

"We got him, all right, but not for long. He's going home to Houston at five A.M. so they can bury him before the Jewish sabbath kicks in."

"That's crazy," I said. "He wasn't into that stuff."

"Doesn't matter. Jewish boneyard won't bury him if he's embalmed, and they won't plant him on Saturday. And you know what they say about relatives and fish—they stink after three days. Hell or high water, Gold's in the Texas dirt by sundown."

I hung up. There's always an autopsy if there's *any* doubt on the cause of death. No autopsy means officially there's no doubt.

Which meant Margaret Hay, Medical Examiner, was never anywhere near the remains of Aaron Gold.

I checked the old phone book for what I guessed was

her unlisted number, then fished out my clearance codes
to call the phone company.

Aaron Gold was shipping out in a refrigerated train car
at five A.M. I had an evaluation hearing at seven.

It was past two.

2:45 A.M. 7809 Deer Ridge Circle

The cedar door creaked open and Margaret Hay stood
glaring at me murderously from a Norman Rockwell living room. A calico cat surveyed me from a rocking chair.
Hay's voice crackled.

"You're out of line!"

"You believe in justice?"

I stood there in my bandages like a battered boxer. Hay
walked back into the house but she didn't close the door
so I stepped in. She spun back, pointed to my feet and
said "Stay!" then went banging around in the kitchen.

Photographs and diplomas decorated the front wall. A
yellowed picture of a worn-out little woman, maybe
taken around 1940. A family portrait of a leathery-
skinned farmer, no wife, and five sunburned kids—four
smaller ones and a tall red-haired boy. A later shot of a
slim Hay in army khakis, circa Korea, with two other
women. I looked back at the family portrait to find which
little girl was Hay, and realized she was the tall one I
thought was a boy. College and medical school diplomas
and a picture of Hay in a cap and gown with her tired old
dad at graduation. And shooting trophies, shelves of
them.

She yelled from the kitchen.

"My job is to find the cause of death. Whether that

brings justice or not is out of my hands. Normal people are in bed by now."

"Normal people weren't trained by Joey Velez," I hammered away, following her into what looked like a farmhouse kitchen.

She glared at me, but with just a little less heat than before. "I told you to stay."

She pounded down a copper coffee pot, slammed cabinets and filled the pot at a butcher block sink, but listened while I gave her the rundown on Aaron Gold's "suicide," leaving out what I knew about TriMondo.

After I finished she said, "The autopsy might show . . ."

"The autopsy won't show anything, because there isn't gonna be one. By the time you get to your office in the morning and straighten it out, Aaron Gold's sleeping through his own eulogy."

"It doesn't matter. We can't do anything without the body."

I leaned over the sink. "Travis County Morgue is open twenty-four hours."

3:15 A.M. 2204 Santa Rita

Jeffries woke sitting in the pimp's dark kitchen, his chair against the outside wall and his bladder full. He made his way up a short corridor, pushed open the bathroom door and flicked on the light, surprising a large white rat as it waddled across the floor, pink nose twitching. Eyeing the dark shower curtain, he drew his weapon and slid the curtain open.

Suddenly a sharp pain like a meathook dug into his gut and ripped upward. He cried out and heard his weapon clatter to the floor as his head hit the tile hard.

He grabbed at his gut, soaked with blood, and felt his insides oozing out. Wheezing, he tried to hold the gash closed, stuff his guts back in. A shadow cut across the bright light in his eyes, and he heard a familiar voice shout, "Fuck!"

He struggled for the word "dying" but couldn't find it as blood poured from his belly.

3:20 A.M. Travis County Morgue

A goon in a white jacket presided over the morgue's cold, white front room with his feet on the counter, reading what looked like a pornographic comic book. When Dr. Hay and I appeared he put his feet down but not in any hurry.

"Dr. Hay. What brings you here this time of night?"

"Got a hot one, Leith. Do you have a Gold, first name Aaron. Came in today. Jumper from the tower."

"Sure do, ma'am. Only I can't let you see him. Sheriff's orders."

She squinted. "Excuse me?"

"Look." He plucked a document with a half dozen signatures on it. "He goes back to Houston at five A.M. intact, by request of his family."

I said, "Are you questioning Dr. Hay's authority?"

As Hay stared him down, her low drone slowly rose like a jet coming in for a landing. "I, *personally,* am the county's final authority in determining cause of death. You have two options." Volume rising. "You can blame me, claiming you followed the most recent order from a higher-ranking official. Or you can *cross* me." She leaned close to his face. "At three A.M. in a refrigerator full of dead people."

The clerk tried to form words, then squeaked, "I'll be right back," and disappeared into the back room. Hay didn't take her eyes off the door, but I could tell she was happy.

"Ever been married?" I asked.

She answered through her teeth. "Lots."

Back at Hay's autopsy room, we unloaded Aaron Gold's body onto a metal gurney. Then she peeled the plastic bodybag off Aaron and hosed him down. A white sheet over a dead body is a Hollywood amenity.

The fall smashed Aaron's skull on the right side along with his shoulder, stomach distended, skin a greenish-white tinge, penis dangling useless between his legs. Hay called out the specs and I marked them on the chart. Massive fracture to right upper skull, temporal lobe protruding. She looked up and down his arms, scoped the lone needle bruise and the area around it. Then with no fanfare she took a scalpel and sliced a diagonal line from Aaron's left shoulder down to the center of his chest, over his heart. Then she made the same incision from the other shoulder, the bloody flesh curling away from the knife as it dug its path. Under the scarlet V she cut a vertical line down to just above Aaron's pubis, blood puffing out of his abdomen as the cuts formed a great big Y.

I watched Hay pull the top flap of the Y up over Aaron's face like a rubber mask, then peel the other flaps open to expose the rib cage. She took her chain cutter and snipped his ribs from bottom to top, up the middle and up both sides. Then she opened the double-doors of his rib cage and laid them out.

She drew blood, bile and urine, the smell of the various fluids melting into one sulfurous vapor that burned my nose and eyes. Then she cut out each organ, neatly slicing the attachments like a butcher. As she reached into Aaron's abdomen and severed the connections to his stomach, I had a nightmare flash of Rachel on the gurney, Rachel's heart cut out and placed on a scale. My boogeyman getting closer.

I shook the image away. There was nothing to worry about. Rachel was fine. Not like it was my business.

Hay cut open Aaron's stomach, dumped his last meal, what could have been steak, and scraped the lining with her scalpel.

"If he ever used heroin before, it probably wasn't habitual. Look at this—no ulcers, lesions, clots."

I pointed out the needle bruise at the crook of his left elbow. "Do occasional heroin users use needles?"

She looked up and down the arm. "Thrill seekers?" Then she squinted at the arm, speaking almost to herself. "I'll tell you one thing they don't do." She hosed down the arm again, then scrubbed it with a white sponge and soap. That didn't work. "Get me that can of turpentine on the shelf." She doused a white sponge with it and as she wiped, the sponge turned beige. Bruises like fingerprints appeared up and down Aaron's arm. She stood straight. "They don't hold their own arms down hard with two hands while they're shooting up, then cover the bruises with mortician's paint."

Hay propped up Aaron's head, cut across the back of it with a scalpel, peeled his scalp up to expose the bone, and turned on the electric saw. "Let's see what his brain says."

The saw revved up and screamed as it cut into Aaron's skull.

5:00 A.M. Pedernales Street

As the gray light of dawn hit Pedernales, Patrolman Dennis Alvarez noticed the familiar white Grand Prix on his second spin through the neighborhood and pulled up close enough to look inside and see the police radio.

He picked up the microphone. "Patrol 21."

"Go ahead."

"White Grand Prix, license plate 353-Victor King Victor, one of ours, sitting on Pedernales all night, near the corner of Santa Rita. Here on business?"

5:30 A.M. Medical Examiner's Office

Hay washed her hands and face, splashing water on her eyes. She didn't like to be rushed but I couldn't wait for the report. "So?"

"He was injected by force," she said. "He put up a good fight."

"Was he dead before they threw him?"

"Ever see a dead man bleed like that? Also the petechiae, the bruises. You don't bruise unless you're living on impact. He was alive when they threw him, but not conscious. The head falls first because it's heaviest. The most determined jumper will hold out his hands in front of him to break his fall. It's a reflex. If it were a hundred stories he'd lose consciousness on the way down, but not twenty-eight. When we get jumpers, the wrists are always broken. Always."

"Cause of death?"

"Murder. No question. That's what my report will say."

"That's gonna piss some people off."

The phone rang.

"I stood up to your chief when she walked in here with a couple of thugs, trying to bully me into changing an officer's cause of death. There has to be some basis of truth operating here." She picked up the receiver, muttering, "Thirty-five years haven't changed her a bit," then into the receiver: "Hay. No, I'm not on call." She cursed quietly. "All right, give me the address. 2204 Santa Rita, got it."

Aaron lay on the gurney, his rib cage open and empty, a bucket of guts near his side. Black plastic wrapped his head, the hood of an executioner, or of the executed. Not a suicide, not an accident.

"Something stinks here, Sergeant," Hay said, her comment stopping me at the door. "Just make sure you're not the next one on my gurney."

I picked the wrong night for an unofficial autopsy, it turned out, two hours I couldn't account for and no alibi. I'd pay for that. But I wasn't the next one on the gurney.

21

FRIDAY

5:45 A.M. 3809 Peck Avenue

Rachel woke with her teeth still clenched from Dan's visit, exercised, showered and ate her toast, fuming as she went over her schedule for the day.

He came over for bandages and comfort, she thought, and as soon as he got them he turned on her. Like it was her fault Joey died. "Where were you that night? Who were you with?" Enough of this. Enough Dan Reles.

Her childhood was nothing but pain—partying was the cure. Then the drink and the drugs turned on her, a chemical re-creation of the agony of home. The way it ended shouldn't have surprised her. Now she was fine: clean, strong, independent, a professional woman. She could do fine without Dan Reles and his kind.

And where did that leave her? A hot twenty-something now turned thirty. Aerobics aside, sooner or later her breasts would sag and her thighs would spread. No friends to speak of. The men she dated liked her outsides and got scared off by her brain. If they stuck around to find out what was going on inside her, the living memories of a hellish childhood and a worse youth, they'd run screaming. But Dan might not. She looked at Joey's real estate brochure.

Dan had potential. Behind his tough-guy facade was a sad kid. She saw it the first time they met. Maybe there was enough there to negotiate.

Dropping off Joey's brochure was as good an excuse as any. She'd stop on the way to work. She'd give him one last chance.

6:15 A.M. Medical Examiner's Office

The sun was just cooking up the empty streets when I left Hay's office, running down the situation in my groggy head.

Aaron thought that university president Bill Oliver was in bed with TriMondo Developing, that together they were multiplying their fortunes building on Barton Creek the way they built on the Blacklands. Everything Aaron said sounded like standard conspiracy theory, except now he was dead. He had photocopies of official documents, but most of those were public record—you could publish them in *The New York Times* and nobody would believe it until the movie came out. So why would anybody care about some kid sniffing around their paperwork in a library? And yet there was Aaron at the bottom of the tower, university cops picking at him like vultures. And someone stripping his apartment and stealing his papers. And Tri-Mondo with a dark history, Torbett said, maybe trying to show a new face.

But Aaron promised me something specific, that he thought he could prove. And he was meeting with someone first, someone he didn't call from home. Who?

I had to shower, shave and make myself presentable for the hearing. And I'd have to present both the Dirty Sally and Aaron Gold cases in a way that made me sound sane. There was no traffic under the hazy sky as I shot up I-35 toward home trying to remember what Aaron had told me. TriMondo had a contract with the university. Bill Oliver had a conflict of interest.

"Homicide 8," the radio crackled as I rolled off the short exit ramp at Forty-fifth Street.

"Homicide 8, go ahead."

"Call Lieutenant Niederwald on a land line. He's at your house."

"What's he doing there?"

I pulled onto Avenue F and saw my front door wide open and a half-dozen unmarked cop sedans parked on my front lawn, along with Rachel Velez's Celica.

22

Miles Niederwald stood in my living room with Milsap and Carter Serio from Internal Affairs, all looking shock-worn. Serio, fifty-five, stood five-foot-six with thick salt-and-pepper hair but the build of a halfback.

Serio said, "There he is!" with something like amuse-ment. Milsap, puffy-eyed, pouted at the floor.

Miles noticed my bandaged hands and said, "Boy, you got some explaining to do."

The ride cymbal from my smashed drums still stuck into the front wall like a shelf by the overturned phone table; the phone cord I ripped from the wall coiled like a snake. The bedroom door hung open and Rachel sat on the edge of the bed in her office dress, crossed legs baring a stretch of sheer black stocking. She was smoking and shak-ing her head slowly at me. And she gave me that look, the one she gave when I first saw her, that said we understood each other. There was everybody else, and there was us.

I breathed in deep. "What happened?"

Miles knocked looks with Serio then pulled me through the kitchen where Torbett and Waller stood like they were waiting for a funeral—even Waller looked somber—then out onto the screened back porch and closed the door.

"You didn't answer the phone, we couldn't get you on the radio so Serio said he was coming here. I had Dispatch tell everyone to meet us. Waller got here first and told your girlfriend to stay."

"She's not my—"

Miles said. "Jeffries got killed last night."

"What?!"

"Looks like a coke deal gone bad. They found a few grams in his pocket and some cash. 'Course we'll say it was a heroic bust and Buck got ambushed, but hell, who we kiddin'?"

The door swung open and Milsap was yelling and pointing at me. "Horseshit! He did it! He killed Buck. Set him up and killed him!"

Serio followed Milsap out to the porch. Miles said, "Carl, shut the fuck up."

Serio asked me, "Where were you last night?"

With Serio, Miles and Milsap staring at me, I thought of explaining how I went crazy and smashed up my drums, then hijacked Aaron Gold's corpse after Miles ordered me off it while Joey's wife somehow wound up on my bed. I turned to Miles. "I was following up on Aaron Gold. I know you told me not to."

Serio wasn't buying it. "Now we have sort of a situation," he said. "Your dead partner's wife is in your house the night a man you're known to hate is killed, hours before he's scheduled to testify at your evaluation hearing.

Your hands show signs of a struggle and you're not quite clear where you were."

Milsap's quivering face looked as close to tears as fire. " 'Cause he was settin' up Buck, that's why!" he yelled. "Buck's lyin' dead with his gut slit open, and he's here fuckin' that spic's whore!"

I flew at Milsap. Serio flung his own two-hundred pounds at me and we landed on the floor hard, my elbow ripping through the patio screen. Miles grabbed Milsap. Serio popped to his feet and dragged Milsap into the kitchen and, from what I could hear, out the front of the house. I sat on the floor of the screened porch and rubbed my eyes as Miles yelled down at me.

"What the hell was that? What do you care what Milsap calls Velez?" I couldn't answer. It was what he called Rachel. And what did I care? "You think I didn't have enough to keep me goin' before? You think I wasn't busy enough when all I had was a bitch chief with her nose up my ass. She's had me over a barrel since Velez died."

"About what?"

"None of your damn business. Plus some Jack the Ripper choppin' up whores—"

"One girl—"

"Shut up! Plus them IAB cocksuckers hangin' on me like stink on shit! Now I got my second dead Homicide cop in six months, first Velez and now Buck. I got Velez's widow who's now *fucking* the partner—"

"Wait a minute—"

"*And* the partner *can't explain* where he was while Jeffries was gettin' his damn gut ripped out the night before he's supposed to give testimony at the partner's damn hearing!"

"He was getting coffee, Miles, I told you that." Rachel was standing in the doorway, trying to cover for me.

"Police business, Mrs. V."

She rolled her eyes. "Oh please." Then to me, "I'm leaving now, Dan. Call me later?" She made googly eyes at me, not the kind of thing she'd do if she really *was* in love, and swayed her hips out the door.

Miles said, "Lemme lighten your load. The hearing's put off till Monday, seven A.M. Sergeant Jeffries being replaced on the panel by Carter Fucking Serio, Internal Affairs."

I dropped my head between my knees. "Jesus."

"Your own damn fault. You pissed Jeffries off every chance you got. In front of witnesses. What do you think Milsap's tellin' Serio right now? Serio's investigating Buck's death. We gotta mount our own investigation and I gotta put Milsap in charge."

"He's a moron."

"He's Buck's damn moron. Who'm I gonna put on it? You? You'll be off Homicide come Monday, face it. You'll be lucky to keep your badge. Torbett's in charge of Dirty Sally."

"Miles, give me a chance . . ."

"I shuffled the damn names to get you out on that bus thing just to give you a chance. Look at you."

"I had half a girl and no face. Now I have a kill site, sketches and dental records. How much did Jeffries ever get on the ice cream thing?"

"You mean after you fucked it up? Fine, that leaves you and Torbett on Dirty Sally. Waller helps Milsap on Jeffries. Lund stays at HQ and helps both teams. I'll catch flack and try and keep our fuckin' jobs. Now get out there and find a killer!" He started through the door.

I looked up. "Miles. Did you say we should find *a* killer or *the* killer?"

He walked into the kitchen. I got up and followed him, but he walked through the house and left.

9:00 A.M. 4612 Avenue F

Waller told me a story before he took off, about his three best friends in Vietnam, how they were like a family, how they looked out for each other, how devastated he was (he said with a glassy look into the past) the day two of them went down in the frenzy of a firefight, and a land mine blew his last friend apart before Waller's eyes. Then he broke his gaze and slapped me on the arm. "But hey," he smiled sadly, "you make new friends."

Waller went after Milsap. Torbett went to HQ. I got a shower, clean clothes, and a headache wondering why I jumped Milsap in front of Internal Affairs just for calling Rachel a whore. I phoned her office to find out what the hell she was doing at my house, but they said she was out. Dispatch called about a DOA on Barton Springs Road related to the Dirty Sally case. How it was related they wouldn't tell me over the phone.

I was out the front door when I heard something shuffling around next to the house. I soft-stepped along the wall, drew my .38 and swung around the corner in time to land my mouth in direct contact with Milsap's fat fist. I recoiled, swung my gun hand and pistol-whipped his jaw. He spun away and braced himself on the wall, pulling something from his pocket. As I swung again he jabbed me in the ribs. The punch sang through me like a slow-moving bullet. Brass knuckles.

I doubled over and he ripped another knuckle shot under my shoulder blade. I winced and pounded him in the groin. The punch wasn't regulation but neither were the knucks. Then I popped up and backhanded Milsap's face with my gun hand, tearing his cheek. Milsap slid down the wall, wheezing. I took his gun and knucks and sat down hard in the gravel, pains shooting through my ribs and down my back. Milsap held his groin and squealed.

"You set him up," he choked. "You hated him!"

"Miles said it was a bad coke deal."

He punched the gravel. "NO!"

I spit blood, thinking what a poor slob Milsap was. A dumb kid who lost his only friend. "Milsap," I said. "Serio's gonna be all over both of us. We'll be lucky to get away with our badges." He got quiet. "How do you know it wasn't a bad coke deal?" I asked.

"He was a bookie! That's all!"

To a lot of cops, bookmaking isn't even a crime. Neither is bribery or assault unless you get caught. I stood up, wiping blood from my mouth. Milsap stayed on the ground still holding his groin. I kept my voice low. "That wasn't all, was it?"

He shook his head.

"What was he doing?"

Milsap closed his fat eyes tight. "Everything."

"But it wasn't a deal."

"It wasn't a deal."

I almost whispered. "How do you know?" Nothing. "Because you would have been there?"

He held his head with his fists. I leaned on the wall.

If a cop was into "everything," everybody knew what that meant. Gambling, graft, beating locals for money or laughs, shaking down whores for services. Covering each other's felonies. Dealing seized merchandise. Plus another million crimes nobody had ever thought of before. And cocaine, the final no-no. A cop could rape a hooker but figure he was okay if he said no to drugs.

And here was Milsap owning up to dealing drugs just to find out who croaked his partner. If there was no deal, that pointed to Jeffries being set up. Why?

"Listen to me," I said. "A lot of cops hated Jeffries enough to kick the shit out of him, but not to kill him. Right?"

He looked at me hard, searching, then nodded.

"You knew his business. You're the man to find out who set him up."

Milsap looked at me long and hard before getting to his feet. He took back his gun and brass knuckles, limped toward his car, then looked back at me. "Watch your back," he said, and headed off like Aaron Gold and me, an orphan out to avenge his partner.

9:45 A.M. Tierra Fuego Apartments

I parked at a distance from the print and TV crews swarming the wood-shingled complex on Barton Springs Road.

Closer to the apartment an acid stink clouded the air. Three days, I thought. Three days dead and no refrigeration. The reporters looked green at the gills. One puked in the bushes while patrols fought the rest away from the building. I grabbed a patrolman. "Tape off the area. No press within fifty feet."

A camera appeared in my face and Lyda Collins, big as life, tried to feed me a microphone. "Sergeant Reles, what's your evaluation of the situation?"

I stared cold into her brown contact lenses. "Obstruction of justice."

"Really? How so?"

"That's the charge for interfering with a murder investigation."

She tried to stare me down, lost and lowered the mike. "We'll wait."

The apartment opened onto the parking lot. Margaret Hay stood outside the apartment door, looking a few autopsies past tired. She pulled on rubber gloves and noticed my fresh fat lip. "What happened now?"

"Just a cold sore. What do we got?"

"Neighbors called in the stench. Patrols figured they hit the jackpot. Don't ask me who called the press." She handed me rubber gloves and a breathing filter and led me in.

The stink hit like an ammonia tidal wave. Flies buzzed in swarms.

"Jackpot," she growled.

The room was a ghoul's paradise. Knives and medieval torture implements—tongs, pikes, spiked clubs—covered the walls, alongside horror-movie stills, news shots of murder victims, and lurid color glazed magazine photos of chopped and twisted bodies, armless, legless, nude.

The victim stared at the TV through maggot-infested eyeballs. I borrowed the remote and hit PLAY, catching the video in the middle. Bad lighting, no music, strictly amateur night.

A naked top-heavy woman knelt in front of a hot plate while a hooded figure penetrated her from behind with something that wasn't attached to him. Her arms stretched out in back of her, palms up, each hand holding a glass of water.

"Spill a drop and you're cooked," the hooded figure yelled.

"It gets worse," Hay said. It sounded like a joke but her face told me otherwise.

The woman on screen must have spilled a drop because he slapped her face down onto the hot plate. Smoke rose up from the plate to the sickening sizzle of flesh and the woman's screams. He pulled her back by the hair. A spiral of stove burner swelled on her left cheek and he ripped a dagger across her abdomen, spilling coils of intestine.

I snapped it off. If it was a fake it was a good one.

"Vice wants the video," she said. "They'll track it if they can and tell you what they find."

Insects blanketed the victim. I borrowed Hay's magnifying glass: beetles chomped on the victim's skin, spiders and millipedes were eating the beetles. Aaron Gold would have called it a microcosm of society. Hay had a different spin.

"The spiders mean he's been dead at least forty-eight hours. His body hasn't started to swell, no blisters or leaks from his nose. No more than three days, if that. The vomitus indicates poison, pending tests. He could have shot up—I'll check the remaining skin. You tell me what the slash across his chest indicates."

I checked the room for a bottle or glass, something he might have drunk poison from, or a needle. Nada. Same for the kitchen.

Back in the sunshine, I ripped off the mask and sucked in air. The patrolman I'd told to tape off the area handed me a letter in a large envelope, a neatly typed and signed note, the patrol told me, confessing to the Jigsaw Massacre. "Dutch act, sir," he said. Suicide. Collins's men tripped two other guys so she could ask me the first question. Four more microphones gathered around.

"Sergeant Reles, is it true that the man who committed suicide here today is the Jigsaw Killer who has held this city under a blanket of fear?"

"Lyda," I said with confidence, ". . . I think people can draw their own conclusions."

Five reporters turned away at once, spinning takes like, "The end of a five-day vigil . . . ," "Peace restored to this happy town . . . ," and my favorite: "Back to normal."

I got into the car, jazzed the engine and sprayed my canister of Skunk-Away under the dashboard, breathing in deep. Then I got the tweezers from my glove compartment, pulled out the note and gave it a read, a full confession that didn't make any mistakes or give away anything the press didn't know. Cagey. And before I pulled out of the parking lot, I took a long look at the signature, wondering about the guy whose name sealed this confession, the nobody whose body was feeding the flies, the sucker who "did the Dutch." I'd heard the name before: Frederick A. Harrell.

11:00 A.M. 2204 Santa Rita

Carl Milsap sat on the back steps at 2204 Santa Rita, looking out over the rusted tin roofs.

His stomach twisted like the French cruller he just stuffed into it. It was his second time at the house that day: the first was at dawn when the call came. A patrol saw Buck's car parked around the corner after one A.M., recognized it and decided to phone it in when he saw it still there four hours later.

They found Buck Jeffries face down in the bathroom, his Taurus 83 on the floor, knife wound to the abdomen, stabbed through the shower curtain, no rounds fired, his skin purplish on the underside. It turned white at the touch and felt cool but not cold. The ME showed at six and said it was a hot night, Buck would have cooled about a degree every hour. Body at ninety-five degrees: that put the death after three. The techs found Buck's prints on the outer knob of the back door and a few grams of coke in his pocket. Planted.

Serio had his own investigation with Milsap squeezed out. Milsap made a fast preemptive strike against his and Buck's closest contacts, heavy with the brass knuckles, to find out what they knew and make sure they didn't pass it on to Serio. Serio would figure out what Milsap and Buck had been up to, sooner or later, and Milsap would be in for it. Did it matter?

Milsap's eye caught a Mexican lady's face in the window of the house opposite him. When he saw her she dropped the curtain. He ran over and pounded the door. "Police!"

"Please! I don't know nothin'!"

He kicked the door open. The woman cowered in a housedress as he backed her into the dank kitchen. "Don' touch me!" she cried.

He cornered her by the refrigerator. "What did you see there? Last night."

"A man."

"What kind of man? White? Black?"

"White . . ."

"What'd he look like?"

She looked down at Milsap's body.

"Fat?! Fat like me?" She nodded. "In a suit? A jacket

and tie?" She nodded again. "When? Talk!" He slapped
her hard to the floor.

"Nine!" She screeched. "After nine last night! Stay
away! He sneakin' around, then he play with the lock and
go in."

"What happened?"

"Nothing. The light stay off. In the morning, ambulance here." He raised his hand again to swing. "That's all!
That's everything!"

"Why didn't you tell the police?"

She didn't answer. Illegal aliens don't call the fire department when they're on fire. Milsap stomped out to the
car and grabbed the mike.

"Homicide 6."

"Go ahead, Homicide 6."

"Find me—" He squeezed his eyes shut. Who could
he tell?

12:05 P.M. HQ

Lyda Collins beat me back to HQ and was interviewing
Denton on the front steps in the middle of what looked
like a Longhorn football-game cheering section: one guy
mouthed "Hi Mom!" into the camera. Denton beamed
sincerity, baking up some crap about top APD detectives
"cracking" the case. We cracked that suicide note, I
thought. We cracked the shit out of it.

Fred Harrell was the owner of record of Live Models on
Fifth Street, where Nikki worked a year ago. Logan told me
that yesterday. I was going to follow up on it when Aaron
Gold turned up dead and I dropped the ball. I'd keep that
to myself.

I asked a few questions at Forensics and then hit the squad room. Miles, Jake and Waller gazed at the tiny TV, Harrell's suicide story taking the place of Jeffries's murder, officially under wraps everywhere but here. Jake said, "Man, Buck was here yesterday."

Waller said, "Could've been any of us."

Torbett stood in the back, holding half a ream of photocopies. Lyda Collins was broadcasting live from in front of the building. If she knew Jeffries was dead she'd have made him a hero. She was doing a *"That's for posterity to decide—back to you, Jim,"* and the anchorman in the studio took over:

"University president Bill Oliver says the state needs to get tougher on crime—"

Miles clicked off the power, raised a ceremonial pint of Scotch and filled paper cups as we sat silently under Jeffries's hovering ghost. Torbett and I begged off; Jake had a cherry soda. Waller gestured to the TV and said, "But, hey, we break a tough one now and then," in a way that I couldn't tell whether he was kidding. Miles and Waller held their cups high for a solemn moment, then tipped and swallowed. Torbett deadpanned me.

"Okay, just a few details," I said. "For starters, Harrell wasn't the killer." Miles's face dropped. "The slash across his chest wasn't self-inflicted. They won't find his prints on the knives unless someone planted them there and Forensics will know the difference. And the signature on the confession is a fake."

"Dutch Act," he repeated, like he was trying to make it true. Suicide.

"Okay, here's how it happened: he's taking a walk and somebody slashes him, so he decides to come home and snuff it." Miles cursed under his breath. *"Or,"* I went on, "he's depressed, cuts himself across the shirt and tie, and then shoots up, *hides the needle* and heads off for the big tomorrow. How far you need me to go with this?"

Miles walked out the door. I followed him into the hall and shut the door.

"Don't you *never* cross me in front of the squad!" he snapped.

"Gimme a break, Miles! This isn't just a set-up, it's a sloppy one. Like they were playing to the cameras."

"File the case."

"This is bullshit."

Miles spat in a fierce whisper, "I been lookin' out for you since Velez died, and you ain't even helpin'! You think I wanna hear this shit with Buck layin' on a fuckin' slab . . ."

He stormed off as fast as his short legs would go, hiding his face. I opened the door and pushed inside. Jake, Torbett and Waller hadn't missed a word. "You didn't hear that. This is my case, you guys are on it, and it's not closed till I sign off on it, or Miles takes me off it *in writing*. Jake, whattaya got?"

Jake looked at the others, then the TV, and shrugged. "Yeah, okay. Logan sent these." Jake gave me Logan's photos of "Vicki" (born Anselma Markus), "Precious" and Natalie—the three missing hookers with A-negative blood he'd found. I looked them over.

"No," I said. "Not her."

"How do you know?"

"I know!" I barked. Torbett gave me a look like *Don't waste your ammo.*

Jake looked to Waller, then said, "Okay, the partial fingerprint from the face package comes up blank, no matches so far in Austin, Houston, the Big D or Washington. Maybe in a year or two when everything is computerized."

Waller added, "And all is pure."

Jake said, "Or maybe he was never busted and this is his first job. Or it's her print and she was never busted." He handed me a black-and-white computer-printed snapshot of a young woman nude down to the waist, with black hair, glowing light gray eyes, high-standing breasts and dark nipples, her skin tanned to what I guessed was a perfect bronze that put me in mind of Raquel Welch. "I borrowed a printer to get it like this. Nice quality, huh?"

I felt my stomach tighten. A phrase crossed my mind, what the hostess from the escort service said. *Too beautiful.* It was Nikki. "Source?"

"This stuff gets passed around. No tracing it."

"Try. Report says Harrell's a ninth-string attorney. His office is over a bail bondsman on Sixth near the tracks." The few blocks of Sixth between the interstate and Red River Street housed day-labor services, bail bondsmen, bottom-end criminal defense lawyers. West of Red River was strictly yuppie bars and frozen margaritas. "And he owned Live Models, where Nikki worked a year ago. Anything else?"

Waller said, "Someone said his clients were pimps and bikers."

Jake said, "Logan says he was the owner of record on a couple of whorehouses besides Live Models." He dug up a message slip. "One for sure on . . . here it is. 907 East Twelfth. The AG closed it down. And 804 Jewell. There might be others, but they started putting the recent stuff in the database and their computers are down."

"Progress," Waller grinned, wiping his glasses. "No stopping it."

I said, "Waller, aren't you with Milsap?"

"He keeps ditching me," Waller said. "He 'has to go see somebody.' Want me to check out the whorehouses?"

Torbett settled in to read the materials he'd copied at the library. Before I headed out to track Fred Harrell's last days I sent Waller to lean hard on anyone busted at Live Models or 907 East Twelfth or 804 Jewell, and find a way—any way—to break into the business that got too hot for Harrell. I should have given him more help.

23

Milsap huffed up the front steps of HQ ignoring the freckle-faced punk from CIB who yelled his first name like they were brothers.

"Carl! Hey, Carl!" The kid ran up to him and cornered him by the door. "I heard about you guys catching the Jigsaw Killer. Good going! What happened to your face?" Milsap turned away. "Too bad about Buck, though. Shit," the kid went on. "I was just talkin' to him last night."

Milsap stopped. "When?"

"Last night. At Homicide."

"What time?"

"I don't know. Nine, maybe a little after. Why?"

"What happened?"

"Nothing. We were talking about the game tomorrow, Buck and one of the other guys and me. The phone rang and he answered it. Next thing, Buck runs off like a bat out of hell. That's the last we saw of him."

Milsap felt his blood rushing again, the first time since he got the call. He ran for the switchboard room.

12:30 P.M. Anderson and Guerrin

Another girl in the break room noticed Tina's salad lunch.

"How can you live on that? I'd starve!"

Two more women came in and descended on the refrigerator.

"Who's on the switchboard?"

"Patty."

A puffy-eyed soap opera starlet fingered the dimple in her chin.

"But Cord, honey! Don't you believe me?"
"No, little lady, you've lied to me one too many times!"

Patty rushed in and flipped the channel.

"Turn it back," someone said.

"Shh! Listen!"

An anchorman was saying something about "a five-day vigil ending with a suicide, as the maniac who stalked the town took his own life . . ." The video showed blurry shots of guns, knives and pornography.

"They got him," Patty said.

The anchorman mentioned the name of a Homicide detective named Reles who was credited for solving the tough case. Tina remembered him, the man who came to see Mr. Guerrin yesterday. Then they mentioned the name of the killer, dead by his own hand.

Attorney Frederick A. Harrell.

Fred, Tina thought. *Oh God, Fred.* She walked quickly

out of the room, fighting back something coming up in
her throat.

1:00 P.M. Sixth Street

I combed Frederick Harrell's ransacked little Sixth Street
law office long enough to guess that anything worth finding had already been found. When I got out, Milsap was
waiting by my car. His cheek was patched and his right eye
half-shut with the shiner I'd given him—it outsized my fat
lip, but not by much. I braced myself for a rematch. "I
gotta talk to ya," he said, breathless. "Coupla CIB punks
saw Buck get a phone call in the office and tear out around
nine o'clock," he said. "A Spanish lady saw him break into
the back of the house not long after that, maybe nine-
thirty."

"Yeah?"

"Only he didn't get killed till after two, which means
he was in the house maybe five hours before someone
killed him."

"Was he with somebody?"

He pounded the car hood. "No, goddammit, that's not
the point! I checked the phone records and no phone calls
went in or out of the squad room between eight-thirty and
nine-thirty. But the phone rang, Buck picked it up and
talked."

"Maybe he was faking," I said. "So he could say later he
ran out on a call."

"Maybe, sure. But the call had to come from somewhere, and it didn't come from outside HQ. And the
phone system don't track intradepartmental calls."

Boom.

"So someone inside HQ called," I said. "Either they were setting him up or they had a deal and screwed him."

He gritted his teeth. "I told you if they had a *deal* I woulda *known* about it!"

"Who the hell in HQ wanted Jeffries dead?"

"Nobody hated Buck enough to *kill* him!" he said. "Except you."

"You think I'm crazy enough to kill a cop?"

"He'd'a killed *you!*" Milsap blurted and then realized what he'd said and backpedaled. "Not *killed* killed, you know what I mean."

"What did he say?"

"Nothin'. You know."

"He's dead, he can't go down for it."

"He just wanted you off the squad. He wouldn't of set nothin' up."

And Jeffries wound up dead, with me his only known enemy on the force.

Jeffries went out on a call and got killed, same as Joey. Only someone set Jeffries up.

Someone inside HQ.

24

2:00 P.M. Homicide Squad Room

James Torbett sat with a pile of photocopies, alone in the squad room—aside from Jake Lund at the computer, which meant alone—following strange orders from a man whose sanity was in question. But Reles wasn't crazy—crazy was Reles's act, like bored was Torbett's.

Torbett looked back at the pages. Maybe somewhere in the pile, two details you'd never notice if you weren't looking, two tiny details, would connect. Like nitro and glycerin. Torbett doing the library work while Waller was out scoping whorehouses. Waller's eyes had jumped at the mention of 804 Jewell. Interesting. Torbett started reading, and reading to the end.

THE AUSTIN ALTERNATIVE TIMES, SPRING 1979

TOWER TOPPLES

A state pilot program, touted as the first effective collaboratively run program between the State of

Texas and private industry, closed this week amid major scandal and allegations of fiscal abuse. *New paragraph*. TriMondo Developing, backer of the program, took no responsibility for six botched and nearly fatal abortions, all performed on black women. However, William Oliver stepped down as CEO, he claimed, to pursue other projects and spend more time with his family in the wake of his wife's demise.

Biographical material on William Henry Oliver III: "Bill." Born Houston, 1928. Private school, Phillips Academy, Andover, Mass. BS, Princeton, 1949, Government. Worked in father's oil company. MBA, Harvard, 1955. More work for Dad. Ph.D., Harvard, Economics, 1963. Taught at Rice. Assorted business ventures, mostly around developing and oil. Foggy business associations. Lands appointment as president of UT Austin, 1982, taking position from Charles Lehane, now retired in Westlake Hills.

Was Lehane enough of an embittered rival to cough up background information?

By 1986 the university is the only sector of Texas state government running at a "profit," several articles comment. Oliver is lauded as economic genius. Nobody questions notion of state agencies turning a profit.

Phone rings. Lund makes no move from keyboard.

"Homicide. Torbett."

A woman spoke in hushed tones. *"Um . . . this is . . . I shouldn't be calling."*

"Can I help you, ma'am?"

"Is Officer Relez there?"

Torbett put on his bored judge voice, talking through

almost-closed lips. "This is Sergeant Torbett. Is there something I can help you with?"

"Yes. Sergeant . . . Torbett?"

"Yes, how can I help you?"

"Yes. The, uh . . . the man they showed on TV, Frederick A. Harrell. The man they said is the Jigsaw Killer?"

"Yes."

"He's not."

The caller didn't get Reles's name right, but she got Harrell's. She knew something about Harrell, and she was sure. "How do you know?"

"I . . ." She started dreamily then blurted, *"I just know."* Her breathing quickened.

"I can't do anything with that."

"Oh."

"Can you come in—"

"NO!"

"Can you meet me somewhere in public? Someplace you feel safe."

"No. No. Not in public." Pause. *"Come to my house. Alone. Make sure nobody sees you."*

She didn't sound like she was playing spy, and she didn't sound crazy. She sounded plain scared.

"Give me your address."

She gasped, then barked, *"I'll call you back!"* and slammed down the receiver. Torbett hit the switchboard number.

"APD Operator."

"This is Torbett in Homicide. A call just came into the squad room. Get me the number and address it came from. And get me the number of Charles Lehane in West-lake Hills. It's probably unlisted."

When they gave Torbett the numbers he had Dispatch radio Reles.

2:45 P.M. 2823 East Oltorf, Apartment 1918

Torbett and I apologized to Tina LaMarque, Guerrin's beautiful brunette receptionist, and said we tracked her down—after she hung up on Torbett—for her own protection. We lied.

I sat close enough to refill Tina's wine glass while I asked the questions; Torbett parked himself off to the side.

"I was a dancer," Tina said with a twang she was trying to cover. "You know. At Gents." She twisted a thin gold chain around her neck. "Fred used to come just for me. He was the only one who didn't expect me to roll over with my legs in the air for a fifty." She reached for a cigarette. "Do you mind?" Torbett got close with a lighter. She jolted, then relaxed as she breathed in the smoke with a forced coolness.

"Anyway, he came in drunk one night and proposed. Any offer that got me out of there would have been welcome, but I said no. Then he offered to hire me as his secretary. He said it was a solid offer and it wasn't for sex. I showed up at his office the next morning in my plainest dress with a steno pad I bought at the drugstore. I must have looked like a whore at a PTA meeting."

"Where'd you learn stenography?" I asked.

"I didn't," Tina said, flushing. "I didn't even know what it was. I'm from Sharp End—" Her eyes flicked at Torbett. "From—from San Angelo," she stammered. "The poor part. If I stayed there I'd be a maid like my mother. So there I was asking for a job with cheap panty hose riding up my pocketbook on a hot day. Excuse me." She tossed back some more wine and held her glass out.

We shook our heads, not a problem. "What happened?" I asked.

"His jaw hit the floor. He forgot the offer till I reminded him. And then he decided to make good on it. Just like that. Titty dancer to legal secretary. Fred paid for my night school. He thought I was making a lot of typos until he found out I just couldn't spell. But I worked hard. Well, he started talking about this Mr. Guerrin, and Mr. Guerrin's clients. Important people Fred was doing little jobs for."

"Little jobs?"

"Oh. You know." She looked away, sucking smoke. "Arrange a lease. Pay a bill."

Torbett asked, "If I mentioned some names, could you tell me if they were Mr. Guerrin's clients?"

Tina looked back and forth between us. "No one will find out I told you?"

"We promise," he said.

She nodded.

"Edward Keenan," Torbett began.

"Engineer. Sure. Girlfriend's abortion."

"Was the girlfriend a hooker?" Torbett asked.

"No, why?"

"Nothing. Herbert Grant."

"Banker. Pay off his daughter's drug debt."

Torbett went down the list of the businessmen who had gotten the meat packs. All dirty secrets. Mistresses' abortions, drug and gambling debts, blackmail payoffs. She knew all but two of them. "They must've been after I left."

Finally I said, "Tina, you know these were the nine other men who received pieces of the murdered woman on Tuesday morning."

The detail hit her but not hard. "Oh."

I tried another name on her: Bill Oliver.

"Oh, no," she said. "No one that big."

"How did you come to work for Mr. Guerrin?"

"That's the bad part. I knew he was, you know, bigger. So one day Fred was supposed to meet with him, I came along to 'help.' I made sure I looked great, and that everything was perfect. It worked. Mr. Guerrin, his eyes popped out. I looked really good. Next day he offered me a job as receptionist."

"How did Fred take it?"

Tina blinked. "Bad. 'How could you do this to me?' and like that. He figured I'd fall in love with him sooner or later."

"Do you think he could have sent out those meat packs?"

"No! That's just the point." Her eyes teared up. "He hated doing the things he did, those nasty little errands. Talk to someone, pay the money. And he wasn't mean. He never even yelled at me, even when I left. And he could have"—dead stop—"*said* things about me after, but he didn't."

I was about to ask "What kind of things?"—her face said it was something worse than being a stripper—but Torbett signaled me to cool it. I took a breath. "Were you with Mr. Guerrin when he opened the package?"

"He didn't open it, I did."

"Excuse me?"

"I screamed and Mr. Guerrin came in and sent me home. I went back to work yesterday. Today I saw the pictures of Fred on TV at lunch and I ran out."

"I'm sorry you had to go through this." I handed her my card. "For your own protection, don't mention this meeting to anyone."

She nodded thoughtfully.

"And Tina." Torbett gave her the stern reverend face. "Don't call us from work."

3:30 P.M. 2823 East Oltorf, Parking Lot

Outside Tina's apartment I said, "So Guerrin forgot he knew the nine other guys who got the packages. I was there again yesterday with her sketch. You'd think that would spark his memory."

Torbett said, "Attorney-client privilege? But he forgot to mention Tina opened his package. So maybe if he opened it himself he wouldn't have called us at all."

I asked Torbett, "What's with the 'shut up' look you gave me? When Tina said Harrell could have said things about her."

He half-smiled. "Ethiopian in the fuel supply."

"What?"

He leaned toward me. "She's black," he said low.

"*What?!*"

"Shut up." He looked up at the balcony running along the back of the second-floor apartments, a row of sliding glass doors. "She's black. Maybe half. Maybe quarter. She's passing."

"How do you know?"

"For starters, when's the last time you saw a white woman built like that."

I thought of Rachel, but I could see the difference.

"Besides," he said. "Ever been to San Angelo?"

"No."

"She said she was from the poor part of San Angelo, that her mother was a maid." Torbett shook his head. "San

Angelo has three parts. The rich white part, the poor white part, and Sharp End, the black part. Where the maids live."

I looked up at the windows. "I knew about Jews passing. I never knew anyone black who did it."

"It's easy," Torbett said. "You just have to look white and lie every time you open your mouth."

I asked Torbett what he got from all his research.

He pulled out two scraps of paper. "Lund tracked the video shot of Dirty Sally to Pleasureland Productions in L.A. Don't ask me how. They had an ID on file, Idaho driver's license, fake. She posed for the promo shots, they think September '87, and flaked out, never showed to shoot the video. Dead end."

"What about Aaron Gold?

"You remember the TriMondo women's health project I told you about, TOWER, collapsed in '79 after the abortions? All hush-hush, no prosecutions, no nothing. Tri-Mondo's CEO, Bill Oliver, steps down. By '82 he's president of UT Austin. Smooth transition." He handed me a photograph of Oliver, distinguished white-haired guy with a Ronald Reagan smile, everybody's dad. "And everybody thinks Oliver is a genius because the university went from deep red to big profits. It's the only state agency to draw a profit. And they keep using that word, 'profit.'"

"So?"

"If a public agency has more money than it needs, they call that a 'surplus.' State agencies aren't *supposed* to make a profit. Only private organizations do that."

"Got any ideas?"

"I know who might." He handed me a scrap of paper with an address in Westlake Hills, where the rich people in Clarksville wish they lived. Then he got in his car and I followed, trying to make a Joey map in my head.

Guerrin employed Fred Harrell to do dirty errands for Guerrin's big clients. Harrell turns up dead and framed.

Guerrin and his friends get meat pack deliveries. Guerrin's the only one who knows everyone on the list. Maybe he wouldn't have called us at all, but his receptionist found the meat pack and there was no covering it up. So he called us and played dumb. But the map pinwheels out to Guerrin's nine clients and their dirty little secrets: Nikki's murder was in a different league. Guerrin wouldn't blackmail his own clients—bad for business. There were forces operating that were bigger than Guerrin. We could brace him, ask him some direct questions and hope for some straight answers. Straight answers from a high-end attorney.

I learned a few things in eight months on the Organized Crime Division. You have choices. Do you reel in the middlemen and call it a day? Or do you take the risk and go after a bigger haul.

And do you know what you're risking?

25

4:10 P.M. 2 Nob Hill Circle, Westlake Hills

I followed Torbett up a paved private road that led from the mailbox on Nob Hill Circle, a quarter mile into the trees, and let out on a grassy front yard no bigger than a concert hall, and a circular driveway in front of a white house smaller than the one in Washington but not by much. Four columns framed the center section, three stories high, and a wing extended sixty feet on each side. On closer look the white was a little dingy, and the wings weren't much bigger than an average house each. Flowered curtains made the joint look less like the president's home and more like Elvis's. Ex-university president Charles Lehane was a man of means.

A black maid in a black dress waved us around the side and let us in through the kitchen to a humble dining room that probably only saw traffic from servants, then up an oak-paneled hallway. She knocked on a door, opened it and nodded us into a darkened den, slices of light between heavy red curtains shining on book-laden walls and a bald, bloated old croaker, hepatitis yellow, in a red silk robe, bent over in a leather chair and coughing up phlegm into a red plastic bowl. He looked up and caught Torbett and me, then turned to me. "Sergeant Torbett?"

Torbett said, "I'm Sergeant Torbett." Charles Lehane, Torbett had discovered, was president of the university right before Bill Oliver. It might pay well but it didn't buy him Graceland.

"Oh," he said, putting his bowl on a side table next to a crystal brandy decanter and snifter. "Well, come in anyway. You want to know about Oliver. I can't ask you to sit down."

Torbett didn't flinch. "You retired in '82."

"Kiss my ass. He retired me. Decided he needed a clean image after the clinic thing tanked. Maybe you read about it." He gave a marked look at Torbett. All the botched abortions were on black girls.

Torbett took a deep breath. "I read about it."

"You don't know anything. Dumped all my stock after that. Who needs it."

"You owned stock in TriMondo," I said.

"We all did. I was on the board of TOWER, just for being a stockholder. Had nothing to do with the day-to-day. Never went to a meeting. Didn't even know they were doing abortions. Wouldn't have let that happen if I'd known. Black *or* white. A human life is worth something."

I didn't press him on it. I showed him Nikki's picture down to the collarbone. Blank. "You said 'We all owned stock in TriMondo.' Who did?"

"Oliver, me, all the big families. Stock in TriMondo, trustees at the university. Go to a hundred goddamn champagne receptions you'll see the same hundred goddamn bluehairs and old cranks like me." He hawked up and spat into his bowl, wiped his chin with a linen napkin. "Oliver went in front of the Board of Regents when I was out of town and pinned TOWER on me. Then he was a chancellor, and then the goddamn president, and me out on my ass. I kept the tuition low and the salaries livable. Doesn't matter. I'm dead by Christmas. Can't even pee anymore."

Torbett said, "About Bill Oliver—"

"You'll never get him. I'd be glad to help. Killed his wife. Not proper, but she was a pill popper and a gossip. She wanted a divorce. She told everybody. A wife can't testify against her husband, but an ex-wife?" Lehane turned away and coughed.

I asked, "How do you know this?"

"I don't. Put it together. He made sure she got all the prescriptions three doctors could write. Thought he'd do better widowed than he would divorced from a woman who liked to talk."

"Better in business or better at the university?"

"It's the same project. You boys don't understand anything. We all knew her days were numbered. When she died, the papers gave him sympathy. Oliver's an oil baby like me. He was born with more money than he could spend in his life. It ain't enough. You can go pretty wild when you're young, cars and women, after a while you need to make something." He poured himself a brandy, sipped it and winced with pain. "Bill Oliver turned dangerous when he decided he wanted something he couldn't have as an oil baron."

"Not money," Torbett said.

Lehane showed his yellow teeth again and sat up as straight as his bent back would allow. "Not money. *All* money. He wanted to change the nature of money in America, John Adams by way of J.P. Morgan. He wanted his face on the dollar bill. Or maybe the hundred. And who's to say he won't have it?"

"Why?"

"My own fault. I'm the one who showed him you could get something from the university you couldn't get from the private sector. Respectability. He took it and ran. Now he wants to be immortal." His yellowing eyes stared square at us. "This isn't Old Man Potter taking over the Building and Loan." He broke off in a coughing fit and ended it gasping for air, finally pushing a button on a cord by the chair. The maid came in followed by a white nurse who rigged up a canister of oxygen. Lehane took a few deep drags from a mask and said, "He'll play TriMondo against the state and wind up running both. Mark my words."

The nurse said, "You have to go."

Torbett said, "But he stepped down from TriMondo. Doesn't that mean he sold his stock?"

Lehane forced something that could have been laughter. "That's just for the SEC, on paper. He has a puppet holding his fifty-one percent now. Puppet CEO." He coughed, sucked oxygen and turned to the nurse. "Who's that ferret he has running around for him? I know. Guerrin."

26

4:50 P.M. 2 Nob Hill Circle, Westlake Hills

I sat with Torbett in my steaming car listening to the radio crackle.

Torbett's jaw didn't move when he spoke. "Guerrin is acting CEO of TriMondo, I can confirm that, holding stock Bill Oliver put in Guerrin's name after the TOWER debacle. That's just hearsay."

"You think Oliver offed his wife?"

"Also hearsay. But why not? Death by prescription."

I said, "Aaron Gold was gunning for Oliver, knew something was up, something shifting, and didn't know what it was. Knew too much. He thought someone was onto him and he was right."

Torbett: "Meanwhile Nikki works for a whorehouse run by Harrell, who ran errands for Guerrin. Odds are he's fronting for Guerrin. Maybe Guerrin fronts the whorehouses for someone else, the way he fronts TriMondo for Oliver."

"So who the hell is Nikki to Bill Oliver?"

The radio crackled. *"Homicide 8."*

I picked up. "This is Homicide 8, go ahead."

"Call from Dr. Hay. I'll patch you through."

More crackling. *"Reles?"*

"It's me, go ahead."

"I talked to Waller," Hay said, *"but I wanted to tell you personally. Harrell's cause of death. It was a needle but it wasn't self-inflicted. Almost missed it, beetles eating the skin. Injection at an oblique angle from the victim's right, not the kind of shot you'd give yourself."*

"That's it?"

"The shot was a heavy dose of heroin, high-grade, uncut. I rushed it through Serology. They say it's the same dope someone gave Aaron Gold."

5:30 P.M. Homicide Squad Room

I headed back to HQ to try and nail real evidence of some of our connections, Oliver to Guerrin to Harrell to Nikki, Oliver to Aaron by way of a double dose of high-grade, uncut heroin. Torbett headed to the courthouse to secure warrants for wiretaps of Oliver and Guerrin. I found Waller alone in the squad room, studying Torbett's photocopies. Jake had headed out for provisions.

"You talk to Hay?" I said.

"Nice work," Waller said, pushing his big glasses back up on his nose. "Aaron Gold and Fred Harrell by the same heroin. Anything else that'll hold up in court?"

"Not yet," I said, and told him what he missed, everything Torbett and I could and couldn't prove.

He flipped his lighter, then dropped more in five minutes than I'd heard from him in six months, all without cracking a smile. "Serio and his boys are all over Jeffries like stink on shit, only it turns out Jeffries was dirtier than shit, surprise surprise. Milsap is in for a reaming and if he sings just the right note he'll just lose his job and his pension but not his freedom. Meanwhile, Miles is running between Denton and Internal Affairs trying to make Milsap look like Jeffries's dupe, but Denton wants to hang someone who's still alive just to show the press when we start to stink. She's got Jeffries in line for sainthood. And Milsap rats you out like a motherfucker to Serio."

"I'm clean."

"Okay, snowboy, but Jeffries got hari-karied while you were fucking your dead partner's wife."

"I didn't fuck her."

"You said you were out chasing Aaron Gold. She said you were with her at your house. What was she doing there?" I didn't answer. "Okay by me," he said. "So Milsap is running around all day beating the crap out of his old contacts and by the time Serio finds them, all blackeyed and lockjawed, he's seeing a trend. Figure by Monday after you get shitcanned at your hearing, Milsap gets busted, Miles gets knocked down because what the fuck kind of squad is he running where everyone is crazy, dirty or dead, and Torbett and I are marked just for being associated with you."

"Ideas?"

"Forget about Oliver. You'll never get him, not with a smoking gun, not with a wiretap on his dick. And if you did get him, no court in Texas would convict him. The best you'll do is Guerrin. Can you keep a secret?"

"Why not."

"I've got my contacts, you've got yours. One of mine is

a host at a very nice whorehouse in South Austin. They call it Heaven's Gate. Strictly to the gentry. Older guy, goes by the name 'Pledger,' knows how to wear a suit, but he can kill you twenty different ways with a fountain pen."

"How do you know him?"

"I came here from Vice, remember? He told me some stories, didn't mention names. I didn't think about it until today, but this whorehouse, it's at 804 Jewell."

It was one of the whorehouses the Attorney General's office told us Fred Harrell "owned." And Detective Sergeant Lonnie Waller was a lot sharper than I ever gave him credit for. "I'm listening," I said.

"By policy, Pledger tries to supply anything his customers want, rich man's privilege. Girls, boys, pro doms. Drugs nobody's seen in years. Opium. Where else can you get drunk on absinthe and get a blowjob from a twelve-year-old?"

"Why didn't you close him down?"

"Texas Mafia. You'd sooner get an indictment against Oliver. But Pledger's always nice to cops."

"How nice?"

"Screw you, you want my help? He also handles heroin, high-grade heroin, just for the guests. Harrell was Guerrin's boy. If Heaven's Gate is Guerrin's whorehouse, what are the chances they killed Harrell with the same heroin?"

"Fifty-fifty. We'll need a warrant."

"Fuck the warrant. He offers it voluntarily. We take him in, tell him we're not busting him for possession but murder, he freaks out and sings. Then we get him to wear a wire."

"Or he's cool as ice and waits for Guerrin to spring him."

"I'll make him freak out. Believe me?" I did. "The heroin, if it matches, Harrell's paper ownership of the house, Guerrin's connection to Harrell and Live Models, plus Pledger's testimony, plus Guerrin on tape. You think that's enough to nail Guerrin for two murders?"

"Maybe," I said, waving away the fog. "Too many details. They could all go wrong."

"All right," he said. "Then we turn it over to the Organized Crime Division and tell them it's too big for us. Or maybe the FBI. OC and the Feds take Dirty Sally, Internal Affairs takes Jeffries, and you light a Yom Kippur candle for Aaron Gold."

I stopped. "I'll think about it."

"Good, and think about this." He handed me a package about the size of an eyeglasses case, wrapped in brown paper, addressed to me at HQ, postmarked and time-stamped at 4:50 P.M. today, the afternoon mail. He'd ripped open one end. I slipped out the package, a black velvet jewelry box, and popped it open. Staring up at me were Nikki's sky blue eyeballs. My vision fogged. "Holy fuck."

I leaned on a desk while Waller took the box. "Meet me at the corner of Jewell and Bouldin Street at eleven tonight. Dress like a cop on the make. I'll clear it with HQ and the Attorney General at the last minute under emergency protocol. And don't tell anyone on the squad. I don't want to blow my contact."

"Fine."

"We'll zip in and zip out. Simplest thing in the world." I got my bearings and watched him, angry at him for showing me the eyes. He flicked the lighter. A spark flew and landed on his gray pants. He brushed it off.

"Shithead," I said. "You ever put lighter fluid in that fucking thing?"

He beamed. "I don't smoke."

27

9:00 P.M. Homicide Squad Room

Torbett had been smoldering since he left Lehane's house. The judge refused warrants or wiretaps for Oliver or Guerrin. Torbett went to campus, asked questions of anyone close to Oliver but not too close, trying to find out who Nikki was to Oliver without giving anything away. Back in the car, there was a radio call from Denton's office telling him to back off. Then back to HQ, where he flipped through phone confessions, follow-up reports, mug shots. Home for dinner and hugs and How was your day, tired smile on his face as he looked at his wife and children and tried to let them rule over his thoughts, instead of Bill Oliver and Charles Lehane and a world of evil pimps. And I have to go back to the office, and Don't go Daddy, please don't go, and I'm sorry, I'm sorry, you don't know how sorry I am, I have to go, baby, I have to make sure one corner of the world is safe for you to grow up.

Jake Lund had faxed the computer printout of Nikki's face to police and sheriff's departments in Houston, Dallas and Kansas City. Torbett called them all and got "Uh-huh, we'll get to it . . ." from everyone except a female deputy at the Houston Sheriff's Office:

"I went through a bunch of mug shots and if you want to put in a good word for me, go ahead. Two years ago, July '86 she's with this guy in his BMW. They're fighting, it says, only he's twice her size. Search the car, two grams of coke, both arrested, booked, released."

"Why?"

"He's from a very good family. I'll send you the pictures and prints. She ID'd as Lorraine Schatz by a Delaware driver's license no one checked out till me, just now. Sweet Lorraine doesn't exist."

Lund's borrowed printer started spitting ink across the paper, line by line. The tops to two female heads took shape, front and side view, black hair, and . . . glassy gray eyes. Match.

"Send me the prints. Who's the male?"

"This part you didn't get from me. Kenneth Lindhauer. He's got eight arrests in Houston alone for assault. All female victims, all charges dismissed. I can give you his new address. His parents sent him to Austin to keep him out of trouble. Funny, right?"

9:00 P.M. 4612 Avenue F

I went home, put on my gray suit and hit three happy hours around the Capitol Building hoping to hear what the cognoscenti might have to say about Bill Oliver, but every cocktail cluster that noticed me shifted away, a big, bruised thug in a cheap suit. I went back home, ate franks and beans and slammed the weights, no music, showered and put on fresh bandages, black pants, a black silk shirt and a blue sharkskin jacket Amy bought me for what turned out to be a divorce present. Then I got in my car two hours before I needed to meet Waller to go bust a dangerous bouncer at a high-end whorehouse. I started driving around and before I knew it I was parked in front of Rachel's wondering what I was doing there.

She opened the door in a loose-fitting black satin blouse, slacks, cigarette in hand, and barefoot, her dark hair brushed back from her face. I stood silently waiting for her to let me in or spit in my face. I noticed how much smaller she was without her heels, not small, just smaller. She looked me up and down, surveying my re-bandaged hands along with my new bruises and fat lip.

"Kid Twist wins by a knockout?" she asked. My dad's boxing moniker. She must have heard it once and re-membered it.

"Too early to tell."

"Big date tonight? Or is that why you have the bruises."

"You're home. It's Friday."

"I just got out of work. I have a date later if that's what's worrying you."

"No, I don't have a date."

"I got you beer."

I leaned in the archway to the kitchen and watched her pull a Michelob out of the fridge, pop it open and hold it out for me. I gave her a long look, then took a cold swig and said, "They think you slept with me last night."

"Was I good?"

"And our stories didn't jive so they know someone's lying."

"I was trying to help," she said.

"Why?"

"I was out when Joey died. You didn't tell anybody."

"All that made you was a lousy wife." The words slipped out on their own, cruel and angry, before I could stop them.

She jolted into high gear. "Goddammit! Every time I'm nice to you, you turn on me. If I were a better wife, he wouldn't have died, is that it? We would have been home making passionate perfect love."

I felt the rage bubbling up. "Why were you at my house?"

She stamped out her cigarette in a glass tray, fumbled with the pack and lit another. "I stopped off before work to give you something but you weren't home, so I was going to slip it under the door, then I saw Waller pull up so I hid it and pretended I was locking up." She opened a drawer by the sink, pulled out a booklet called *Buying Rental Property* and shoved it at me. "Here!" On the back some notes were scrawled in Joey's handwriting.

"So?"

"He was planning on buying some," she said. "His notes say he had eighty thousand dollars."

I read it: *Seized property on Ulit: 150G. Less 80 is 70G. Ten units at $200/mo.*

" 'Less 80' doesn't mean he had eighty grand," I said.

"Maybe they were going to knock off eighty thousand out of the goodness of their hearts. I don't know when he wrote that. The only account I know of was our checking account, and that had about six hundred in it when he died. If he managed to buy property, he didn't do it under his own name. If he had the cash and hid it, I'd like to know."

"For what? So you can buy a marble toilet?"

"Screw you. It's my money. I'm next of kin. You said so the night he died. I'll have trouble forgetting it."

"Is that what you care about? Eighty grand in a tin can somewhere?"

She trembled. "I gave him my twenties. I'm *thirty*."

"My heart's bleeding!"

"Go to Hell." She stomped past me into the living room. "You and your drunken friend. He came home from being out with you stinking of tequila and wanted to get romantic after six months of highs and lows, him going off on secret missions to New York or Juarez or wherever and coming back coked up and smelling of crack whores. I said no and he got mad and punched me in the eye. That's why I had sunglasses and heavy makeup on. And that's why I left."

So Rachel stopped using drugs and Joey started. And I didn't see it. "I didn't know," I said.

She powered away from me and I trailed her into the bedroom as she yelled, "I don't have time for this. I have a life. I have a career. I'm working and staying clean and he's out screwing whores!"

I'd never thought about Joey from anyone else's point of view. To me he was a hero. To her . . . I grasped at something. "Maybe he wasn't—"

"Fuck you. Fuck you and your blue wall of silence, all you brave silent knights, 'Woe is me, no one understands the horror I've seen, no one understands my pain. I haven't got a friend in the world.' You think your pain is so goddamn unique, you think you're the only one who's alone . . ." A sob choked out in her anger.

I walked closer and held her shoulders to calm her down. I knew why I jumped Milsap when he called Rachel a whore. I was glad Joey was gone. I hated myself for it. That's why I felt guilty when Joey died. But he was dead, and Rachel was right here. I thought she'd shove me away but she didn't.

She said, "You're just like Joey."

"I'm not," I said. Joey betrayed her. I wouldn't. I leaned close enough to feel her breath on my face and smell her skin.

She muttered, "Your tantrums and your brooding silences. Bunch of fucking bad movie actors. That's all you are."

I wiped her tears, wrapped my arms around her. I smelled her smell close, felt desire rise in me. I wanted to pull away and I couldn't. I owed Joey. Or did I?

"If you came here to find Joey, he's gone," she said.

"I know. I came for you."

"You're a mess," she said.

"You drive me crazy," I told her.

"I hate you so much."

"I'm gonna kill you one of these days," I whispered. "I swear to God."

She turned her face to mine. Our lips pressed together, warm and wet. We separated, then kissed again, harder. Her tongue pushed through my lips. I touched the gentle curve of her waist, felt the softness of her face, her skin against my cheek. Then I lifted her up off the floor. She wrapped her legs around me and squeezed my breath out.

We fell on the bed and she pulled my jacket and shirt off, unbuckled my pants, then slid her black satin blouse over her head, slipped off her slacks and lay on the covers naked. She held me close as I buried my face in her neck and slid inside. I opened my eyes wide and saw Rachel, only Rachel. I rose and fell inside her over and over. She squeezed me close with her legs, moved with me, slower, then faster.

Just Rachel. No innocent girl chopped up in the sand. No Joey flying off a cliff.

Just us in a room, making love.

28

10:00 P.M. 6009 Mount Bonnell Road

Guerrin in his den, looking out over peaceful homes, husbands who came home at five o'clock, loving wives, devoted children. How many of his neighbors were worried about suddenly winding up in prison? How many had killed to prevent that contingency?

He'd had more people killed in a week than in his whole previous career. Or at least more people he knew by name. The little sleep he could get was racked with nightmares. He couldn't take much more of this. He kept a revolver in the drawer. It was looking like a very attractive option.

Guerrin jolted when the mobile phone rang. He clicked it on, took a breath and said, "Yes."

"It's arranged." It was Payne.

"Good."

"But the medical examiner tracked your gopher's death to a particular long-haired kid."

"What?!"

"Two victims with the same dope. Why didn't they just leave an address? And they know he worked for you. I disappeared the paperwork. That'll buy you a day."

Guerrin tried to suck in deep breaths but he couldn't. His rib cage closed in on his lungs and kept them from filling up. "Take care of it," he wheezed.

"Take care of it yourself. We're even."

Guerrin took a deep breath. He needed to sound powerful. "After these two, we're even."

"When I'm done, no one will listen to anything this guy says again. But I can't clean up after those assholes. I'm through."

"You cost me three thousand dollars to that poor girl's family every month," Guerrin hissed. "You're through when I say you're through."

"You're crazy."

"Crazy is a cranked-up vice cop who cripples a whore and thinks he'll walk away scot-free. I own you, 'Payne'!"

Payne was silent. Guerrin could hear him flicking that stupid Zippo lighter.

Guerrin had crossed the line. He threatened the man, and claimed control he didn't know if he had.

Suddenly everything was different, and clear, as if a light switch had flicked on and the darkness of the last twenty-five years was gone. No more stress. No sucking revolvers for him. He didn't even feel tired anymore. He might never sleep again. He could see sharp as day what he needed to do: call Oliver's men, tell them how they screwed up, put it in their court to fix it. All he had to do was stay in control. Everything would be perfect. But he'd already threatened Payne.

Finally, Payne said, *"I'll take care of him because I promised. The next one I take care of is you."*

The line clicked off.

10:45 P.M. 3809 Peck Avenue

Rachel woke in time to see me button up my silk shirt and put on my sharkskin jacket. She sat up in bed and looked me up and down like she was trying to photograph me for later on. I kept expecting her to pull up the sheets to cover her breasts but she didn't. She reached for a cigarette and lit it without looking. "Where you going?"

I shook my head.

"Official police business," she said. "I probably wouldn't understand. Is Torbett your new partner?"

"No."

"From the shine on that jacket I'd say this has something to do with drugs and prostitutes."

I smiled at her. "You assume the worst of me."

"No," she said, serious. "You assume the worst of *me*."

I holstered my .38. Rachel put out her cigarette and lay down, pulling the sheet up over her shoulders and turning away.

I asked, "Can I see you tomorrow?"

"I have a date tomorrow."

11:00 P.M. 2107 Bridle Path

Torbett parked in the trees and waited until the sky was black and he could see occasional movement in Kenneth Lindhauer's windows. Reles was not to be found and Torbett wasn't about to approach a rich maniac in his house, not alone. Lindhauer finally walked out the front door in a sports jacket and slacks: twenty-eight years old, six-foot-two, reddish hair, build like a tree trunk, a football player gone to pot. He climbed into his red Aston Martin and buzzed off into town, Torbett following at a safe distance, looping Lake Austin Boulevard, up Lamar, past Pease Park and Al's Guns to the Yellow Rose.

Torbett watched Lindhauer go in, waited a few minutes and followed. A bouncer greeted him with a dirty look. Torbett gave him a twenty and passed inside. A woman stood on the stage, half-heartedly moving her feet to the music, step-touch, step-touch, while men drank and groped the waitresses. Torbett couldn't make out Lindhauer's prominent physique in the smoke. He found a spot at the bar near the back, ordered a Scotch and soda from a surly bartender and watched the room as the smoke burned his eyes. After about five minutes he noticed a man follow a young woman through a curtained arch near the stage. He weaved through the crowd and followed.

Behind the curtain Torbett found an unmanned door. He opened it and a broad bearded biker with a shaved head suddenly filled the doorway, showing no signs of letting a single man pass. Torbett flashed his badge and the biker announced, "We're clean here, officer. All girls a minimum of twelve inches from the men at all times—" Torbett found the light switch by the door and flicked it up, the white fluorescent light cleansing the room of sin. From three corners, three women in pasties and G-strings straddling three seated men, two fumbling with their zippers, one of them Lindhauer, all looked in Torbett's direction, squinting like moles.

Torbett announced, "A word with Mr. Lindhauer." Lindhauer's squint turned angry. "The rest of you clear out." Scramble of feet to the door as Torbett stepped toward Lindhauer, whose powerful hand now clamped the arm of the pigeon-toed peroxide blonde standing over him.

"No, you stay," Lindhauer ordered her.

Torbett put on his tired voice, hid the anger pounding beneath. "You can call her back in a few minutes. I just have some questions." Lindhauer didn't let go. He'd stopped blinking and could see Torbett's face. "Suit yourself," Torbett said, and unfolded the printout of Nikki, mugshots from front and side. "You know this girl?"

Lindhauer looked hard at the printout and at Torbett. "I don't have to answer anything."

"Here or downtown."

"Kiss my ass, nigger. The last two cops who ran me in wound up out of work."

Torbett pocketed the picture, checked his eyes at half-mast and took a deep breath. "So my career's in the toilet. So I have nothing to lose by cuffing you wrists-to-ankles and throwing you in the queens' tank."

Lindhauer's eyes opened wide, then squeezed at the intrusion of light. He released the girl, stood slow as if to say, *Ya got me,* then took a sloppy roundhouse swing at Torbett. Torbett dodged, grabbed Lindhauer's wrist, twisted it behind his back and pinched the pressure point. The playboy groaned through gritted teeth.

Torbett dropped the sleepy tone, snarled in Lindhauer's ear. "Assault on a police officer. Felony. Hours in the tank before I get you your phone call, MAYBE. Fifty angry motherfuckers taking turns on your ass. You *will* get AIDS. You will die like a dog and nothing your rich daddy does will buy you out of that one. And then you will know how the other half lives."

Lindhauer winced. "Houston, a couple of years ago. At a party."

"What kind of party?"

"Guys. Girls. A party."

"Did you pay them?"

"No, you buy them stuff."

"Rich boys buying things for pretty girls?"

"Yeah. Shit. What's that, some kind of nigger karate? Ow!"

"What happened?"

"Nothing. We went out, went for a ride, pulled over, one thing leads to another."

"You hit her."

"She was asking for it."

"How?"

"Didn't talk, didn't say nothing."

"That's how she asked for it?"

"Man takes a woman out, spends some money on her, he expects a little appreciation."

"Did you have sex with her?"

"The first night, at the party. Not the night we got busted."

"When did you see her after that?" Torbett leaned around to see Lindhauer's eyes from the side.

"When they booked us."

"You never saw her again?"

"No."

"What's her name?"

"Beats me." Torbett pinched Lindhauer's wrist and twisted his arm harder. "Aaugh! What are you after me for?"

Torbett leaned toward Lindhauer's ear. "Because you prey on the weak." Torbett shoved Lindhauer over the chair and walked out.

11:00 P.M. South Austin

I'm with Rachel now, I thought. I waited years for her. I felt guilty, like I was betraying Joey. But Joey used coke, cheated on her, beat her. Living or dead, he had no claim on her. I spent the last six months chasing Joey's ghost. I had to stop.

But I had to bury him first. At a pay phone, I dialed Hay at home.

"Yes."

"It's Reles. You told me Denton tried to make you change the cause of death for some cop. Was that Joey?"

Hay let out a breath. "No."

"You're lying."

"All the specifics are in the autopsy report."

"I never saw it."

"Of course you didn't. Nobody did. When I wouldn't change the cause of death they buried the report. I just write the reports," she said. "I can't make anyone read 'em."

"What was the cause of death?"

"Unknown."

"What does that mean?"

She rumbled, "It means unknown. Maybe it was an accident like they said. Maybe he was drunk and they were hiding it from the press. And maybe it was suicide. You were with him. How drunk was he?"

"Unknown. What do you know about him using drugs?"

No answer. If she knew something else about Joey, she wasn't telling. "I spent the day with Jeffries," she said. "The ranks are thinning. Remember what I said about the gurney."

I drove the few blocks to the corner of Jewell and

Bouldin. Waller got in the car, the air still hot and soupy thick even this far into the night.

"You're late," he said. He was wearing a Hawaiian shirt—against his plastic frame glasses he looked even more like a geek—but he seemed wired to the teeth, a marine on a mission. "You think this is a game, come whenever you want?" I didn't answer, and he smiled like flicking a switch. "Relax, we'll have fun. I scored some meth from Narco. We'll use it as bait. Everyone knows bringing dope in kiboshes a drug bust."

"Isn't there some rule about not being impaired while undercover?"

He handed me a pint of Jack Daniel's. "Drink this and shut up."

I had bruised ribs and a split lip from my fight with Milsap, bandaged hands from the drums, Rachel's smell on me and hot new ideas bubbling in my head about Joey flying off that cliff drunk and coked to the rafters, and me glad he's gone so I can have her to myself.

No time to think. I took a swig: it made me shudder but it rippled down and warmed my insides. I scoped the street.

Waller said, "They're strictly by appointment here. Pledger said they're not expecting anyone important until four, they'd be glad for the company. Don't expect them to put out the good china. You didn't tell anyone about this, did you? I don't want to blow my contact."

"No," I said. "You square it with HQ and the AG's?"

He nodded. "Ready?"

11:10 P.M. 7809 Deer Ridge Circle

Margaret Hay hung her robe in the closet and climbed into bed, pulling the sheets up to her neck. She couldn't sleep without something over her, no matter how hot it was. A truck rolled up the quiet street. She listened to the silence, then rolled onto her side and closed her eyes. Not much of a night's sleep last night thanks to Reles, and a long day today: Aaron Gold the hippie, Fred Harrell the fake psycho killer, and Buck Jeffries the cop. And all before breakfast. She'd sleep tonight.

11:15 P.M. Jewell and Bouldin

I rubbed Nikki's charm in my pocket as Waller and I walked from the corner to the house, painted a faded brown to keep it from drawing too much attention. Working against the effect of the paint was the house's three stories, two more than most buildings in the balmy Southwest. Four stone steps led up to the front door, the parlor level, with windows a good ten feet high. We climbed the steps and knocked, and Pledger opened the door, a gray-haired fiftyish guy about five-ten in an English suit, with the bearing of a nineteenth-century stockbroker. Antique wood and paintings decorated the detailed-wood corridor, a high-fallutin' old-time whorehouse—ass with class.

"Come in, gentlemen. The party's just beginning."

29

11:15 P.M. Heaven's Gate

Half a dozen women, assorted sizes and shapes, glanced up as Waller and I walked in. Red velvet wrapped most of the furniture and silk wrapped most of the girls, Frederick's of Abilene. White breasts swelled over the tops of black teddies.

Someone said, "Tonto!"

It was Vita, the Latina hooker I saw Monday at Casa Rosa Apartments, familiar face from the Joey days, with black hair tinted red, and green eyes, bosom filling out a skimpy white silk dress that zippered down the front, no indication of anything underneath. She jumped up and stood close to me. I pulled back and she held her ground.

"Small town," I said.

She said, "Sooner or later everybody fucks everybody."

"I thought you worked alone."

She breathed into my ear, "I freelance."

Pledger said, "Vita, why don't you get your friend a drink." I glanced at Waller who grinned, the amiable guest. My eyes followed Vita to the bar.

Rachel Velez stood by the window wrapped in a sheet, looking out over the darkened yard and the public golf course beyond it. She deserved better than this, frantic intimacy then, "I gotta go and I can't tell you where." And yet with all that, there was an honest strain in Dan, something about him that made her feel safe. She hadn't felt safe on her own, hadn't felt it for years with Joey, as he stepped from father figure to lover to stranger to nemesis. Hadn't felt it with anyone before him. And certainly not with her father.

So Dan went off to meet somebody, on police business, and it wasn't Torbett. Jeffries dead, Milsap out of the question. Miles and Jake not the stuff of midnight missions. That left Waller, the other new guy.

Waller was the first one who showed at Dan's house that morning, before everyone else. He was the one who spotted Rachel about to leave the pamphlet. His look made her jolt—he caught her doing something, but his face read like she'd caught *him*. She watched Waller circulate with the other detectives as they showed up, Waller flashing understanding nods when the others looked at him. The rest of the time he scanned, surveyed the squad, evaluated. No, Waller wasn't part of the squad, it took an outsider like her to see it. Maybe he was an Internal Affairs mole, on Serio's team. Or maybe he was on his own team. There was a reason Waller was at Dan's house first, Rachel thought. And it wasn't official. Then something hit her hard.

Wherever Dan was going tonight, if he was with Waller, it was a trap.

30

1:30 A.M. Heaven's Gate

Nine ball cracks against the eight ball. I leaned over a pool table by myself, rolling balls around. The walls were maroon, dark like blood and fuzzy. Velvet. The table stood in an alcove off the hall. I found my drink, watched my feet stumble in front of each other to the dining room, leaned against the wall watching through my haze, a fuzzy vision of Waller at a dining table with Pledger and the girls, spinning tales about his travels.

"In Amsterdam they're not so tough on the girls. They have picture windows set up right out in the open like a department store."

Vita followed me into the living room.

"What's the matter, baby? Not having a good time?"

My face felt hot, my head was pounding and something vibrated from my throat down to my stomach. There was something I was supposed to do—what was it?

I babbled, "There was . . . a girl."

"What kind of girl, baby?"

I remembered a picture. "A brunette."

She pursed her lips. "I'm a brunette."

I couldn't take my eyes off her breasts. She unzipped the white silk dress slowly down.

"You can touch 'em if you want. That's what they're for!"

A buzzing ran up and down my legs, my spine, circled around my pelvis and groin, my bruised ribs, my swollen lip. A small voice called to me from a distance, *You can't, you have a girl,* and got lost in the haze. Helplessly, I wet my lips and leaned over.

The second rule of going undercover: No sex.

I tried to think. What was the first rule again?

I heard a bunch of voices chorus, "Sna-agged!" and I pulled away. Waller and some girls were wagging fingers at us from the kitchen doorway.

Vita said, "Thanks a lot," then turned back to me. "Don't mind them. Let me freshen that drink."

In the doorway Waller ran his hand along one girl's shoulder. She stiffened as if his hand were ice.

The room got darker like someone dropped a veil over it. I couldn't feel my legs.

"I'm sorry, Mrs. Velez. Sergeant Reles isn't answering the car radio. But he's not on call. Have you tried him at home?"

"No. No, I will. Thank you."

"I'm sure sorry about Sergeant Velez. He was a wonderful man."

Rachel didn't recognize the Dispatch operator's voice, just another woman at APD who knew the legend. "Yes," she said absently. "He was."

"But I'm sure you're all right," the woman added slyly.

Rachel slammed the phone down. Then she called information and got Jake Lund's home number.

"Leave a message . . ."

She hung up again. She shouldn't have called HQ. She paced up and down the room. She didn't have a friend she could call in the middle of the night. Jake was out. Miles Niederwald? He'd be blind drunk, but he'd be home. She sat on the bed and dialed.

He answered on the sixteenth ring. *"Yeah?"*

"Miles, this is Rachel Velez."

"Yeah." No recognition.

"Miles, this is Rachel. Rachel Velez. Joey Velez's wife. He died. Remember me?"

"Who?"

She gritted her teeth. "Rachel Velez. Joey Velez's wife!"

Niederwald broke out of a cloud. *"Velez is dead."*

"I know he's dead!" she shouted. "He was my husband. This is Rachel Velez, Joey's wife. I'm in trouble and I need your help! Splash some water on your face, Miles!" Then she took a deep breath and yelled, "WAKE UP!"

Niederwald coughed and sputtered, then spoke with something like clarity. *"Fuck you, lady. You called me!"* He hung up. She dialed him again and the phone kept ringing. Niederwald was down for the count. Who was left?

I watched Waller sitting at one end of the table, telling stories and cutting crystal meth on a mirror he passed to Pledger. A chunky woman slid her hand down to Waller's crotch. He grabbed her hand and twisted it hard enough that she buckled.

"Ow!"

He let go with a grin. "I'm a *ba-a-ad* boy. So I pull the guy over and . . ."

I saw parts of things, hands around drinks, lines of meth, breasts, asses. The skinny waist of the girl on my lap. I was singing along with what sounded like Bob Marley.

"Lifting you in your despair . . ."

"You sing real good," she said. "I used to wanna be a singer when I was a kid."

I tried to follow the traffic around the hazy room, knocking imaginary drums with my battered knuckles, my arms circling her tiny waist.

"You play drums?" she asked in a high curious voice. "I bet you play real good."

"How the hell would you know if I'm any good?!" I yelled. This wasn't the same girl. What did she want from me? She ran small fingers along my bandaged hand.

"You got good hands," she said. She'd scratched the polish off her own battered fingernails.

"Right."

"I mean it. You got muscles in your hands like a bodybuilder, but you don't use 'em hard, you use 'em like . . . you use 'em gentle."

She brought my hand to her naked baby-soft thigh.

Damn, I thought, I'm supposed to be doing something. What *was* it?

Somebody passed her a joint. She flicked off the ash, put the joint in her mouth backward and blew smoke at me.

I breathed in deep.

◆

Hay jolted awake and lay still in bed. She had a definite sense of movement somewhere, maybe in the garden. A raccoon? The last thing in the world she needed was some APD clowns coming over, finding nothing and spreading it around that she was a paranoid old crank.

She lay perfectly still and listened. A shuffle, maybe a scratching.

Then she heard a small click.

I was watching a movie, a guy standing and a girl sitting on the edge of a bed.

He lifted her white dress. Her soft tan skin looked clean and fresh in a crazy dirty world. She laughed a low rumbling sound.

He pulled off his pants. Whatever he left behind was gone. All bets were off. His powerful hands squeezed her hips.

He felt everything more intensely, both the moistness and the throbbing in the back of his head and his lip. He started slow, then moved faster and harder, giving in to the buzzing in his head, mouth, skin, his own pelvis a blur before him, one sizzling firecracker all over, building and building and finally rushing through him, a warm torrent flowing, still flowing, more, harder each moment, as he squeezed her, a final thrust, until there was nothing left, just a few drops, drops, hold her tight for good measure, squeeze, squeeze, and just as I was fading into darkness I got it, that the man in the movie was me. And it wasn't a movie.

31

3:30 A.M. Dreamland

I zero in on the gearshift, three-on-the-tree, on the steering column of Joey's Chevy Caprice. He's alive, driving wild-eyed up 2222, the road swinging roller-coaster right and left, a hundred miles in the air and straight back down.

"Joey, you're dead," I say.

"No," he laughs. "Pretty near."

I want to ask what happened and what comes out is, "I never touched her." He grins wide.

I'm making love with Rachel.

A dim overhead lamp shines its yellow haze on two men, one white and one brown, behind a table in a smoky room. Gold coins clank down in a pile. The clanking echoes in my ears.

A shadowy figure looks at me. I turn and he turns. I draw my revolver but I can't move fast enough. I know I'm going to die. I realize I'm looking into a mirror but I already pulled the trigger.

The shot thunders and my face fades into Joey's. He smiles, takes the bullet and shatters to the ground.

I woke with a start, a narrow beam of light hitting me from the hall as someone walked away. I blinked a few times, focusing my foggy vision on the light, then rolled over on my chest and found the floor with my feet. Where was I? It was still dark out, I was still here, in the house. What house? Wake up! I slapped my cheek. Everything hurt. What house? I remembered women and dope. The whorehouse. South somewhere. Texas. South Texas. No, South Congress maybe. I slapped my face again, hard, braced myself on the post of the bed, pushed down with my legs and stood up straight.

Too fast. My vision went black and I crashed to the floor. I kept slapping my face to keep from passing out. I rolled onto my knees, then using steady pressure on my trembling legs, I pressed down on the floor and slid my hands up the splintery wall until I was standing. I got my balance, sliding my hand along the wall until I found a light switch, and braced myself for the light.

Margaret Hay put on her robe, checked the loaded Colt .45 Single Action Army Pistol in her nightstand, walked with it all around the house, turned on all the lights, checked the locks and made herself a bowl of oatmeal. She sat and read two more chapters of a novel, drank a cup of chamomile tea, checked the cat's water dish, and when she was still wide awake but too tired to stay upright, headed back to bed.

She lay the Colt on the nightstand, got a fresh glass of water from the bathroom, brought it back and stood it next to the Colt. Two nights of interrupted sleep in a row. Still, it was Saturday and she could sleep as late as she wanted, not that she would. Forty years off the farm and she still woke the roosters. But she could lie in bed late if she wanted to, or maybe take a long nap in the afternoon. As she kicked off her slippers, she turned to see the reassuring sight of the Colt. Old Security, Dad called it. Old Second Amendment, provided you didn't look at the wording. She took off her robe.

Then she noticed the closet door was closed. She'd left it open.

I was alone in the room, but I hadn't been alone for long. I had a dope hangover, still half high, bladder fixing to burst.

And I made it with another woman, a prostitute, the very night I first got with Rachel. Slipped a mickey, so stoned I thought I was dreaming it. Committed my crime in a half-blackout. The prisons were full of guys just like me.

I had to get out, find Waller and make a break for it. It would all blow over, I kept saying as I pulled my clothes on. Where was my gun? Music floated up from downstairs, the only noise in the hall.

"In his effervescent Grace . . ."

I shuffled my way along the empty corridor to the bathroom, tried to find the light, failed, left the door open a crack while I used the toilet. I was stoned, hungover, sweaty and sticky. I needed a shower, steak, eggs, coffee, enough Scotch to forget what I'd done, and a real night's sleep. But first I needed to get out. I ran water in the sink and splashed it on my face, then reached for a towel.

My hand landed on the toilet tank, on the warm muzzle of my .38.

I blinked and swung the door wide open to let the light in.

The intruder stood still in Hay's closet.

He'd unloaded her old revolver while she was in the bathroom. He would let her get into bed before he opened the door—easier than chasing her around the room. He heard her come in, sit on the bed, cough. She got up, opened the window, moved around the room, coughed, closed the window, prayed—was she kidding?—and then settled into bed.

He took a deep breath, opened the door silently, raised the silenced Magnum and fired twice—a whispered *Choop! Choop!*

I gaped at Pledger lying in the bathtub in a pool of his own coagulating blood, his eyes shining back at me, a bullet hole puncturing his forehead. I heard the gunshot in my dream. Killed in a bathtub like Jeffries. I picked up the weapon carefully, my weapon, hoping to save any fingerprints, and popped the chamber. One shot fired, only one.

They left him in the tub with a bullet in his skull from

my gun. They got close enough to get my weapon, but then let me live. Set-up time.

And where the hell was Waller?

The killer stepped out of the closet toward the bed. As he bent over to check his work, a thin ghostly figure rose behind him, raising the butt of a Colt .45 in the air.

I stumbled through the house pushing doors open. In one bedroom a sleepy blond girl, a thin teenager, sat up naked and said, "Hi." I remembered her sitting on my lap earlier. I didn't notice before how young she was. I ran down steps I didn't remember climbing, clutching the banister for balance.

A tape deck on the floor blasted Bob Marley. The dining room was empty, the people and bottles and dope were gone. I checked the other rooms and found the same: the party had cleared out.

I lurched down another flight of stairs and followed light to the back of the house and the kitchen. Waller in his Hawaiian shirt was wiping the back doorknob with a handkerchief. He spun around with a start.

With all her might, Hay smashed the lightened Colt like a sledgehammer down onto the intruder's skull. As he fell he fired blindly behind him. One shot hit her in the hip. She threw herself on his back with a yell more fury than pain, raised the Colt again and bashed him tomahawk-style, breaking his temple with a loud crack and leaking fluid. He dropped the Magnum and rolled her off him, holding his head and shrieking as he ran out into the street.

Hay rolled onto her back, propped herself up on her elbows and looked at his weapon and her wound: nine millimeter, high impact. Perforated bone and artery. Hold arterial pressure point. She dragged herself to the phone, almost chuckling at the medical examiner calling her own ambulance. She picked up the receiver.

The line was dead.

The blood rushed to my head so fast I thought I'd pop. I flew onto Waller and slammed him against the wall, shouting, "Why, why, why?!" I pounded him in the face twice, didn't get an answer and didn't knock the grin loose from his lips. He dropped his head forward, bit my left shoulder and sank his teeth in. The pain shot down into my arm, and I cursed and kicked him three times in the groin before he loosed his grip enough for me to tear him off, my shirt soaking with blood. I rushed him, landing jackhammer blows to his face that broke his glasses and knocked his jaw loose. He didn't flinch, instead shooting lightning shots to my gut and ribs too hard for someone his size, still grinning with my blood running down his crooked chin. I head-butted him by the counter. My skull buzzed and my shoulder stung and I grounded myself and put all my weight into a knockout shot Waller dodged as he grabbed a handful of something white from a plate and threw it into my eyes, then whacked me in the face with a liquor bottle.

Bones crunched, blood vessels popped and the blood flowed from my nose. I dropped to my knees, snorting blood, blinked and tried to focus on Waller. He loomed ten feet tall. I tried to get up but my knees buckled and I was on all fours again, choking out, "Why?"

A sharp pain shot through my left hand and I saw that Waller had nailed it to the floor with a kitchen knife. I yelled and tried to break free, but the knife was an inch into the wood. When I could see, Waller's bloody jaw hung slack on one side, the other side still grinning as he spooned up a tiny bit of white powder from the plate, snorted it and licked the spoon. He lifted his broken jaw, tried to relocate it, screamed briefly and left it locked in place. He spoke through his teeth.

"Sorry about Jeffries. He was fat and stupid but a man of convictions. That was meant for you."

"You killed Jeffries. You called him from inside HQ."

"It was a mistake, I own that," he said. He found his glasses on the floor and tried to reattach the missing arm. "But think larger. The world is in disarray. Every year it gets worse. We need a change."

"Dirty Sally?"

"A sign of her times. No, I didn't do that, they brought me in later." He gave up on the glasses and pocketed them.

"Who?"

"You know who."

"What *are* you?" I asked.

He leaned over me. "I'm a soldier. What are you?"

Helpless with my hand nailed to the floor and my eyes half-blinded, I struggled against Waller's arm with my free hand as he pressed my broken nose. "You know what's wrong with you?" he said through gritted teeth, pressing down. "*You . . . lack . . . DISCIPLINE!*"

A familiar voice shouted, "Waller, move away from him."

Torbett stood in the back doorway, aiming his automatic. Waller laughed, let me go, leaned himself over the stove. I worked the knife back and forth in the floor and pulled it loose, taking a chunk of my flesh along with it, then struggled to my feet.

Waller slurred, his back to us, "The gang's all here. Who's up for pancakes?"

Torbett said, "I got fingerprints coming from Houston. Two years ago Nikki worked a party there, maybe several parties. Rich boys, pretty girls, expensive gifts. Waller, anything to add? Before we take you in."

"You miss the point completely," Waller said through his sealed jaw. He faced us, grinning, and wiped my blood off his chin with a dishtowel. "We can't go on like this. Social services draws the dregs of the state to Austin. Vagabonds soiling the streets. Women in positions of responsibility. The police force itself is run by ethnics and mongrels," with a look at Torbett and me. "We need to clean up from the top down." He looked at the bloody towel, tossed it into the sink. "I did my part," he said, and stood grinning by the stove.

I noticed the knobs were turned up and gas was hissing out. Waller reached into his jacket pocket with a bloodstained hand and pulled out his lucky Zippo lighter. I didn't wait for his final words, instead running toward Torbett and the door and flying fists first, the image in my mind of the half-asleep teenage girl trapped upstairs, as Waller flipped the lighter open and flicked, and a cataract of flame and glass blew overhead as the blast chased a heartbeat behind us.

PART THREE

THE WAY OF ALL FLESH

32

SATURDAY

1:00 P.M. Anderson and Guerrin

"I don't appreciate being treated like a criminal," Guerrin said to Oliver's two men where they stood over him. Even past their sunglasses Guerrin could make out a crumbling illusion of control. His senses were growing more acute by the minute. Last night he hadn't even bothered trying to sleep. He didn't need it.

"Our operative made it back to us this morning with his last breath," the tall one said. "Don't underestimate our commitment."

Guerrin said, "I haven't heard from Payne."

"What about Harrell?"

"That's on you," Guerrin said, gaining courage. "You used the same heroin on Harrell and Aaron Gold. I told you that. I didn't tell you to kill the fucking Medical Examiner!"

It was hard to see past the two men's sunglasses, but their silence said they were in trouble too.

The tall one said, "There was no paper trail between Harrell and you. How did they know he worked for you?"

"Think hard," the one with the crew cut said. "Who could have pinned you to Fred Harrell? Who could have given that information to Reles?"

Guerrin thought, and the thought caught his breath. Tina. Oh God. Tina!

1:00 P.M. Brackenridge Hospital

A ball of white light shined in the blackness, went out, shined again. I blinked and the white was everywhere. My nose felt like it was about to explode. My left arm throbbed from my hand to my collarbone. I was alive.

Rachel's face appeared out of the light as she approached the bed. "They said if you keep it immobilized you might get full use out of it again." My bandaged left hand was strapped into a fiberglass splint.

"Why am I here?" I remembered diving through the back door but I didn't remember landing. I remembered an ambulance.

"You were pretty messed up," she said. "They doped you to work on your hand, not that you needed it."

If I concentrated I could tell the pain was coming from my hand and shoulder and not my whole body. I could move my sore legs. Gauze and tape mummified my left shoulder where—the moment came back with a shot of agony—Waller had sunk his teeth.

"And they gave you half a dozen shots for that bite. Everything they had. You'll need more tests. Are you okay?"

"Sure," I said. I grabbed my briefs from the night table,

slipped them under the bedsheet and tried to pull them on with one hand. "How are you?" I was ready to pretend I didn't remember what I did with the girl in the house, Vita. I remembered plenty.

Rachel was wearing a cream-colored dress, like a nurse's uniform only warmer and showing more skin. But there was no warmth in her face. "I got a call from Houston."

"Yeah?" I tried to move my left arm against the throbbing pain.

"Jack O'Connor. Houston Police. He said you called about me."

I froze.

She went on. "I can fill in the blanks. Or did you read the whole report?"

"I'm sorry—"

"For what?" she said. "Investigating me? You think my marriage was loveless? It was! You think I want Joey's money? I do. Jack O'Connor was my friend. He knew my history. Only he never used it to hurt me."

"I didn't want to—"

"You want to see the worst in me?" She leaned close to me, trembling, and whispered fiercely. "The night I met Joey, I killed a man. He followed me home from a club and got into my apartment and attacked me. I was high. I killed him with a kitchen knife. Now every time I hold still I think about the horror, my hand on a knife plunging into a human being's throat. That's my life. Tell me now."

"I . . . Tell you what?"

"Tell me you trust me."

I wanted to answer, wrap my arms around her, tell her it was okay. I couldn't.

She stood up. "If Internal Affairs comes calling I'll know it's a real investigation. Anything else is just you chasing ghosts. I gave you one last chance, and you ran my rap sheet." Torbett walked in. Rachel's eyes locked on him then snapped back to me in a final, surveying motion. "This is where I came in," she said, and walked out.

Torbett said, "You want me to go?"

I imagined Rachel walking down the hall and away, and shook my head.

"Waller's dead," Torbett said. "I palmed his badge when the firemen hauled the bodies out."

"Suppression of evidence."

"It'll turn up Monday with the paperwork. Murder-suicide. Slam dunk."

"Murder?"

"One male, one female. Any ideas?"

I turned away. The host and the blond girl. "Waller killed Jeffries by accident. He was after me."

"Why?"

It was coming back. "Waller had an idea to go to this whorehouse to bust someone close to Guerrin, make him wear a wire."

"You didn't tell anybody."

"Waller was gonna clear it with HQ and the AG's office at the last minute." I tried to sit up to cover how stupid I sounded. I caught a glimpse of my face in a mirror, swollen nose and two black eyes.

Torbett breathed in deep through his nose. "I don't know if Waller could have cleared that particular maneuver if he'd tried. The judge wouldn't authorize wiretaps for Guerrin or Oliver. You picked the wrong man to trust. I searched his house this morning. There was nothing there, I mean nothing. Clothes, soap and a Bible. Whatever life he had he didn't keep at home. I sent Nikki's prints and mug shots to Dallas, Houston and D.C. I haven't tracked any busts for her in Austin yet. I'd say we'll have an ID by Monday. Which doesn't tell us why a fifteen-year cop tried to kill you."

"He said I shouldn't go after Oliver, I'd never catch him, I should try for Guerrin."

"When?"

"Yesterday, in the squad room, after we talked to Lehane and you went out to Warrants."

"After the heroin connected Harrell's death to Aaron Gold's."

I froze.

"So Waller takes a swipe at you Thursday night after you brace Guerrin and gets Jeffries by accident because he stabs through a shower curtain. Then he takes a second swipe at you Friday, only smarter, tries to set you up, after we connect Harrell's death to Gold's."

I sat up painfully on the edge of the bed and tried to pull on my pants.

Torbett said, "Lie down. You're half dead."

"Waller knew evidence wouldn't just go away if a cop got killed. But if I got caught with my pants down, all bets were off. Who's left? Guerrin?"

"You think Guerrin's scared enough to talk if we corner him?" Torbett asked. "If he had Waller and somebody else at 804 Jewell and two of them are dead?"

I checked for Nikki's charm in my pants pocket, plucked it out and squeezed it in my fist. Joey's words came back to me. *Three people can keep a secret if two of them are dead.*

I said, "Get two patrols and go pick up Guerrin. I have to talk to somebody."

I blew it with Rachel. I'd be a good cop. I didn't have anything else.

1:30 P.M. Brackenridge Hospital Entrance

A car service dropped me at Jewell and Bouldin ("Pal, you sure you're all right?") and I got into my Impala, cruised north and turned right on East Twelfth, past the overpass where Rick Schate got flattened, where I first found Nikki, sliding slow and scanning both sides of the street, up to the pink stucco walls of the Casa Rosa Apartments where I started the investigation, and pulled up in front of number 5 as the door opened.

One of the boys stepped out and pulled the door shut behind him, before he saw me and ran for the alley. I was in no shape to chase him and I yelled, "I wouldn't run." He stopped dead, turned and walked to my window.

"What now?" he said and saw my bandages. "Fuck!"

"I need a favor."

Ten minutes later, blasted on the powder from three capsules of what I was pretty sure was pharmaceutical-quality methamphetamine, I tore up the outer stairs to number 11, each step rippling through my arm and shoulder, and pounded the door with my good fist. I clutched Nikki's printout picture in my bad one.

Vita, the bodacious Latina who served me my first drink at Heaven's Gate, opened the door in a white terry cloth robe, rubbing her wet hair with a towel. Her green eyes lit when she saw me.

"What happened to you?" she said, half amused, and let her robe fall open. I pushed her into her small living room. A big mirror hung on one wall to make it look spacious, liquor bottles on a side table. I shut the door. "Cool it," she said. "Jesus!"

"Three people can keep a secret if two of them are dead!"

"What?"

"What happened last night?"

"Oh, that."

"You gave me a drink. What was in it?"

"I don't know. Pledger mixed it. You were crazy last night."

"What'd I do?"

"Nothing. Goofy shit. Something about a brunette you were looking for, and then you fell down. But you made it upstairs all right."

I showed her Nikki's picture. She said, "Shit."

"You know her?"

"Nikki."

I nodded. "Nikki."

"Yeah, with two *k*'s. Like Nikki Sixx. Sure I know Nikki. Will you calm down? Jesus!" I stepped back and she closed her robe. "I used to run around these parties in Houston a couple of years ago. Rich boys. Anyway, this guy, he had me bump into her, pretend to make friends. It was a crazy set-up. I figured somebody just spotted her and wanted her for the circuit. I felt bad. But someone introduced *me* to the circuit." She glanced skyward. "And I turned out all right."

"What happened to her?"

"She started on coke like most of the girls. Got too strung out and switched."

"When's the last time you saw her?"

"I don't know. A year and a half? More?"

"The guy who had you do this, what was his name?"

"Roy."

"Roy Guerrin?"

Her jaw dropped.

"Get dressed," I said. "I need a statement."

She flashed shit-scared. "I'm not going anywhere."

"I can bust you."

"You can't make me talk. I'm independent. I don't know anybody, and I don't remember faces."

I grabbed a liquor bottle and threw it at the big mirror, smashing it to shards. Vita jumped from the flying glass and I cornered her with the picture.

"A girl just like you, dead. You helped get her there. Testify and we can stop the men who killed her."

"Mr. Wonderful. Who's gonna look out for me? You?"

Vita could nail Guerrin to Nikki and wouldn't. No one could nail Waller to Guerrin except Waller, and he was dead. Who knew anything about Guerrin and was still alive to testify? His receptionist, Tina LaMarque.

But if I knew it, Guerrin knew it too.

I hit the gas and tore down I-35 back toward Tina's place.

33

2:00 P.M. 2823 East Oltorf, Apartment 1918

I got to the door of Tina's apartment and heard men's voices, one of them Guerrin's, and a woman whimpering, "I didn't know, I didn't know!" Tina.

Clock ticking on Tina. I remembered the running balcony along the back of the second-floor apartments, all with sliding glass doors, and headed back for my car. No time to call for backup. If there was more than one guy, I couldn't approach from the front door. My eyes were okay but my left shoulder was half-immobilized and my left hand practically useless; I couldn't handle two weapons at once. I dug out the Ruger automatic I keep locked up under my car seat, checked the clip, locked up my .38, walked to the apartment two doors down from Tina's and knocked. A chunky woman in a housedress answered and gasped at the black-and-blue sight of me. I flashed the badge and she clutched her buttons. "Good morning, ma'am, I hate to disturb you but could I possibly step out on your balcony for a moment?"

"Is something wrong?"

I talked calm over the rising storm in my chest. "Call of a disturbance two doors down and I thought I could scope it better from the window. Just to make sure everything's all right."

I climbed over to the balcony next to Tina's and crawled close. Nothing but a waist-high railing separated one balcony from the next, so I could climb over or slither under pretty easily, which I did, laying on my left side on the concrete balcony, pain shooting from my shoulder in all directions. Squinting through the screen and the glass door, I saw two guys in black suits holding automatics—a tall guy and a guy with a flattop haircut, *and* Guerrin, and Tina tied to a chair. The couch has its back to me. Guerrin, near tears, says something about ". . . lied to me after everything I've done for you . . ." Tina beyond-terror babbling, "I didn't, I swear, I didn't . . ."

I bet Guerrin isn't armed, and if he is he can't shoot. But the other two are pros. If I shoot one, the other will let loose on me. I have to get both of them fast without hitting Tina. Fuck Guerrin. I shimmy backward on my back, inching into position, draw the Ruger on Stretch, making ready, ready . . . Suddenly the neighbor's door slides open and she yells across at me. "Excuse me, Officer, would you—OH MY GOD!" She screams at fifty decibels. Stretch, Flattop and Guerrin all turn like a chorus line.

I think, *NOW!* I fire twice. The glass shatters, some of it sprinkling me. I shield my eyes. I can't see the men. Shots firing over me, seconds before they see me on the floor. Someone fires lower, shots whizzing past my head and arm. Guerrin's screaming, "No, please, for the love of . . ." Three shots and Guerrin's down. I can see. There's glass everywhere, something moving under the couch, I fire under the couch and twice through it. Movement stops, blood running, ringing in my ears.

Blood-splattered Tina screaming. Is she shot? Did I shoot her? My heart's pounding, everything's shaking. Focus: Tina screaming ". . . the other one, the other one!" Suddenly, *Choop! Choop!*—two silenced shots hit Tina through the chest, her heart gushes royal red. I fire through the couch—*BLAM!* And keep firing as I jump up to see Flattop crouched over Stretch and bleeding and turning to me, still armed. I fire two more shots into him. He falls back, fires *Choop! Choop! Choop!* into the ceiling as he hits the floor. I hope to hell there's no one upstairs as the echo settles, ringing sharp in my ears.

Oh God, Tina.

I slide open what's left of the door, case the apartment, closets and all, then go to Tina, hanging limp in the ropes. No breath, no pulse. I untie her, lay her on the couch. Her mouth hangs open and her eyes stare dead ahead in terror. The pounding in my chest comes up into my throat. I stroke her forehead the way you would a sick child, whispering, "I'm sorry. I'm so sorry." I put my mouth against her ear. "Please. *Please* . . ."

"Please, please . . ."

My head jerks around at the echo of my words. Puffy, corpulent Guerrin lays on his side on the rug, bloody steam puffing from a hole in his chest, begging for something I can't give him.

"Please, please . . ." he mutters between tiny breaths.

I crouch close to him. "Tina's dead," I whisper. "You killed her. I know you worked for Oliver."

"Please, please . . ."

"Help me prove Oliver ordered this. Make him pay."

"Please . . ." Then his mouth opens for one last gasp as he sees something important far away, blood gushes from his mouth and he stops breathing. I check his carotid to make sure he's dead before I stand up.

Then I kick his ribs in.

2:45 P.M. Interstate 35, Frontage Road

I radioed Jake from the road, with half an explanation of the East Oltorf incident, how I'd left "in hot pursuit" and they should identify Stretch and Flattop, if they could.

I pulled off into a parking lot and leaned my head on the steering wheel. Tina and Guerrin were dead. Somebody big was scared. But nothing real I could pin on anyone. A million leads, a million dead ends. I stared at the dashboard, at the gauges—zero, empty, cold—my mind drawing blanks.

Rachel was gone.

Dashboard cracked by the heat. Microphone cord reinforced with electrical tape. Old phone book lying on the seat. Ruger in my holster. Flip through the phone book and start over or blow my brains out? I sighed and hoisted the book onto the steering wheel, idly flipping open to the butcher shop pages where the printout was.

I ran my finger down the tattered computer paper and the Yellow Pages entries for butcher shops. Then I started to see differences: there were two new places listed on the printout that weren't in the book—and four old ones from the book that we never checked.

Click, click, click.

I drove to a pay phone and dialed the Health Department.

Someone expecting a call answered with a full mouth. *"Sweetheart?"*

"This is Reles, APD Homicide. I need you to look something up for me."

"Oh, sorry." He swallowed and blew his nose. *"We're closed. It's Saturday."*

"DO I GOTTA COME DOWN THERE?!" I yelled.

"No, no. Shoot, go ahead," he said.

I gave him the names, and he took about five minutes looking them up before he came back to the phone.

"Okay, that's one 'moved,' two 'bankrupts.' Last one . . ." he said, *" 'ritual sacrifice.' "*

"What?"

"The chicken dies for your sins." I froze. *"Who's gonna complain, the chicken's family? But you're sure not supposed to do it in a state-certified butcher shop."*

I thought about the meat packs. "Any hint of *human* sacrifice?"

"Not according to this. Anyway it reopened a few months ago under the name Tejas Meats. Ha! 'Friendly.' They're not in the phone book yet." He gave me an address on North Pleasant Valley Road. *"New owner of record, Emmett Tejani. Anything else, buddy?"*

I floored it to Pleasant Valley, ignoring calls on the radio for a patrol to go to 2823 East Oltorf.

34

Bells jingled as the door closed behind me, my sweat disappearing in the chill of the brightly lit shop. The stout, dark man behind the counter tallied change for a customer. I browsed through the cases and waited for her to leave. The handle of a carving knife stuck out from a shelf under the cash register. The butcher looked over my bruises and raised his chin, asking, "What do you need?" Black circles cupped his eyes.

"Chicken."

He nodded at the chicken case.

"No," I shook my head, "I mean a white girl. Around twenty. Gimme a thigh and a leg if you have one left."

The butcher's eyes bulged, and he bolted for the door. I sidelined him and we crashed to the floor. Then I grabbed his hair and smashed his face down, cracking his nose on the ceramic tile. He cried out. I hoisted him with my good arm and hurled him against the register shouting, "Where is she?!"

He hit two buttons on the cash register and the drawer rang open.

"Take it," he cried, blood streaming over his mouth. "There's more."

"Where's the GIRL?!"

His eyes twitched to the freezer. I cuffed him behind his back, grabbed the carving knife from under the register with my bad hand and pushed him through the swinging door.

I shoved the butcher into a hanging beef carcass. He was wearing layers under his bloody apron: I was only wearing a shirt but I wasn't cold. Finally I saw a metal locker the size of a steamer trunk with tubes and wires attached to it. The butcher fell to his knees. I took a bloody rag from his pocket, grabbed the lid and lifted. Vapor poured out, rolling away from the remains of a woman, detached arms and legs cut into pieces and frozen solid in orange Styrofoam packs, and to clinch it, the faceless skull with long black, frozen hair, empty eye sockets staring at me. I dropped the carving knife. Nikki.

I turned to the sobbing man. "You did this." He shook his head as blood dribbled down his chin. "You cut her up." He nodded. "But you didn't kill her." He trembled. That was my big mistake. I took for granted the killer and the cutter were the same person. It was the butcher's print on the face package. "Okay, who did it?" Nothing. I backhanded him to the floor then rolled him onto his back on top of his cuffed wrists.

"You're facing serious charges. Accessory after the fact," right cross, "obstructing justice," right cross. I picked up the knife, sliced his apron straps and cut open his shirt. "You ever done time? I didn't think so. They put you in a little concrete cell, a six-foot cube, toilet. No window. They feed you through a slot in the door. The cell is built for two guys, but when it's crowded, there could be five. The steel door slams on you, boy, you *know* you're in jail. Sometimes they lock five guys in, only three walk out. They're not civilized like you and me."

"Tejani," the man dribbled out.

"What?"

"Armand Tejani. My b-brother."

"Your brother killed this girl." The butcher nodded. "Why'd you send the packages?"

"I'm so tired!"

I looked at the remains in the freezer, and started soft. "Emmett . . . Mind if I call you Emmett? I've seen lots of dead bodies before. Never a frozen one. They should keep them all frozen, it would keep them from stinking. Of course you couldn't cut them up . . .

"But this one body," I went on, "his name was Joey. You know what they do, they take a scalpel, smaller than this. Hey, does ice sterilize things like fire does?" I ran the blade along the freezer's edge. Vapor rose and the knife screamed a high-pitched squeal.

The butcher rolled his head side to side, tears streaming down his face.

"I don't know how you cut this girl up. The first thing they do in an autopsy," I said, "they cut a big Y in the chest. Is this cold?"

I touched the tip of the blade to the butcher's chest. He yelped and the blade hissed. "You can hear the knife *chop-chopping* through his flesh, that's what's so spooky about it. Wanna hear what it sounds like?"

He snorted blood. "No . . . no . . ."

"I guess it's easier if you don't know them, huh? I wouldn't mind them cutting him up like that," I seethed, all psycho Jew. "But the thing is," I snarled, *"I don't make friends so easy!"*

The butcher cried out, *"NO!"* and the knife clattered to the floor.

I dropped to a whisper. "You made me drop it. What's the matter with you? Somebody could've been hurt."

"You think I want to do this? I got a wife and kids! I can't sleep! Every time I close my eyes I see her face."

"Why didn't you turn him in?

"To who? The cops? He *was* a cop."

Bingo. "What?"

"Vice. Atlanta. He was crazy from being a cop. After prison, shit. He had friends. He could kill me remote control. He'd do anything."

"When was that?"

"Friday maybe—a week ago. He couldn't stop talking, said a lawyer paid him thirty K to do it. I'm so tired."

"What lawyer? Harrell?"

The butcher dropped his eyes. I reached for the blade.

"Guerrin," he said suddenly. "Don't tell my wife, please. Harrell hired Armand, but Guerrin was Harrell's boss. Armand smoked him out for more money. He left her," he stammered, "t-torso to scare them. He figured the cops could never track us from that. He dropped the slices at all the guys from Harrell's files, tapped Harrell's phone to figure out who called in. That's how he found Guerrin. He said they tried to kill him, he was turning the heat up. Said he'd cut my heart out if I let on I'd seen him. Tuesday night, that's when he came for her f-f—"

"Her face."

He turned away.

"Have you heard from him since?" He shook his head. "I'm gonna take you in now," I said. "If you don't tell the stenographer what you told me, *I'm* gonna cut your heart out. You believe me?"

He nodded. "Yes."

I thought about it. "So do I."

I tossed the butcher face-down in the back seat and radioed Dispatch as I drove.

"Homicide 8."

"That you, Sergeant Reles?" Martha Nell asked.

"Yeah."

"Son, people been looking for you."

"In a minute. Dial Margaret Hay at home and patch me through."

"Just a second," she said, then later, *"Got the machine. Leave a message?"*

"No, send me to her office."

The ME office phone rang. *"Medical Examiner."*

"Dan Reles for Margaret Hay."

"Dr. Hay can't come to the phone right now—"

"I've seen her patients. They can wait."

"She—she's not in."

"Tell her I have the rest of her Christmas present in the freezer at Tejas Meats, 764 North Pleasant Valley, off East Seventh. You better pick up the body right away." I told Dispatch to find Torbett, tell him to do a search on an Armand Tejani and meet me at Central Booking.

At Central Booking, four guards fought a raging barefoot prisoner. They cuffed him and beat him to the ground. I pushed the butcher to the counter. Behind the counter, Aguinaldo with the Sheriff's Office saw me and lit up. "Reles!" she said. "About time you showed up."

"Why?"

"Shit, man, don't you watch the news? We got seven homicides since yesterday!"

"Seven?!"

"Yeah, new record—four in a shootout on East Oltorf, three at this fire on Jewell." She turned to the butcher. "What's this? Resisting arrest?"

In five minutes, Emmett Tejani was booked and placed alone in a cell by me personally. "Don't talk to anybody," I said. "I'll be right back."

He said, "I'm so tired," as the iron door slammed on him.

I tore out of Central Booking, across the parking lot, down the concrete stairs and into the back entrance of APD. Carl Milsap tried to stop me with a "Where the hell you been? There's shit going down—"

"I know," I yelled as I passed.

"You *know*?"

I ran past Forensics and into the skeleton-staffed typing pool. One woman sat at a desk, reading a newspaper.

"Can I help you?"

"I need a stenographer, fast."

"Ginny's in today but she's transcribing—"

"Where?"

She pointed to a door and I burst in on a chubby, short-haired woman in front of a tape recorder, steno pad and typewriter, eating a Twinkie. She looked up in mid-bite. "Dan!"

"I need you to take a statement right now."

"I'm kinda busy—"

I thundered, "Just fuckin' do it!" She froze. "Look, I can't explain. Please. A hundred dollars if you come with me now."

Ginny gauged me a moment, then took up the

recorder and pad, slipped a fresh cassette into her pocket and stuffed the last of the Twinkie into her mouth. I grabbed the recorder and her wrist. We ran through the typing room, down the hall, outside and up the concrete stairs.

"Slow down, will you!" she whined. "I can't keep up." She stood still, straightening her skirt as seconds ticked by.

"Okay, I'm ready." I reached for her wrist and she pulled it away. "I'll *follow* you!"

She followed me up the second flight, across the lot and into Central Booking where Aguinaldo buzzed us in. I nodded at the cell block entrance guard, who looked to Aguinaldo for verification as I pulled Ginny past him.

Another guard stood at the opening to the second cell block, the butcher's block, and unlocked Emmett Tejani's door.

Emmett Tejani had solved his sleeping problem.

35

4:00 P.M. Central Booking

In his short stay in the cell, Emmett Tejani unhooked a spring from the bunk, hooked it around his carotid artery and yanked. He didn't want his wife to know his crime. And he was tired, so tired. I knew how he felt.

One day he was innocent, the next an unwilling accessory. A week later he was dead.

Emmett Tejani the butcher lay on his side on the concrete. Heavy dark drops of blood from his throat plunked down in a thick puddle.

Armand Tejani checked out as a jailbird ex-cop from Atlanta, no address, only a Buick registered in his name. We put out a search on Tejani and the Buick but I didn't expect to find either of them. Armand crossed the wrong crowd.

When I got back to the squad room, I found Carl Milsap

sitting alone with a pint bottle of J&B. "Buck's," he said, and passed it without looking at me. My arm throbbed and my teeth chattered. I took a long pull, swallowed and felt it ripple down. I flipped through copies of the printout of Nikki's topless promo shot, and her mug shots.

"Find anything?" I asked.

He shook his head. "Three dead at a house on Jewell. Waller AWOL. Four dead in a shootout on East Oltorf. Torbett went there. I'm suspended."

"What are you doing here?"

He turned angry. "You don't like me bein' here?!" I handed him the bottle. He drank and said, "Margaret Hay's in Brack Intensive Care with a bullet in her hip."

"What?!"

"They said she walked in on a burglary."

"Is there a guard on her?"

"No. Why?"

I rushed out the door and Milsap followed. "Nobody tried to rob Margaret Hay," I yelled running down the hall. "They tried to kill her. Now they'll try to finish the job."

I tore the three blocks back to Brackenridge.

4:20 P.M. Brackenridge Hospital

I badged my way into Intensive Care. When Milsap caught up I sent him up and down the halls checking for trouble.

Hay was out of surgery and I found her in a white private room with oxygen tubes up her nose, an IV drip and a beeping EKG. Bedside, I spoke just above a whisper.

"Dr. Hay?"

She opened her eyes. I couldn't tell if she knew me.

"Margaret?" I said.

Her eyes focused angry. She knew me.

"Who did this to you?" I asked.

She pointed to my holster, then cupped her right hand near her heart.

"A cop?" I asked.

She crossed her fingers.

"Cross?" I guessed. "Ex? An ex-cop?"

She tossed up one hand to say, you finally got it.

"How do you know?"

She looked at me as hard as she could. After a career of working around cops, their square haircuts and hard faces, she knew what an ex-cop looked like. Guerrin's men? She started to shake. I found an extra blanket and laid it over her. In a minute, she made a gesture like writing. I found her a pen and pad. She wrote two words.

"Killed him."

"No," I said. "He wasn't even there. He walked away."

She started to move her lips. I put my ear close to her. Whispering took all her strength.

"Dead. Occipital . . . fracture. Deep. Colt. Forty-five." She mimed swinging a hammer. "Dead. Twenty minutes."

I looked her over, impressed. "Listen," I said, "Waller had something to do with this but I don't know what yet." She nodded but I could tell it was too much for her.

An older nurse came into the room. "Dr. Hay shouldn't have visitors."

"I was just leaving."

"Now."

I leaned back to Hay. "I'm keeping a watch on this room. You'll be safe. Just rest."

Milsap came back. "Looks clean."

"Can you set up a twenty-four-hour armed guard on this room?"

"I got no place to go."

I left him alone in the hallway, like any cop, his misery and loneliness buffered for the moment by having something important to do.

36

8:00 P.M. Austin City Limits

I unholstered the Ruger automatic and lay it on the seat beside me, then drove all around town, up Interstate 35, across 183 and back down Highway 1 toward Westlake Hills and the rich people as the sun set, looking over my life. Time to think. Just my luck.

Last night I finally held Rachel close. Today she was gone from my life.

Hay said she wouldn't rule Joey Velez's death an accident. Suicide? Maybe, but why? A loveless marriage? He could have bailed. And a real estate scheme doesn't spell suicide. Especially if he did have eighty grand like Rachel said. Likely conclusion: just plain drunk.

But where would he get eighty grand? A few dollars aside every week? Not a chance. Graft? *Once a cop is compromised, he isn't a cop anymore. A cop who does well doesn't do good.*

I glanced at the Ruger lying on the passenger seat beside me, the way you look over a cliff, thinking, "Hmmmm . . ."

I holstered the Ruger, radioed Dispatch and asked for Torbett's home address.

8:30 P.M. 1205 Walnut Avenue

Off Martin Luther King Boulevard, on a humble but well-kept street, I found Torbett's humble but well-kept house, and knocked on its steel front door.

From inside: "Yes?"

"It's Reles."

Torbett opened the door, allowing me to nod at his wife, and her to smile back with polite suspicion. Torbett, wearing a tennis shirt and slacks, stepped out and closed the door behind him, then walked me down the front path. When he stopped at the end of the path and faced me, I said, "What do you hear?"

He casually scanned the lamplit street as we spoke, avoiding my eyes. "I hear Waller is officially AWOL. You're bleeding through your bandages like you took a bath in the briar patch. I hear four dead bodies on East Oltorf at Tina LaMarque's apartment, including Guerrin and Tina LaMarque. He was fuming. Plus Waller and the two unidentified on Jewell. I got no problem taking orders from a man on a mission, but seven bodies is out of my safety zone. And why did one of them have to be Tina LaMarque?!"

"I tried with Tina, man. I—"

Now he looked at me. "HOW HARD?!"

"How—" I drew the Ruger and popped the mag so he could see how many rounds were gone. "*This* hard!

Okay?!" I snarled, "Is that fuckin' hard enough? Or you want me to come back in a bag so you'll know I *really* tried?!"

Torbett looked down. "I was responsible for her. I brought her into it. I promised her . . ."

"I know. Me too."

"It's different."

Long silence. "Why do we do this?" I said.

"Do what?"

"Some big guy wants a little whore out of the way. We don't know who she was or why. A week later everyone who could connect them is dead. And we can't get a wire-tap on anyone important because they belong to the right country club."

He looked down the street, shrugged off whatever he was holding against me and let his breath out. "Man, there's always something you can do. As long as you're suckin' air."

I reached Nikki's charm out of my pocket, stared at its busted tooth.

Maybe I could put Nikki to rest. And if I could put Joey to rest, I wouldn't get Rachel back but I'd sleep again.

"Have faith, Daniel," Torbett said. "You're not so bad. You'll make something happen." He walked back to the house.

He should have told me *what* I was going to make happen. I'd have quit right there.

37

I popped the lock on the Democracy in Academia office, cubicle 14E in the Student Union, and sat at Aaron Gold's desk. At the top of the bulletin board hung a quote scrawled on a torn half-sheet of loose-leaf paper:

> "Get the thing straight. The policeman is not there to create disorder. The policeman is there to preserve disorder."
>
> Mayor Richard Daley
> Chicago, 1968

Under the quote hung the snapshots of Aaron and his disappeared friends. Among them hung the picture of Aaron, Rick Schate and two other longhairs in Rasta hats, passing a pipe around a coffee table. I peeled it down and held it under the light.

Aaron smiled at the camera, full of life. Rick smiled shyly, his face down. I ran my fingertip over the photo to

elp focus on details. I could see the face of one of the
other two longhairs, white, male, older than the others,
maybe thirty or more, with glasses and a ratty goatee, a
twisted braid sticking out from the cap. A white guy with
dreadlocks.

On Monday, we kept hearing the same names, some
we couldn't track: a girl named Tula or Lula. And a pimp
named Ray, a white guy with dreadlocks.

I'd seen him before, but where?

I couldn't see the last kid's face, only his thin neck. I
went through the desk drawers looking for a magnifying
glass, found a broken old pair of glasses like Aaron's and
held the picture under the light.

I followed the contours of the dark thin neck and the
ratty wool shirt the kid wore. The collar was open, just
wide enough to reveal a narrow neck, an inch of hairless
chest, and a slight recession. A girl. Along the collar ran a
piece of thread or string. At the end of the string, almost
hidden in the collar of the shirt—I raised the glass—hung
a little something, a little charm. I looked closer: a small
black skull. The charm I had in my pocket. *Click.*

Then I remembered where I'd seen the dreadlocks.
Click.

I ran to the car, hit the siren and tore down Guadalupe,
past the orange-lit tower, past bloated cheering preppies,
past the river and into the parking lot at Mag's, clutching
the snapshot and the printout picture of Nikki.

I burst through the entrance and headed for the
kitchen. Paul tried to head me off.

"You got a lot of fuckin' nerve coming in here!"

I pushed past him and through the kitchen doors. A
teenage busboy sat on a counter kissing a standing blond
waitress. In the corner the cook stood at the griddle flip-

ping eggs. He was wearing glasses, a ratty goatee and Rasta knit hat. The white guy with dreadlocks in the photo. I yelled to him.

"Ray?"

Ray turned to me. His eyes flashed fear.

He flattened against the wall as I cornered him and pulled off his cap, spilling patchouli-stinking dreads. I heard his name Monday: Ray the white pimp with dreadlocks.

"What do you know about Aaron Gold?"

"I'm clean, man, I'm clean. You can search me."

I tore his left sleeve open to the elbow, baring fresh tracks. "Hey!" he protested.

"I could bust you for what's in your blood right now and plant you in a cell you won't walk out of." I showed him the snapshot of him and Aaron together. "What do you know about Aaron Gold?"

"He was a guy. He went to school."

"He didn't use with you?"

"He smoked a little grass. Leave me alone."

"Who's this girl?" He twitched. I dropped the picture, twisted his arm and held his face over the griddle.

"No!" he screamed.

"Who!"

"She was my girlfriend."

"You took her to the prom?"

"No, man, I crashed at her place on South First. She'd go out and turn tricks and score dope."

"What did *you* do?"

"Nothing, I was too fucked up. I'd just lay there and wait till she came back."

"You were her pimp!"

"I was just there for show. So she could tell the real pimps she had someone."

"That's all?" I shook him by the collar.

"I was only with her a few months. She had good dope. Aaron got me this job. He tried to get her into rehab, but she wasn't buying. Then she took off. No note, no nothing."

"What was her name?"

"Nikki."

I pushed his nose down for a split-second, just long enough to sizzle in the grease. He screamed.

"Her *real* name!"

Ray was crying, his nose running on the griddle. "Stacy. Stacy Piel."

"Why'd she come back to Austin?"

"Man, I don't even know why *I'm* here."

"She have any family here? Friends?"

"Just me and Aaron and this old boyfriend."

I held Ray's face closer to the griddle. "What old boyfriend?"

"Aaah, no! This rich guy. She—she tried to hit him up for money a couple of times, but she couldn't get near him. John Oliver, that's the boyfriend. You know him. His father's gonna be governor. I guess John dumped her. We're both all fucked up, and she's turning tricks and trying to get near John for money, says she has something on his father. And then she split. That's it. That's everything!"

I let him go. He hit the floor, crumpled up against the wall. I thought for a second, then ran out of the kitchen.

Paul stopped me. "They were here," he said.

"What?"

"Aaron and John. Wednesday night. Turned into a showdown."

"Aaron Gold and John Oliver?"

"They were kids together. The Golds and the Platinums."

"How do you know that?"

"Everyone knows everybody. Aaron was my pal. I hired griddleboy for him."

"What do you know about Stacy?"

"The three of them. Childhood friends."

Aaron Gold. Stacy Piel. John Oliver.

Bill Oliver.

"You know where I'd find John Oliver?"

"First game of the season. Tailgating party for the masses, Aaron used to say. The trustees toast champagne at the Old Austin Club on Neches."

I jumped back into the Impala and zoomed up Congress. The traffic along Fifth wasn't moving, so I double-parked and ran east on Sixth, zigzagging between beer-fattened teens in designer shorts, toward Neches and the Old Austin Club.

38

Blacklands

10:15 P.M. Old Austin Club

I approached the Old Austin Club, a stone building with wide balconies across the second and third floors. I stood outside a while trying to think of a way to get inside. I didn't need one. The door swung open. "Will you be coming back, Mr. Oliver?" someone said in an accent straining toward England.

A young man answered, "If the rest of the world is more boring, yes, Oscar, I'll be right back." He bounced down the steps—mid-twenties, slim, blondish, about six feet, in a tailored suit—and swaggered with a champagne-boosted lightness toward the football game revelers on Sixth Street. I followed.

The tailgate party from campus crept west along Sixth, horns squealing from BMWs painted with the school mascot, the castrated longhorn steer. Young drunks made the sign of the devil, crying the school motto, "Hook 'em Horns!" Meanwhile, a crowd of about three hundred people hauling "Barton Springs Eternal" signs, protesting Tri-Mondo's development of the springs and surrounding area, tried to break across Sixth Street at Red River, disrupt the parade and, likely, crash the party at the Club. The preppie kids weren't hip to it. Two cops on horseback tried to navigate the narrow path between the parked cars and the ones trying to move, where only a daring few risked walking.

"John! John Oliver!" I shouted behind him.

John turned around, smiling artificially at his name.

I ran to him. "Dan Reles."

He sneered at my bruises and shook my hand with a visible thought about where he might wash up. "Nice to meet you, Dan."

"Hey, John. Do you know Stacy Piel?"

His face lit up bright and sad. "You know Stacy?"

"Aaron Gold was a friend of mine."

He turned somber. "Yes. Excuse me." He walked away.

I followed. "What did you and Aaron talk about Wednesday night? Was it her?"

"You should have seen them when they were kids," he said as he walked. "They were a team. Nobody could get between them, not their parents, not . . ." He trailed off.

"Not you." No answer. "Who knew that you met with Aaron?"

"Anyone at that dopey hippie hangout. Why?"

"Did your father know?"

He stopped walking. "Who are you?" he asked.

"A friend of Aaron's, I told you. You were in love with her, I don't blame you."

John gave a weak smile. "When I was six I asked her to

arry me. I asked her again when I was in Austin two
ummers ago, after my first year of law school. She said
s but then the Blacklands happened." He stared over the
owd and saw something that happened long ago.

I knew TriMondo had squeezed out the local black
opulation to turn the neighborhood into an extension of
ae campus, but anyone could know that. "What hap-
ened in the Blacklands?"

"Didn't Aaron tell you? He was there."

"He told me bits and pieces." No answer. I took a shot.
s that when you dumped her?"

He looked at me hard. "She dumped me."

"But I heard—"

"You heard wrong," he grinned, bitterly. "She cleaned
p that summer. I came back from Boston and we got a
lace by the lake. But she started using again after the
lacklands. A lot. We fought over it. She said I was just
ke my father. She was right. By then I just wanted
loney. I didn't care how I got it." He softened. "Law
hool changes you." He shook off the sentiment. "Aaron
lled me out of the blue on Wednesday. He wanted to
low some crap about my father's companies. Old story.
is father used to hit my father up for stock tips. My fa-
ler finally gave him one and like an idiot, Mr. Gold in-
sted everything he had. He lost it all and blamed us."
e half-grinned. "You might say it caused a rift between
le families."

"How long since you've seen Stacy?"

"Two years? Has it been that long? Yes, two years. Dad
tid, 'Let her go.' Then *we* had a big fight. Didn't matter—
le was gone."

"Gone?"

"Left town. Los Angeles, I guess. She used to talk about

it. Aaron didn't know where she was for sure, or h
wouldn't tell me, anyway."

John didn't know Stacy Piel was dead. I put it to
gether. Stacy left John after the Blacklands, when she sa
just how greedy the Olivers could be. That was fine wit
Daddy Oliver. He arranged her move into party-girl ci
cles, had Guerrin hire a girl, Vita, to introduce he
around. Figured she'd hang herself given enough rop
Drugs brought her down, from party girl to the street
Heavy odds she had a family somewhere and a reason fo
not going to them. She drifted from town to town, bu
then she drifted back to Austin. Oliver knew about it bu
John didn't. Maybe Oliver found out she was trying to ge
to John. Maybe she really had something on Oliver, h
was thinking about his political career and couldn't a
ford his son's cokewhore ex-girlfriend selling dirty secre
to the press.

I said, "I'm going to your father's party. You coming?

He looked me over with a smirk. "Do you have an in
vitation?"

"Not exactly."

He rolled it around. "Why not. It'll create a stir."

We wove through the sidewalk crowd. The proteste
squeezed into the street and the revelers booed an
shoved them. I tried to keep my footing. John got jo
tled, then pushed someone back. I saw the movemen
ripple across and then the reaction, the mass pushin
back in the other direction. Waves swept through th
crowd and a woman fell in front of a Jeep. The Jee
screeched to a halt as someone yanked her back into th
melée. People swarmed between the parked cars just t
get off the sidewalk.

Across the crowded street and a few storefronts dow

I saw a helmeted cop on horseback point his club at a blonde woman in a tan dress, the cop saying something like, "Get out of the street." She was arguing, pointing to the packed sidewalk.

I started to make my way over but it was impossible. A dozen other walkers forced off the sidewalk by the shoving surrounded the horse.

The cop repeated the gesture with more emphasis. People around her yelled something like, "Leave her alone!" Someone jostled the cop's boot.

He swung his club blind. People ducked out of his way and he missed, then swung again at the only thing he was sure he could hit, the blonde. His club connected with the side of her head and she fell.

Terrified looks and shouts from the people around as they edged away from the mounted cop, but the crowd behind pushed them back. The cop kept swinging. John Oliver's face read fear. I raised my badge and shoved through the crowd, trying to get the mountie's attention.

"Hey! APD!" Not a blink, and the crowd didn't or couldn't let me pass. I thought of shooting the ground, then imagined a stampede at the sound of gunfire. I jumped into the bed of a pickup and waved my arms and badge at the cop like it was *Let's Make a Deal* and he was Monty Hall. "Hey! HEY!"

People near the mountie tried to get him to look at me, but he took their jabs for attacks and swung harder. His horse swayed into the crowd, cornered by a parking meter. Then I watched the mountie slow-mo reach for his holster and draw his gun.

I pulled the Ruger and took aim. I could clip him, maybe, and keep anybody from getting killed. Or I could

hit wide and high, kill him or maybe an innocent. Screams
around me, "Don't shoot!" "No!"

Something happened to the horse and it reared up
flipping the cop backward. He crashed through the
plate-glass window of a hair salon. Two cop vans with
sirens screaming pulled up on the north leg of Red
River and opened their doors, spilling two dozen patrols into the crowd. I holstered the Ruger and elbowed
back to John, perched atop a BMW and grinning at the
spectacle.

"Let's go!"

"You're a cop," he said, then climbed down, stumbled
and headed back toward Neches as the crowd spilled up
the street past him.

A woman tripped and hit the ground. I helped her up
and went after him. "John!" He didn't turn around. "Do
you know how Aaron died?"

"Heroin."

I jumped in front of him. "He was killed."

Wild shock. "What?!"

"He was unconscious when they threw him off the
tower. Somebody held him down hard while someone
else shot him up with a deadly dose. They left bruises on
his arms and painted them over."

"That's crazy!"

"I can show you the autopsy slides." John knew the official word on Aaron's death. I was willing to bet Daddy
Oliver had kept the details from his son. I said, "I need to
talk to your father."

"I don't understand."

"He's probably trying to protect Aaron's family. But he
knows something about Aaron's death."

Thoughts spun around his head. "How . . . why . . . why would someone kill Aaron?"

"I don't know. I'm just asking you not to talk to your dad until I talk to him. Can you do that? Please."

He walked away and I followed him. At Neches, we pulled off the main street with the rushing refugees and jumped up the steps of the Old Austin Club. When the Club was a nineteenth-century whorehouse, the girls stood on the balcony and propositioned passing men. Now guests enjoyed an expensive cocktail while they watched the rioters get trampled. We pushed through the front door, pulling it shut behind us.

The tuxedoed host greeted John in front of a smoked-glass wall separating the front foyer from the main ball-room.

"Glad to see you back, Mr. Oliver. And who is this?"

John at least was in a suit, if a rumpled one. I was wearing a dirty shirt to go with the splint on my hand, two black eyes and a freshly broken nose. "Dan Reles," I said.

"Dan Reles. He's a friend of mine." The host checked the list on the podium. "It doesn't matter if he's on the list, Oscar. He's with me."

John led me past a riled Oscar, through smoked-glass doors into a room packed with tuxedos and summer evening gowns. Across the crowd, Daddy Oliver was making a speech that was supposed to be spontaneous. The whole room was tuning in, men standing on their toes to get a look at the Great One. A few heads spun in our direction but not enough to make a difference.

". . . the federal government has proven it can't handle . . . anything." General laughter. "Privatization has always made all the difference. We've proven that at the university. We've wiped out waste and fraud, and we're turning a profit. Why not the welfare system?"

On one wall hung a banner reading, T.O.W.E.R. and in smaller letters, TEXAS OFFICE OF WORKFORCE ENROLLMENT. Oliver had balls of steel. Instead of burying TOWER, the women's health program that nearly buried half a dozen young women, he was recycling the acronym to wipe out public memory of its last use.

A crackling hillbilly voice shouted from the opposite corner, "Why not the prisons?"

Heads spun. Instead of bouncing the cracker out, they tried to get a better look at him too. Oliver, in a white dinner jacket, responded goodheartedly, "Why *not* the prisons, Frank?"

Frank Pollard shouted back, old-timey stump speech, "Why not the schools?"

"Why *not* the schools? Why not the gas and electric?"

"And if it works in Texas," Pollard crackled, "then what?"

Oliver froze the staged tennis match and held the room rapt. "When it works in Texas . . ." his voice resonated optimism, ". . . the sky's the limit." They couldn't buy this, I thought. No one would buy it.

The audience cheered. Champagne flowed. People turned around to make toasts and congratulate one another.

Chips fell into place. Billionaire Franklin Pollard had teamed up with Bill Oliver. Oliver was using Pollard's money to fund his planned campaign, and Pollard's down-home accent to make him seem accessible to a broader base of support. Pollard used Oliver to get a bigger piece of bigger action: The welfare system, the schools, the prisons, public utilities, social services, all under corporate ownership. Private control of everything public.

And if it works in Texas, it'll work in Washington. And if it works in Washington?

Guerrin hired Harrell who hired Tejani to kill Nikki/Stacy.

Stacy probably had enough dirt on the Oliver family to tarnish Oliver's image, or at least make a stink he thought he could do without. Killing her was like swatting flies. Except that John loved her. But John didn't know where she was, and he didn't know she was dead.

Bill Oliver was clean as a whistle on paper. Everyone who could nail him to the killings of Tina, Guerrin, Tejani, Harrell, Stacy or Aaron was dead. Oliver was headed for the governor's mansion and maybe the White House, unless he found something bigger—with the Blacklands, Barton Springs and God knew how many dead bodies in his wake. Smooth sailing from here on in.

The crowd spread out, and John and I got close enough to catch his father's eye.

"John!" Oliver sang. "And Sergeant Reles! Glad you could make it!" The elder Oliver addressed the cluster near him. I was surprised that he knew who I was, more surprised he admitted it. John found a drink and I saw him slam it down. Oliver's entourage reassessed me from vagrant to curiosity when he said, "Sergeant Reles solved the Jigsaw murders!"

I said, "Murder."

"Excuse me?"

"There was only one," I said, adding, "Right?" His expectant smile didn't flutter. "Bill, can we speak privately." It wasn't a question.

Oliver weighed the refusal against the scene I might make. "Of course!" he boomed. "Anything for the boys in blue." Oscar was at his side. "Oscar, see Sergeant Reles to my office and get him a drink."

"Yes, sir."

Oliver added with a wink, "And something to wear!" The cluster around him chuckled. Oliver whispered something to a flunky who quickly vanished into the crowd.

As I passed John I slipped Nikki's skull charm into his palm.

Oscar led me up a broad staircase and into a room of dark wood paneling and orange leather chairs, a podium, and a huge oaken desk, behind it an antique gun collection on the wall. Heavy brown drapes swathed sky-high windows. I guessed doors opened behind some of the drapes. If someone wanted to shoot me, not much would stand in his way.

"And what will you be drinking . . . *sir?*"

"I won't be drinking."

He sniffed twice. "I'll bring bourbon," he said, then retreated through the double doors, letting Oliver in and closing the doors behind him. Martini in one hand, a large manila envelope in the other, Oliver opened with his usual jovial style.

"So, Dan, what's keeping us from the party?" He placed his envelope on the podium.

"You're under arrest."

He beamed. "Am I?"

"For the murders of Stacy Piel and Aaron Gold."

He laughed like he'd just enjoyed a full meal. "People say worse things about me every day."

I faced him, showdown style. "You didn't want Stacy

near John, you couldn't afford her badmouthing you to the press, so you had her killed. But your hired gun found out how much money was in it and he went into business for himself, dropping pieces of her around, figuring we'd find them and turn the heat up on you. So you killed him and everyone in between."

Oliver pursed his lips thoughtfully. "I'm a very bad role model."

"You killed the girl your son loved because she got in your way."

"She was a prostitute," he snapped back. "She wasn't an appropriate wife for an Oliver."

"You killed your wife." Long silence. I jumped on it. "She wanted a divorce. You were afraid for your career so you fed her all the pills she could eat."

He pulled on a smile. "Shall I come along quietly? Or would you rather I take the honorable way out?"

"Man, you knew Stacy when she was a little girl."

"Sacrifices were made."

"By who?"

He raised his glass. *"Whom."*

He sipped and waved the matter aside like cigar smoke, then walked to the podium, setting down his drink and slipping something from the envelope. "But enough about me," he said. "Let's talk about you." He flipped a few switches on the podium, dimming the lights. A curtain hummed open, revealing a four-by-six-foot white glass screen. A beam of light from the podium's front hit the screen with a blurry image of Oliver's hand steadying a photograph. "You'll have to excuse me," he said. "I was never any good with these things." He settled the photo and focused the projector. "There!" The shot was a black-

and-white of my late partner Joey Velez and another guy, shooting pool. Joey has the bloated pre–heart attack look that marked his last months. He's lining up a shot, and the other guy is grinning off to the side. He's a big, dark-skinned guy with a build like Joey's but his face is a lunar landscape of pockmarks and crevasses. A crisp professional photograph, and a candid one. "I wonder," Oliver said, "if you can identify the gentleman with Sergeant Velez."

I stared at the picture. Dark velvet walls. It was the poolroom in the house on Jewell, Heaven's Gate. Waller told me they were friendly to cops. I played cool. "I won-der if you can tell me who was snapping candid shots of my friend shooting pool in a whorehouse."

"How do you know it's a whorehouse?" he asked. No answer. Heaven's Gate was Oliver's, of course. And the pictures he took of his clients, big and small, helped him keep his hold on Austin, on Texas, on the world. If he didn't have shots of me it was only because Waller torched the place. Oliver went on. "Your friend isn't that important. This gentleman is." Oliver took some effort pronouncing the name. "Mohammed Rashid Nadiri brought his product into the country by way of Mexico, I'm told, but the heroin originated in Afghanistan. Nadiri's Texas connections made distribu-tion here possible."

If the Nadiri story was true, Joey was in a whorehouse shooting pool with a dealer and never told me about it. Partners know each other's business. He was hiding some-thing. If Joey did have eighty thousand dollars as Rachel thought, I got a sense of where it might have come from. "Interesting," I said. "Only how would you know that? Unless you had a contact on the force." Waller. I watched him and I tried to look cool.

Oliver's eyes lit up. "You had no idea. You didn't know what he was doing. Well, it doesn't matter. If he was in it, you were in it. That's what everyone will think."

"Fuck you."

He watched me, then said, "I see! He was your hero."

"You have the right to remain silent. If you give up that right—"

"When they prosecute us, me with a staff of the most powerful attorneys in the world, and you with a public defender, who do you think will get the longer sentence? The university president who may have had some financial indiscretions? Or the dirty city cop with the Afghan connection? Any evidence of *my* crime? Witnesses?" he said with a glimmer. "I see. And when testimony surfaces about your behavior in a particular brothel last night, the very brothel where Velez did his business, do you think that will sway public opinion in your favor?" My jaw dropped. "Your lady, Vita. Do you think she stands by her police friends? A whore with a heart of gold?"

I looked at the slide of Joey. Oliver walked over and put a hand on my shoulder.

"Feeling bad doesn't make you moral," he said. "Only unusual. Good intentions aren't enough. And thus," he spread his palms like Jesus over the dinner table, "the myth of the moral cop goes the way of all flesh."

A bourbon and soda clinked down on the glass table beside me. Oscar smiled coldly, handed a fresh martini to Oliver and retreated with his tray. Oliver raised his glass.

"A toast. To the multiple triumphs we're celebrating this evening. First, the Barton Springs Planned Urban Development bill has passed."

I gulped my drink. "How'd you swing that?"

"Quietly. Second, Police Chief Lucille Denton is

leaving Austin, having secured an appointment with the Justice Department in Washington. An agreement was made between the present administration and"—he beamed satisfaction—"the future ones. And on a lighter note, we won the big game against the Okies, our arch rivals."

"You don't give a flying fuck about Oklahoma."

"People need enemies, Dan. How else will they know who their friends are?" He strode across the floor. "Austin needs a boost. We need new schools, new highways, new buildings!"

"Half the buildings downtown are empty."

"They won't stay that way. Within five years, Austin will see another boom, dwarfing the one it saw in the early eighties."

"I remember that big boom," I said. "When it was over, there was a big bust, lots of empty skyscrapers and home-less ex-yuppies."

"This time we'll be ready." From the podium he flipped off the opaque projector and flashed a slide with the words MISSION: SUCCESS! and a 1950s logo of a soaring jet, the familiar signature of Orion Aircraft.

"In thirty years," he boomed, "seven corporations will run the world. Why not Orion? Good old Orion. They won the war for us. If it weren't for Orion, we'd be living under Fascism." He showed slides of suburban homes and happy suburban families. "Orion Aircraft has meant pros-perity in the American mind since 1941, first in military supply, then in civilian aircraft, and tomorrow," he said with pride, "in public service.

"Take Joe Taxpayer, for example." The screen showed a cartoon of a schmoe punching a clock. "Joe works hard at the plant all day. He doesn't want his tax money spent keeping some freeloader in cigars and beer." A cartoon of a bum sitting on a couch with his feet up, watching TV with a beer and a cigar butt. "Orion takes the responsibility off Joe's back, and puts it back where it belongs!" The last slide is a split screen. Half has the freeloader getting kicked out of his house with his ratty suitcase; the other half shows Joe giving the "okay" sign to the camera. The screen went black, lights rising on Oliver's triumphant face.

"No one'll buy it," I said.

"They're buying it already. The police department is already set up for profit," he said. "Don't try to argue otherwise. Austin is a trial market for everything from movies to junk food. Why not privately run public services?"

Bourbon made me bold again. "And if it works in Austin, you'll take it on the road. Maybe to Washington? You already have a friend in the Justice Department."

"Government *should* be run like a business, Dan. The university is in the black for the first time in years."

"Half the kids in Texas can't afford public college anymore."

He showed his dimples. "There are always jobs for caddies. Dan," he said in comforting tones, "Americans prove in every election that they love millionaires. They want more power and more money in fewer hands, they just keep thinking their own hands will be among the lucky few." He sauntered across my path, martini in hand. "You've learned more than you were meant to. I'm not worried about an indictment, but I won't have a scandal. I see two possibilities. You can ride the gravy train with us. Be the hero cop who brought to justice the murderer of poor Stacy Piel, whose death will be blamed on the lack-adaisical crime-fighting policies of the current governor. I'll give you a state-appointed office."

"As watchdog for you and your friends? I can eat shit and bust any streetwalker who crosses you?"

"What do you do now?" He didn't change his tone. "Maybe you'd like something closer to home. Head of Homicide?" No answer. "Or, alternatively, you can die tragically in some accident or other. In case you're having martyr impulses, you can first have your otherwise brilliant career derailed by the exposure of the brothel incident and your heroin connections, followed by . . . let's see." He picked up an index card from the podium and read it. "Of course! It all makes perfect sense now. Followed by the tragic and unexplained death of your dear friend"—he looked at the card, then at me—"Rachel Velez!"

Somewhere a heavy steel door slammed shut.

I tried to keep my head up as I skulked toward the door. Then I turned to Oliver with my last drop of defiance.

"Winning doesn't make you right."

"I have a staff of scientists and historians. Writing the histories—*that's* what makes me right. Consider my offer."

"Is it true what the building says," I asked, "that the truth shall make you free?"

He raised his empty martini glass. "If it doesn't kill you."

I turned away.

"Oh, and Dan?" Standing under a burnt orange lamp, he let the corners of his mouth curl up. "Hook 'em Horns."

As I headed out, a higher, younger voice spoke from

the shadows. "Sergeant Reles, would you stay a minute?" I spun around in time to see Bill Oliver's jaw drop and his ever-placid face turn white.

John Oliver spoke again, stepping into the light. Tears streaked his permanent sneer. He'd been there a while.

I kept my eyes on Oliver, saying, "I don't think your father wants me to stay."

"Nobody stays when Dad wants them to leave, right Dad? You saw what happened to my mother. And to Stacy."

Oliver turned on his calming voice, reached a hand toward John. "Son, that was a long time ago. There'll be other girls."

John raised a revolver, an old one from his father's collection, and pointed it in the direction of his own head.

"John, put that gun down. She loved herself. She didn't love you."

"You don't know that!" He pointed the gun at Oliver.

Oliver talked faster. "She left you."

"She would have come back."

I spoke up. "Don't do it, John. Prison is forever. A concrete block, always watching your back, not a minute's peace."

"You think prison is worse than this?!"

Pretending to smile at the weapon, Oliver said, "John, put that down. You're my own blood! Don't give up your future over an old wrong. We'll be on top of the world." Then slightly faster, "And when I'm gone you'll take over the throne. You'll have more women than you know what to do with. And parties, and friends."

John spoke to me but he kept his eye and his gun trained squarely on Dad. "I don't have friends. I have flunkies, like Dad does."

"You don't have *peers*," Oliver blurted. "I was breeding a prince!"

John went on. "Two years ago they had to clear the Blacklands, so Dad paid off who he could and had the houses flattened in the middle of the night. Only one family didn't get out. The parents were deaf, they didn't hear the bullhorn, is that right, Dad? The mother and daughter got out, but the father and son got stuck in the building and crushed. The mother cried, this horrible, inhuman gut sound. Dad made a cash settlement on the spot—he had a country club to build—fifty thousand for the father, another thirty thousand for the son. They had her sign a contract right there. She was crying so hard she couldn't see. My father is such a shrewd businessman. Two lives for under a hundred thousand. Is that what a son is worth, Dad? Thirty thousand?"

"A son is invaluable," he said.

"That right? I thought it was thirty thousand." He turned to me. "Dad saw Stacy there with me that night. Pretty soon she was gone. You talk to her, Dad? Pay her off?" Oliver stood silent. "Aaron was like my brother. You killed them both. You killed my *mother*. Everybody I cared about. Everything you ever wanted, you took. You could be president without breaking a sweat."

"So could you."

"All I wanted was Stacy."

"She was a whore. She did it with everybody."

"I don't care!"

"She did it with . . ." Oliver stopped dead.

John said, "With who?"

Oliver didn't answer.

Jesus, I thought. Oliver made my old man look like Father Knows Best.

Oliver reached to him desperately. "John, she didn't love you. *I* love you!"

John yelled "SHUT UP!" and tightened his body just enough to squeeze the trigger. The pistol blast shook the room and landed in the heavy drapes with a thud.

39

11:30 P.M. Old Austin Club

It was a very old gun.

The backfire ripped open John Oliver's hand and scorched his arm. Bill Oliver and the medics were able to walk John down to the ambulance. I signed the accident report.

Bill Oliver had strip-mined South Africa, leveled ghettoes and parks to build country clubs and sports facilities, starved people out, poisoned their water, destroyed their homes. He'd killed whoever stood in his way, while he tried to turn the federal government into a superstore.

Stacy Piel was dead, along with Aaron Gold. Tina, Harrell, Guerrin, Waller, Jeffries and half a dozen more in the aftermath.

And no one I could arrest except maybe some flunkies, if I could find them. Might as well bust the waiters and the cab drivers. If I passed the evaluation on Monday—and I guessed Oliver and Denton had already fixed that—I'd still have my job: errand boy for the Corporate Mafia, just like my dad. A mobster's lackey.

I could even have the bone Oliver offered to throw me. Head of Homicide. Why not? Maybe I could do some good.

Joey's words: *A cop who does well doesn't do good.*

The last of the medics and onlookers followed the Olivers down, leaving me alone in the still, empty room, holding the glossy of Joey and his dealer friend. They'd cut John's jacket off him and left it in a twisted heap by the podium, with his wallet. The drapes soaked up every drop of sound. When I held still I couldn't hear a thing. Perfect silence.

I pocketed the glossy and flipped through John's driver's license and credit cards. I pulled out a white rectangle, the words "Aaron, Stacy and John, at 6, 8 and 10," written in pencil, and flipped it over. Someone's back yard, six-year-old Aaron, close-cropped hair, is sitting in a foot-deep inflatable pool, laughing, loving the world. Stacy stands behind him in a one-piece pink bathing suit, her black hair in a short bowl cut, her sky blue eyes gleaming. She wraps her arms around Aaron's shoulders, cradling him loosely. Yellow-haired John stands next to her in the water, bent over like he's about to splash someone, jaw tight from the cold water. Stacy's skinny little body doesn't show a hint of what will drive men wild later. A string around her neck is twisted to the side, holding a charm she'd keep all her life. I remembered the time I saw her remains, and the last time I saw Aaron alive. I remember the last time I saw Joey Velez, waving goodbye across that parking lot before he gave it up and, by accident or on purpose, drove off that cliff. I hadn't saved any of them.

Something rose inside me. I ran from the building, down Fifth Street toward Congress. I poured on speed, the back of my head pounding. I tightened my fists through the pain of bandages and stitches and pulled with my arms to run faster, shoulder screaming with pain, heart pumping in my throat, trying to beat whatever was coming up inside me. At Congress I jumped into the car, started it and hit the siren and lights.

I leaned on the horn as I floored it up Congress, running red lights, sending other cars into skids. I cut across to Lavaca, then headed north and cut across again to the Drag, roared up the western edge of campus, up through Hyde Park, and across Thirty-eighth Street, hollering and pounding the dash.

I raced the wrong way up a one-way street, sent a Corolla careening onto a lawn. Then I pulled up with a skid at Rachel's house, ran up the path and pounded on the door. She opened it, her eyes wide, mouth open. She wore a man's button-down shirt hanging to her thighs. The news was blaring from the television, Lyda Collins saying something about an accident at the home of Bill Oliver, someone interviewing the vice president on the campaign trail, and then jets flying over the flag and a smiling crowd of Girl Scouts with Oliver waving from a podium.

Then I looked back at Rachel's face, her shocked concern softening to a smile. She wasn't afraid of me. And the angry cop in me broke. My rage crumbled away, and all I felt was sad. Sad for all the victims I'd seen in eleven years of police work. Sad for me at ten years old, alone and motherless in my parents' apartment, waiting for my father to come home from prison. Sad for Aaron and Stacy, for Tina, and for Joey—I hadn't put one of them to rest, hadn't brought justice to one perpetrator. Sad to admit that I had failed.

And in that sadness was my first moment of peace.

Acknowledgments

I wish to thank the crowd who helped me in this process, in particular:

My agent Nat Sobel, who invested his thirty-plus years of experience in a story he believed was worth telling. And his partner Judith Weber for her insights.

My editor Ray Roberts at Viking, who saw it through.

Anna Bliss and Catherine Crawford at Sobel Weber, and Clifford Corcoran at Viking, for making things happen.

At the Austin Police Department: Sgt. Will Beechinor, formerly of the Homicide Squad; Mike Burgess (formerly) and Laura Albrecht (currently) of Public Information; and Lt. David Crowder, formerly of the East Austin Substation.

Ron Urbanovsky, Director of Texas Department of Public Safety Crime Laboratory Service; Mike Johnston, Manager of the Headquarters Laboratory, Texas Department of Public Safety (retired); the late Curtis Weeks of Central Booking; Rick Morrisey and Robert B. Ybarra, both formerly of the Texas Attorney General's Office; and Frank

Passarella, formerly of the New York City Department of Investigation.

Elizabeth Peacock, M.D., Deputy Medical Examiner, Travis County (Austin).

Rob Key, formerly of Just Guns, Austin.

The staff and clients of Travis County Adult Probation, East Austin Unit, for inspiring me.

My friends Troy Dillinger, Dolores Witkowski, Dennis Ciscel, Billy Roberts and Randy Bruin, patriotic Austinites all, for their guidance and insight into the heart of this beautiful town. My beloved friend and colleague Samantha Webber for lending me her camera, her car, and her couch, and for steaming my gray suit so I could interview cops.

My all-weather friends Jeffrey Robles, David Johnson and Calvin Chin, for sticking by me through this long process.

Three gifted readers and writers: Nan Mooney, Jason Eaton and Dionne Michelle Bennett, for their painstaking reading and invaluable suggestions. My sister-in-law Tanya for her feedback on crucial points.

My father, Robert Louis Simon, who made all things possible.

Above all, my brother Richard Simon, for inspiring me to write and teaching me how.

Finally, to the people of the City of Austin, for giving me a safe place to hole up for a few years while the heat died down.

FOR THE BEST IN PAPERBACKS, LOOK FOR THE

In every corner of the world, on every subject under the sun, Penguin represents quality and variety—the very best in publishing today.

For complete information about books available from Penguin—including Penguin Classics, Penguin Compass, and Puffins—and how to order them, write to us at the appropriate address below. Please note that for copyright reasons the selection of books varies from country to country.

In the United States: Please write to *Penguin Group (USA), P.O. Box 12289 Dept. B, Newark, New Jersey 07101-5289* or call *1-800-788-6262.*

In the United Kingdom: Please write to *Dept. EP, Penguin Books Ltd, Bath Road, Harmondsworth, West Drayton, Middlesex UB7 0DA.*

In Canada: Please write to *Penguin Books Canada Ltd, 10 Alcorn Avenue, Suite 300, Toronto, Ontario M4V 3B2.*

In Australia: Please write to *Penguin Books Australia Ltd, P.O. Box 257, Ringwood, Victoria 3134.*

In New Zealand: Please write to *Penguin Books (NZ) Ltd, Private Bag 102902, North Shore Mail Centre, Auckland 10.*

In India: Please write to *Penguin Books India Pvt Ltd, 11 Panchsheel Shopping Centre, Panchsheel Park, New Delhi 110 017.*

In the Netherlands: Please write to *Penguin Books Netherlands bv, Postbus 3507, NL-1001 AH Amsterdam.*

In Germany: Please write to *Penguin Books Deutschland GmbH, Metzlerstrasse 26, 60594 Frankfurt am Main.*

In Spain: Please write to *Penguin Books S. A., Bravo Murillo 19, 1° B, 28015 Madrid.*

In Italy: Please write to *Penguin Italia s.r.l., Via Benedetto Croce 2, 20094 Corsico, Milano.*

In France: Please write to *Penguin France, Le Carré Wilson, 62 rue Benjamin Baillaud, 31500 Toulouse.*

In Japan: Please write to *Penguin Books Japan Ltd, Kaneko Building, 2-3-25 Koraku, Bunkyo-Ku, Tokyo 112.*

In South Africa: Please write to *Penguin Books South Africa (Pty) Ltd, Private Bag X14, Parkview, 2122 Johannesburg.*